THE EXPOSED SERIES

PART ONE, PART TWO, PART THREE & PART FOUR

DEBORAH BLADON

ISBN : 9781500624019
eBook ISBN: 9780993721687

Book & cover design by Wolf & Eagle Media

deborahbladon.com

PART ONE

CHAPTER ONE

HE WEARS THE TUXEDO WITH THE UNCOMPLICATED GRACE OF
a man who is comfortable in a suit. I stare at him as I walk
slowly down the staircase. He's talking to Maria, his hands
waving through the air as the words pour from his moist, full
lips. The lips that I imagine would glide across the most inti-
mate parts of a woman and bring her pleasure that is difficult
to match. They complement his vibrant blue eyes and rich
black hair. He is striking. I stop to watch the way his broad
shoulders dip as he leans in close to her. He knows how to
use his body even if it is during something as seemingly
insignificant as a conversation about the weather. He understands the impact he has on others. He owns it.

"Ms. Lockwood." Maria rushes over as I put the last step
behind me. "I'm sorry to disturb you, but Mr. Reynolds forgot
his overcoat."

I smile at her and run my hand down her shoulder. "It's
fine."

"Thank you." She bows slightly and I instantly feel a pang
of awkwardness. She works for my parents. I don't want her
to think that she has to submit to me. "I'll finish cleaning up."

"No." I point towards the kitchen. "You'll gather your things and you'll go home for the night."

"You're sure?" she asks, her face brightening at the suggestion.

"Go," I say insistently.

"Thank you, Ma'am." A wide grin covers her face pulling on the wrinkles that are beginning to form around her eyes. "I'll see you tomorrow."

"You'll see me the day after tomorrow and it's Sadie." I correct her. "Take tomorrow to play with your grandson."

"Thank you." She turns to leave but stops herself. "Have a nice evening, Mr. Reynolds," she says. I catch her expression and I swear she's swooning over him. I can't blame her. I did it earlier for hours from afar during the benefit dinner. I couldn't keep my eyes off of him, even though he arrived on the arm of one of the most stunning and generous benefactors of my mother's charity.

"It's been a pleasure and it's Hunter." He nods as she pads off down the hallway.

"Your overcoat?" I question as I walk towards the coat room. I wish I hadn't taken off my heels or pulled my hair into a ponytail. I had no idea he would be waltzing back into my life or my home mere moments after the party ended.

"I don't normally do this." His voice resonates. It feels as though it rushes through me. The tone is deep. It pulls desire from within me with each syllable he speaks.

"Forget your coat?" I stop in place holding the handle of the door in my grasp.

"Pretend to forget my coat so I can seduce a beautiful woman," he says smoothly.

I take in the words, repeating each in my mind. He didn't just say what I think he said, did he?

"Excuse me?" My hand drops from the handle and bounces against the silk of my dress.

"How old are you, Ms. Lockwood?" he asks assuredly.

"I'm twenty-one." My face flushes.

He's standing next to me now. There's energy moving between us. I can feel it and sense it. It's bouncing off my body, tearing my inhibitions away from me. "Old enough then." His lips brush against my ear.

"Old enough?" I glide one small step to the left, just far enough that my ear is out of his reach. Keeping my composure when I can literally smell the scent of his skin and almost taste his lips is an impossible feat. I need distance and maybe another glass of the champagne I was drinking earlier.

"I don't need to spell it out for you, do I?" he asks, amusement skirting the question.

He's so confident it's maddening. He was much more attractive hours ago when he was just a man with a gorgeous face. My best friend, Alexa, and I had spent virtually the entire evening drooling over him from afar trading fantasies about what we'd do with him. "You don't and yes, I'm old enough." I pull a faint smile across my lips. "I'm old enough to realize that you're trying in some roundabout way to get me to sleep with you."

He stands in silence, his eyes running from my face, down the black shift dress I'm wearing to my bare feet. I'm suddenly aware that I'm still sporting the same red, white and blue toe nail polish that I have been since the fourth of July, a week ago. I try in vain to curl the toes of my left foot under the right but it's not working.

I'm startled when he abruptly jerks his head back in rolling laughter. His eyes squint as the enjoyment slides over his face. I feel a blush rush through me and I take a deep breath to try and curb it.

"You're lovely, Sadie." The way he says my name is different. He pulls it across his tongue so that it lingers there just a touch longer than it should. "I was talking about a woman I saw at the benefit dinner. I was hoping you could tell me who she was and give me her number."

"B...but you said I was old enough," I stutter. "So I thought you meant."

"Old enough to understand discretion," he whispers as he places his index finger over his lips.

I stare at it mortified that I'd made such a ridiculous assumption. What was I thinking? How could I have thought he wanted me? Look at him. The man can scoop up any woman he wants with a flash of that smile. Men like that want nothing to do with girls like me.

"She was tall, blonde and she was wearing a stunning red dress." His words bite through me given the fact that I'm barely over five feet tall, brunette and my fashion choices are limited to whatever will fully cover the large scar that transverses my chest.

"I'm not sure," I say softly now wishing that I would have asked Maria to stay. She would have been able to handle this conversation much better than me. My mother's maid has been a part of our family since before I was born and she knows everyone's business. She'd know exactly who Hunter was talking about and he'd be out the door by now.

"You couldn't have missed her." A grin pops back up on his face. "She was the center of attention."

The moment he says those words I'm immediately aware of the woman he's talking about. "That's Petra. Petra Monroe." Petra stole the audience in any room she walked in to. She was captivating and I wasn't surprised that she'd be the one he was fixated on.

"Have you got a number for her?" he asks the question so easily.

I'm more than slightly tempted to bring up the woman he arrived and left with but I don't know her name. Besides, what he does and who he chooses to do it with is none of my business. Although I have to admit I'm envious of any woman who gets to do anything beyond talking with him. "I don't," I lie. "I'm sure her husband has it. You can ask him. He's Eric Monroe."

"The senator?" he asks bluntly.

"One in the same." I brush past him with the hope that he'll follow my lead. I reach to open the heavy oak door of my parent's townhouse. "If that was all, it's getting late."

He glances at the silver wristwatch he's wearing. "The night is still young."

I know it must be nearing three by now. "I have an early morning and I'd like to get to bed." I motion with my arm towards the street where a car is idling. "Your ride awaits."

"What are you going to be doing so early on a Saturday?" He's standing in front of me now. His presence is imposing. It's not just his height, which is near six feet. It's the raw charisma that is oozing from him. I wonder briefly what it would feel like to just reach out and kiss him.

I sigh heavily. "I have to be at work in a few hours."

The corner of his brow cocks upwards. "You have a job?" he spits the question out. He clearly isn't trying to mask the surprise in it.

"Yes and I'm very tired." I gently start to close the door but it resists once it hits his shoulder.

"You're a Harvard student, aren't you? And your parents obviously aren't pinching pennies." The way he casually gestures around us irks me.

"What does that mean?" I'm annoyed and I hope he can

pick up the subtle clue I'm trying to hit him over the head with.

"You don't *have* to work, do you?" It's obvious by the way he stresses the word '*have*' that he thinks I'm a trust fund baby. I am but that's not his business and besides he can't be that much older than I am and that Rolex on his wrist suggests that his daddy is probably paying his way.

I wrinkle my brow as I search for the right words to politely tell him to fuck off. My mother left me in charge of her charity dinner and if I piss off someone who might have written her a nice big check I'll never hear the end of it. "It's late and my work isn't really your concern." I know that sounds snappy but I'm too tired to care what he thinks.

"Where do you work?" He stands his ground and I feel a slight chill course through me as the cool night air creeps through the open door.

"At Star Bistro." I cringe when the words leap from my lips. Why am I telling him this? "I really need to get to sleep."

"You're a barista?" he asks, looking baffled.

"You say it like it's a bad thing." I'm losing my patience quickly. Maybe his date contributed to the charity and he was only arm candy. I pull my fingers to my lips to cover my smile at the thought of that.

"Well…no…it's just that…" his voice trails. "It's just that I assumed…"

"I'm going to bed." I push on the door with both hands now forcing him to step onto the porch. "Good luck with Petra."

I hear him mumbling through the crack of the door as I slam it shut and lock it. Any lasting fantasy I had about him just evaporated into thin air.

CHAPTER TWO

"YOU SAID WHAT?" SMALL PELLETS OF COFFEE COME shooting out with the words from my best friend's mouth.

"Thanks for the shower, jerk." I laugh as I pull a napkin across the nameplate on my chest. "I thought he wanted to sleep with me." I wince knowing that she's never going to let this go.

"Christ, Sadie," she shrieks. "Why would you think that?"

"Um…thanks." I playfully shrug my shoulders. "I mean I know I'm no Alexa Jackson, but the way he said it. I just thought he was talking about seducing me."

"Don't beat yourself up." She runs her hand down my back. "You're gorgeous, Sadie. I didn't mean it like that."

"I'm not." I laugh. "I made such a fool of myself."

I watch the expression on her face change from glee to pity. I hate that. Alexa has been my best friend since grade school. She was there when I was sick and after my heart transplant. She was always the pretty one and I've always been the smart one. It's just how it's worked. I've watched her date every boy I've ever had a crush on. How could I blame any of them? She's beautiful. She has everything I've always wanted. The long blonde hair, the beautiful blue eyes, curves in all the right places and a body that is whole. It's flawless.

My mousy brown hair, big brown eyes and thin frame have always paled in comparison to her. The only part of my life when I haven't felt insecure in her shadow is in school. It's where I belong. It's where I can hide away from the world.

"I think we had too much champagne last night." She reaches to level the nameplate on my shirt. "You weren't thinking clearly."

"I'll go with that." I push my elbow into her side. "It's almost seven. Time to put on a happy face and serve some coffee."

She rolls her eyes as she adjusts the plain white dress shirt that she's wearing. That along with black pants and a red apron is our required uniform at Star Bistro. I giggle as she unbuttons the shirt so her cleavage is just barely visible.

"You're such a tease," I say as I walk past her into the already bustling bistro.

"HE'S HERE. Oh my fucking god, he is here," Alexa hisses into my ear as I'm trying to take the order of a man with a very thick Russian accent.

"So that's a large, quad, half-sweet, caramel macchiato?" I repeat back hoping that this time I've finally got his order right. The dozen people standing behind him waiting for their java fix don't look too amused by my lack of translation skills.

"Yeah, yeah." The burly Russian exclaims as he claps his hands. "You right!"

I smile as I take the cash he offers. I ring it through and

drop the remaining few cents into the tip jar at the edge of the counter.

"Sadie," Alexa pulls me to the side as she whispers my name. "The guy. That guy. He's here."

"Good for him." I can't focus on what she's saying. Josephine, our manager, is staring a hole through both of us right now. I may not need the job, as Hunter Reynolds pointed out last night, but I love this job. I can't lose it.

"Not now." I pull on Alexa's apron to get her attention. "We're so backed up. Whoever he is, you can talk to him on your break."

"Pay attention." She grabs both of my shoulders and gives me the slightest shake. "That guy. The one you thought wanted to fuck you in the coat closet. He's here."

I stare at her lips. Is she saying that Hunter is here? He's in the bistro? Now? I search her face for some clarification but she's fixated on something past my shoulder. I'm frozen. I can't turn around.

"Shit. He's waving to me." She drops her hands and I get a glimpse of her fingers wafting through the air next to my head.

"I feel sick," I whisper. If I have to be subjected to Hunter Reynolds picking up my best friend, I'm going to hide in the back room with the ground coffee and paper cups for eternity. When did my life become this humiliating?

"He's motioning for you to turn around." There's confusion woven into her words. Why wouldn't she be confused? She looks like she just stepped off a fashion week runway show for baristas and I look like I've been dragged under a truck. I have spilled milk, a combination of espresso and cocoa and something that resembles chewing gum stuck to the front of my apron.

"I can't." I try to barrel my way past her to the refuge of

the office at the back of the bistro. "I need to help Josephine do up next week's schedule."

"Alexa." As if on cue, Josephine's shrill voice carries over the buzz of the customers. "Take an order."

"Fine," Alexa barks back. I cringe when I see the expression on our manager's face. I've saved Alexa's ass from being fired so many times I've lost track and if she doesn't change her attitude soon, I'll be working here without her.

"Excuse me, Sadie." I hear his deep voice calling out from behind me. I know this is the moment when I'm supposed to turn around and act all nonchalant about the fact that he's in the middle of the bistro I work at. Given the fact that it's just shy of eight o'clock on a Saturday morning and I only saw him a few hours ago, I'm guessing that he has an ulterior motive. It's likely he's looking for the number of the redhead who was bartending last night or maybe that blonde who was handing out canapés before dinner.

I turn slowly, trying in vain to wipe off my apron. He's standing near the counter, his left hip leaning against it. He's wearing a pair of jeans, a light blue dress shirt and a navy suit jacket. I drink him in. He's more gorgeous than he was last night, if that's even possible. The way his hair is falling casually onto his forehead gives him a boyish charm. The sharpness of his formal look has been replaced with a softness that makes him even more stunning.

"Sadie, it's me. Hunter Reynolds," he says with a grin.

I nod. Of course I know his name. I searched for it online after he left last night but what little I found didn't amount to much. He's elusive and that makes him even that much more appealing. "Yes," I whisper.

"Can you talk for a minute?" he calls over the hum of the crowded space.

I shake my head as I look at the crowd of people waiting to place orders. The line is out the door now. Working at the busiest bistro in downtown Boston certainly had its perks. You couldn't beat the tips and the steady throngs of people passing through meant each shift flew by. "I don't have a break until ten thirty."

He glances at his watch. "I'll just wait."

I scowl at the thought of him waiting more than two hours in this crowd just to talk to me. I shake my head. "No. That's okay. Did you need someone's number?" I walk over to where he's standing. Maybe if I just give him what he wants he'll leave and I can get my heart beat back under control. How can any man possibly be as beautiful as he is?

"Someone's number?" He smiles sheepishly. "What do you mean?"

"You're looking for a woman's number, right?" I glance over my shoulder at Josephine. She's standing right behind Alexa watching her every move. I sigh. I'm grateful for the gentle reprieve.

"What woman?" He throws the question back with a quizzed look.

"Petra's replacement," I offer. "I assume you're here to get a number from someone else you met last night."

His eyes wander over my face while he contemplates my words. "I'm not looking for any numbers." He gazes down at the counter before he continues, "I just wanted a few minutes to talk to you."

"To me?" I almost scream the words. Dammit. I have to temper my reactions to him. He may be the best looking man I've ever met but I can't keep acting like an inexperienced fool when he talks to me.

"I'll order a coffee and wait." He throws a smile over my shoulder. I assume it's in the direction of Josephine. She may actually be the only person alive his charm won't work on. He quickly darts his gaze back to me. "Ten thirty it is."

I watch him walk to the back of the line as I pull in a deep breath. Hunter Reynolds is going to sit in this crowded, over heated bistro for more than two hours just so he can talk to me. I wish I had a clean apron.

CHAPTER THREE

"CAN I GET YOU ANOTHER CUP OF COFFEE?" I REACH FOR THE empty, stained paper cup sitting in front of him on the small circular table.

"No." He chuckles as he waves his hand over the rim. "Three cups is my limit for the morning."

I nod silently as I place a chilled water bottle on the table before taking a seat across from him.

"I wanted to apologize." He leans just a touch forward in his chair so his elbow rests on the table. "I didn't handle myself very well when I came back to your place last night."

I can feel Alexa's eyes burning a hole in my back. The quick pep talk she gave me in the storage room before my break only made me more nervous. Her advice for flirting left me laughing in her face. I can't think about that now or I'm going to start giggling and Hunter is going to think I'm more of a childish brat than he already does.

"I misinterpreted what you said," I offer. I still feel embarrassed over assuming he was talking about seducing me.

"I'm not usually such an asshole." A thin grin slides across his lips.

I smirk. "I would call you more of a dick than an asshole."

He throws his head back in laughter. I stare at the shape of his jaw and the soft stubble that is covering it. None of the boys I've dated in school have been anything like him. He's different. Maybe it's his confidence or maybe it's just that fact that he knows how to carry himself. Whatever it is, it feels like a magnet that is pulling me into him.

"That's fair." He picks up the paper cup and lightly taps it against the table. "I shouldn't have come back that late and I sure as hell shouldn't have been a *dick* about your work."

The way he emphasizes the word dick makes me smile. "You were hot for Petra," I say casually.

His eyebrows shoot up and a smile once again floods his face. "I was?"

"You must have been." I shrug my shoulders while I try to stifle in a giggle. "Why else would you come back in the middle of the night to get her number?"

"I lost track of time?" He poses it as a question.

"Wrong answer," I tease.

"I was in the neighborhood?" He runs his tongue along his lower lip and I almost melt.

"Strike two," I whisper.

"I'm a dick?" He playfully punches his fist lightly on the table.

"We have a winner." I giggle before taking a small sip of water from the bottle.

"I came to apologize." His voice has taken on a more serious tone. "It was wrong of me to show up at the door that late and I had no right to ask about where you worked."

I'm surprised. I'm sure that he can tell by my silence and the stunned look on my face. This guy sitting across the small table from me isn't the same guy I was talking to a few hours ago in my parent's house. This man seems genuine and the charm has slipped into the background.

"Apology accepted." I glance at the clock on the wall to the right. "I need to get back to work."

I feel his hand reach for mine as I start to stand. The electricity that flows from him into me startles me. I look directly into his eyes to see if he feels anything and I see something that I just can't place there.

"Wait," he says quietly. "Maybe we can grab a coffee or lunch sometime."

I sit back down in silence. I can't process what he just said. I don't want to humiliate myself again by misjudging his words.

"I thought it would be good to learn more about your mother's charity." He drops my hand. "I was impressed by what I heard last night and I'd like to know more."

I breathe in a heavy sigh. "My mom would be the best person for you to talk to about that. She's away in Europe right now but if you give me your card I can have her call you."

"Can't you tell me more?" He cocks his head to the side.

"I guess," I say dispassionately. Although my mother started her charitable endeavours when I was ill, I've never been directly involved with it. Last night I was pushed into hosting her dinner because she had scurried off to Europe with my father to put out another fire started by my older brother, Dylan.

"What about later today?" He stands as he picks up the empty paper cup.

"I have plans." I push myself from the chair.

"Plans?" he questions.

I wish I could read him better. He's being almost as pushy

as he was last night. "A birthday dinner for a friend," I cautiously offer.

"A boyfriend?"

The question startles me. Why is he asking me if I have a boyfriend? That is what he's asking, isn't it? Maybe he means a friend who is a boy? It's obvious that he sees me as a girl and not a woman.

"A friend." I push back. "I need to get back to work. If you drop by the house late next week my mother will be back and she'll be more than happy to tell you all about her charity work."

He doesn't say anything. He just nods as I turn and walk back towards the counter and Alexa's grinning face.

CHAPTER FOUR

"HE COULD BE YOUR SUMMER FLING." ALEXA LOOKS AT ME IN the mirror. "It'll be all hot and heavy until you have to go back to school, then you go your separate ways."

"You must be hard of hearing," I say as I point at my ears. "He's not interested in me. He wants to know more about my mom's charity."

She spins around so she's facing me now. I don't move from my place on my bed. She's almost ready for Kayla's birthday dinner and I don't even have the energy to take a shower. I'm still tired from last night and spending the evening with a bunch of catty girls from Alexa's sorority doesn't seem that appealing at this moment.

"Get up lazy bones." She pushes on my leg with her hand. "We need to be there in forty five."

"When have we ever gotten anywhere on time?" I tease as I sit on the edge of the bed. "You can't make a grand entrance if we get there early."

"Smart Sadie to the rescue." She smirks before continuing, "I'm going to finish with my makeup. Get in that shower."

I begrudgingly do as I'm told and within the hour I'm dressed in a shimmering, short metallic brown dress, nude heels and I've pinned my hair up into a messy upsweep. Unlike Alexa, I opt for minimal makeup. She's always on display and I'd much rather fade into the background. I smile as she walks back into my bedroom. The pink dress she's wearing is cut almost to her navel. The black very high heels she's chosen to wear look impossible to walk in but she breezes through the room with ease.

"I called a cab." She scans the room looking for her purse. "Let's go."

I follow her out of the house and into the waiting taxi. I don't say a word as I watch her expertly palm her way through countless messages on her phone.

"I'm going to meet up with Danny after we're done with the dinner," she says casually as she tosses her smartphone back into her purse. "I need to get laid."

I laugh out loud at her boldness. I envy it but I've never told her that. She's the same age as I am and has had more lovers than I can count. I've only had two and both were quick to leave my life after we had sex. My last boyfriend, Will, told me he loved me but that all changed after we made love. He broke up with me in a text the following day. Alexa has it all figured out. She's the one fucking and then leaving. I don't know how she does it, but she seems happy. Judging by the wide grin on her face at this moment, Danny must be the best of the best.

"I don't remember you mentioning Danny before." I try to stifle a chuckle. I don't remember any of the names of the guys she sleeps with.

"He's new." She gazes out the window. "I met him at a club two weeks ago. He fucked me in his car. Christ his cock is huge. I need that tonight."

I shake my head and don't respond. I'm actually not sure what I could possibly say after that.

"We're here." She throws a few bills through the small window in the glass divide between the driver and us. "Get out, Sadie."

I feel her hand pushing my leg towards the door so I open it and step out into the warm night air. "We're having dinner here?" I glance towards the long line of people awaiting entry into Axel. "H...how?" I stumble over the word. This is *the* restaurant in Boston at the moment. Everyone wants a table here.

"Kayla knows someone who knows someone." She twists her hips so she can pull down the hem of her dress. "Let's get inside."

I follow her lead and we enter a beautifully decorated space. I look around the room breathing in the exquisite ambiance. There are groups of people all huddled together around small tables, enjoying glasses of wine and plates of food that look like works of art. This is definitely going to be a treat.

"This way, ladies." The hostess hesitates on the word ladies and I wonder instantly if it's a cheap barb at the way Alexa is dressed. I can't blame the woman for judging her. She does look a little underdressed for the occasion.

"Alexa, Sadie." Kayla bounces to her feet, almost falling over in the process.

I cringe as I realize she's already a bit tipsy. "Happy birth-day." I reach to give her two air kisses, one on each cheek. The girls in Alexa's sorority have never tried to veil the fact that they don't like outsiders. I didn't pledge so I've always gotten the brush off whenever we hang out with them.

"Kayla," Alexa shrieks her name loud enough that several people at the tables near us crane their necks to see what's going on. "You look gorgeous." I recognize the slight edge of sarcasm in my best friend's voice. I vaguely remember a few days last summer when Kayla was the enemy because she was dating someone Alexa wanted. I smile knowing I'll never be pulled into that.

I sit down and pretend to listen to their conversations. A waiter appears and takes my drink order. If I'm going to get through a few hours with this bunch I'll need something stronger than sparkling water so I order a dirty martini. I heave a heavy sigh of relief when he doesn't ask to see some identification. I get carded so often I'm shocked when it actually doesn't happen.

"I'd do him in a heartbeat." Kayla's slurred announcement perks up everyone at the table and we all instantaneously follow the path of her index finger as it waves in the air towards the restaurant's entrance. "Have you ever seen anyone as hot as that?"

I careen my neck trying to gaze past a group of women who are gathered a few feet away. I'm greeted by the sight of a gorgeous man. He's tall. His brown hair is pushed back from his face revealing a strong jawline and deep brown eyes. He glances briefly in our direction before his gaze is pulled behind him.

"I should go talk to him." Alexa pushes herself into a standing position, her breasts almost spilling out of her dress. "Fuck Danny. I'm going to fuck that." She waves her half full wine glass in the direction of the entrance. She shrieks when the wine comes spilling out, splashing onto the table and her dress.

I grimace at the sight of her standing there so disheveled. I try to catch her eye to motion for her to sit back down but it's to no avail. Mr. Gorgeous from the front door is now walking in our direction.

"Holy shit, he's coming over," Christie, one of Kayla's friends tries to whisper but her tone is so loud that I'm sure everyone waiting outside the front door can hear her.

I hang my head down focusing on the napkin sitting in my lap. I don't want to be a party to watching these women trip all over each other trying to get that man's attention. Maybe I can pretend to go to the ladies' room and I can bolt out the door and catch a cab home. I debate the move as I hear the frantic voices of Alexa, Kayla and their friends arguing over who gets to go home with him.

Suddenly, they all quiet. There are faint whispers and I know that he must be standing at the table. "Sadie? Sadie Lockwood?" A deep voice breaks through the low hum in the room.

I pull my gaze up to see Hunter Reynolds standing right next to Mr. Gorgeous.

CHAPTER FIVE

I CAN FEEL EVERYONE'S EYES ON ME AS I STRUGGLE TO respond. "Hey," I say. Hey? Really? That's all I can come up with? All of these girls I've secretly envied for years are now staring at me because one of the two hot guys standing in front of our table actually knows me.

"Sadie. I didn't know you'd be here." His eyes scan the faces of the other girls before they settle on me again. "Which of these lovely ladies is celebrating her birthday?"

"That's me." Kayla bounces from her seat. Her hand pops out and reaches towards Hunter. I have no idea whether she's about to shake his hand or grab his crotch.

"Happy birthday to you." Hunter takes her hand in his and brings it gently to his lips.

Kayla giggles and flashes us all a look that screams *this one is mine.*

"Sadie, aren't you going to introduce us to your friends?" Christie snarls.

I shake my head slightly at the irony of the situation. How did I suddenly become the one with hot male friends? What alternate universe existed inside Axel? It's no wonder everyone is scrambling to get a table here.

"This is Hunter Reynolds." I motion towards him. "And this is…" my voice trails. I have no idea who the man with Hunter is.

"Jax Walker," Hunter interjects. "He's a business associate from Manhattan and an old friend."

Jax nods and locks eyes with me. "It's great to meet you, Sadie." His voice is warm and calm.

"You could join us." Alexa is standing now too. "We can make room." She motions for all of us to scoot our chairs over. The other girls gleefully comply and I'm suddenly shoulder-to-shoulder with two very ample chested friends of Kayla's.

"Thanks for the invitation." Hunter motions for a waiter. "But we've got some business to discuss."

"What is it, Mr. Reynolds?" The waiter taps his foot anxiously. "What do you need?"

"Whatever these beautiful women want is on me." He waves his hand over the lot of us.

"That's kind of you." Kayla reaches for him. I think she's about to kiss him. I stare in stunned silence as Jax steps aside to give Kayla uninhibited access to Hunter. The grin on his face mirrors the one on mine.

"Any friend of Sadie's is a friend of mine." He skillfully steps aside skirting Kayla's roaming lips. "Now, if you'll excuse us. We have business to discuss."

I swear I hear Kayla moan in utter disappointment as they both turn to leave.

"Sadie." Hunter stops and turns back around. His eyes latch onto mine. "Come see me at my table before you leave."

I nod and smile. The sheer delight of imagining what

these girls are thinking is going on between Hunter and me has given me a huge appetite.

"You heard the man. It's on him." I reach one of the menus in the center of the table. "Let's eat."

CHAPTER SIX

"THAT WAS INCREDIBLY GENEROUS OF YOU," I SAY OVER MY shoulder as Hunter pulls out a chair at his table for me to sit in. "Thank you for that."

"It was my pleasure." He pats my hand as he sits down next to me.

"It was also unnecessary." I frown. "You barely know me and you don't know Kayla at all."

"I know you're college students," he says with a grin. "I remember my limited budget back then. Did you enjoy your dinner?"

"It was delicious," I say the words with a sigh. "It may be the best food I've ever had in Boston."

"I'd agree with that." Jax pushes the plate containing the remnants of his dinner away from him. "Hunter tells me you're a student at Harvard."

"I am." I feel a bit flushed from the second dirty martini I had with my dinner. "It's a great school."

"She's going to be a doctor," Hunter states boldly.

I turn my head to look at him. How does he know that?

Someone at the party last night must have told him. I blush slightly knowing that he was curious enough to ask about me.

"What do you do?" I focus my gaze back on Jax. I can't look at Hunter right now. The martinis, combined with the fact that he knows more about me than I realized has me worried that I'm going to misread him again and make a fool of myself.

"I work with my girlfriend, Ivy, right now." His face lights up as he smiles. "She's a jewelry designer." He reaches into the pocket of his suit jacket to retrieve a business card.

I run my hand over the embossed lettering. *Whispers of Grace* it says along with an address in Manhattan. "That must be very exciting," I mumble. "I'm not creative at all."

"You're just a genius." Hunter's voice is low and composed.

"That's not true," I chuckle. "I'm just a good student."

"It is exciting," Jax interjects. I'm grateful for the escape from Hunter's unexpected compliments. "I'm unsettled though. I've got some other irons in the fire. Some with this guy." He nods in Hunter's direction and I suddenly realize that I know absolutely nothing about what he does for a living.

"What kinds of irons?" I direct my question at Jax who is throwing Hunter a quizzed look. It's the same look I shoot at Alexa when I don't want her revealing my entire life story to someone.

"Restaurant irons." Hunter straightens in his chair. "I do consultations for new restaurants."

Jax chuckles and I toss my gaze in his direction. He takes a long drink from his wine glass and darts his eyes around the room, avoiding mine.

"Consultations? What does that mean?" I know I don't

sound worldly but now I'm curious about what exactly Hunter does with his time. "You help new restaurateurs?"

"Yeah. Exactly." Hunter nods. "I help them before they open."

"How did you get involved in that?" I'm going to push the issue. He's a mystery and any tidbit of information I can gleam from him or his friend is a jewel.

He shoots his eyes across the table towards Jax before he answers. "My dad owns a few restaurants. I grew up in the business. I know what works and what doesn't. It's a good fit for me."

"That makes sense," I whisper. "Did you help with this restaurant?"

They laugh in unison and I immediately feel like the outsider in an inside joke. Why am I even having this discussion with him? How did I end up sitting at his table?

"Not this one. No," Hunter tries to regain his composure as he answers.

I'm overcome with uncertainty and I realize that this is my cue to leave. I've thanked him for the dinner and met his friend so it's time for me to make my timely exit. My bed is beckoning me anyways. It's been a very long couple of days.

"I'm going to say goodnight now." I stand to leave, reaching for my purse on the table. "It was great meeting you, Jax." I offer my hand and he takes it gently in his.

"It was great, Sadie." He smiles. "If you're ever in Manhattan stop by Ivy's store and say hi."

"Definitely," I say as I run my thumb over the card. I can't recall the last time I was in New York or anywhere other than Boston. Since I've started school, studying and working has been my entire life. Adventures aren't a part of the picture at this point.

"I'll get you home." Hunter reaches for his suit jacket,

which he lazily shrugged off his shoulders during dinner. "You shouldn't be wandering the streets alone at night."

I furrow my brow. "Wandering the streets?" I ask. "I'm going to walk out the front door, get in a cab and go home." I turn to leave.

"I'll take you." The insistent tone of his voice causes me to stop in my tracks.

"That's silly," I sigh. "Stay here and visit with your friend." I nod towards Jax who is now leaning back in his chair listening to our game of verbal tennis across the table.

"We'll catch up tomorrow?" Hunter doesn't wait for Jax's response as he takes my elbow guiding me towards the restaurant's entrance. Why do I feel as though this is an evening I'm not soon going to forget?

CHAPTER SEVEN

"WAIT HERE FOR ME JOE." HUNTER TELLS THE DRIVER AS WE pull up to the curb in front of my parent's townhouse. "I won't be long."

I feel disappointed by his words even though I knew that he'd likely drop me off before he made his way into the bed of another woman. Why do I keep torturing myself into wanting him when he's made it clear he views me as some helpless waif who can't take care of herself?

"I can make it to the door myself." I open the car door and dart my right leg out. "Thank you for the ride."

"Don't move." Hunter taps my forearm as he jumps out of the car and races around to my side. I smile as he holds out his hand, helping me exit onto the sidewalk.

"How gallant are you?" I tease.

I'm rewarded with a bright smile and it catches my breath. He really is handsome. Being this close to him makes me realize just how powerful an attractive and confident man can be. The boys I've dated couldn't measure up to him in any way.

"I better get inside." I break free from his gaze to fumble

through my purse for my keys. "Thank you again for dinner and for the ride home."

I turn to walk up the concrete steps towards the front door and I sense that he's right behind me. I cannot only smell the sweetness of his cologne but I can hear his measured breathing. Everything about him is appealing. I haven't touched myself in so long but tonight I'm going to find my release while I think about him. I curse inwardly at myself. Why am I thinking about that right at this second when the man is not more than a few inches behind me? I have to calm down. I have to stop thinking about him that way.

"You want to kiss me, don't you?" His breath trails across my neck as I reach the door.

I drop the keys in response. I know I didn't hear that. I wanted to hear that. He must be on his phone making a booty call. That has to be it. Don't overreact Sadie. Don't make a fool of yourself again like you did last night.

I crouch in silence to pick up the keys in the dim light. I hold my breath waiting for him to continue his conversation but I'm greeted with barren stillness. All I can hear is a dog barking somewhere in the distance and the shrill screech of a car alarm. I raise myself back to my feet slowly and try to push the key into the lock to no avail.

"Sadie." I can feel him pressed against me now. His body is strong, the weight of it pushing against my back. I want to feel more of him. I want to know what it feels like to feel his hardness pressed against me.

"Yes?" I ask in a hushed tone as I finally push the key into the lock and turn it.

"Turn around," he commands. His breath flows across my neck as his hand lightly grazes my waist.

I close my eyes and pull the cool night air into my lungs. This isn't really happening. It can't be happening to me.

"Do you have a boyfriend?" He leans in closer as the words leave his lips.

I don't speak. I only shake my head from side-to-side.

I flinch as his index finger finds my chin. "Do you have a lover?"

A pink blush races through my skin. I've never had a lover. I've made love but those men weren't lovers. "No," I murmur under my breath.

"No?" he questions as his lips hover over mine.

"No." I repeat back wanting to grab the back of his head with my hand so I can taste his breath.

"Have you ever had a lover?" The hand on my waist traces a path from my hipbone down my thigh. I'm already wet. My panties are so wet just from being this close to him. I can't let him feel me there.

"Yes." I push back into the door breaking the contact between his hand and my leg.

He counters by taking a step closer to me. I can sense the strength of his chest pressed against mine. He's aroused. I can feel his hardness through his pants. I want to push the door open and pull him into my bed and into my body.

"You want to kiss me, don't you?" His lips are so close to mine. All I have to do is lean forward and claim them with my own.

"I need to go inside." I reach back with my right hand and clench the doorknob.

His hand instinctively covers mine. "You're scared of me." His tone is stern and composed.

"I'm not." I shake my head as I try to turn my hand to no avail. "I'm not scared."

"I'm going to kiss you." I jolt when I feel his lips brush briefly against mine. "And I'm going to have you in my bed."

"No," I whisper knowing that the word betrays what my body is feeling. "You're not."

"I will." He pushes his body closer to mine and I can feel the outline of his cock. It's large. It's hard. It's all I want. "If not tonight, soon."

I shiver as I try to push myself further away from him. The resistance of the door is forcing my body further into his. "No," I repeat. "I can't."

"You can't?" I feel a small chuckle course through him. "Or you won't?"

"I can't," I say as I finally manage the strength to twist the doorknob in my hand. I stumble backwards as the door swings open. "I can't."

"Sadie." He reaches out to grab me as I almost tumble off my heels. "Stop. Wait."

"I'm not like all of them." My throat tightens as I speak. "I don't do that."

"Sadie." His voice is softer now. I know he wants me to look at him. I can't. I won't.

"I don't. Go find someone else," I say quietly as I pull free of his hand and slam the door.

CHAPTER EIGHT

"TELL ME YOU'RE FUCKING KIDDING ME." ALEXA POPS A piece of orange into her mouth.

"Don't swear." I wave my index finger in the air across the dining room table. "Maria hates swearing."

"Newsflash, Maria," she screams in the direction of the kitchen. "Sadie is an adult now."

"Shut up," I bark back at her. "Maria is an angel. Don't tease her like that."

"Whatever." She picks up a strawberry and dips it in the yogurt cup on her plate before she eats it. "You're saying that Hunter Reynolds wants to do you?"

"I guess?" I shrug my shoulders.

"You guess?" She waves her fork in the air. "There is no guessing, Sadie. Did the man say he wants to fuck you or not?"

"He said he wants me in his bed," I say slowly wanting to repeat what Hunter said word-for-word.

"Holy shit." She playfully fans herself. "He's so hot and he wants you. When are you going to do him?"

"Never," I spit back at her. I'm slightly annoyed that

she's not seeing the magnitude of what happened to me last night. Why can't she understand the emotional pain I'm in? A man, a real man finally wants me and it's more than likely that he's interested in nothing beyond me warming his bed for a night before he moves onto someone else. Besides that fact, the moment he'd get a glimpse of the enormous scar on my chest, he'd be pushing me out the door.

"What?" She's on her feet now. "Are you crazy? Men like that don't come along every day?"

I close my eyes as I work to steel my breath. "Alexa, you know I can't sleep with him." I tilt my head as I look at her lowering herself back into her chair.

"Don't say that." She reaches across the table to cradle my hand in hers. "Not all men are going to run away screaming because you have a scar, Sadie."

I smile at her attempt to reassure me. She's the only person who knows how things ended with Will and I. She held me when I cried over his rejection. She knows exactly how I feel about my scar. "I can't risk it again."

"You don't know how he'll react until he sees it."

The level of masked reassurance in her tone is matched only by the doubt in my mind. "He's gorgeous. He can have any woman he wants. He's not going to want me anymore if he sees the scar."

"I think you're selling yourself short." She presses on, "I'd give him a chance. You've got nothing to lose."

She's wrong and I want to point it out to her. I have every-thing to lose. I'm on track right now to fulfill my dreams. I want to honor the person whose heart is beating in my chest. I can't do that if I'm sleeping with a random guy. My heart gets too invested and I'll spend weeks crying about him when he moves on to the next girl. I won't risk that.

"Give him a chance." She covers another piece of strawberry in yogurt. "If you don't, I might," she teases.

"Speaking of you, how was Danny?" I need a change in subject and her sexual escapades last night are just what she needs to focus on to get her mind off me and Hunter.

"Not like I remember him." She pushes her empty plate to the corner of the table. "I'd give him a D minus."

I burst out laughing. "That's why you're studying to be a teacher. You've got that grading thing locked up tight."

She giggles so hard so almost spits out the orange juice she just sipped. "Funny for you. Not funny for me. No orgasm for Alexa last night."

I laugh even harder as Maria winces at that statement as she walks into the room.

———

"YOU'RE A LIFESAVER, SADIE." Josephine pulls her arm around my shoulder. "Thanks for coming in on such short notice."

"It's not a problem," I lie. It was a problem. I had planned on staying in this dreary Sunday evening and watching a movie. When Alexa bailed on her shift after calling another guy in her quest for sexual fulfillment, I was the go-to gal. I couldn't say no when she asked me to cover for her. I could never say no to her. That's what best friends were for.

"It's been pretty quiet all day." She grabs her purse from beneath the counter before walking towards the entrance. "Lock up and I guess I'll see you tomorrow?"

"Bright and early," I call to her as the glass door shuts behind her.

I spend the next hours busying myself with making beverages for the few customers who do stream in amid the rainstorm that is currently pelting the city. Between that and finishing up next week's schedule, time flies and soon it's just fifteen short minutes until closing.

"I'll have a mocha latte." I recognize the smooth tone of his voice before I turn around to face him.

"Hunter," I whisper his name as I punch in the order. He hands me a twenty dollar bill and I make change, never once looking up to meet his gaze.

"Keep it." He motions with his hand towards the tip jar and I push the few bills and coins into it before turning to make his order. We stand in silence while I take my time preparing the latte, hoping that he'll be taking it to go. I need him to walk out of here as soon as I hand him the paper cup.

"Here you go." I try to sound gleeful. Instead it translates to overly enthusiastic which makes me feel even more humiliation.

"You're almost done, right?" I catch a glimpse of him gazing at his watch out of the corner of my eye.

"I need to clean up after closing." It's not a lie. I do have a few minutes of tidying before I can take off. Tonight, I may stretch that to a few hours to avoid him.

"I'll wait." He settles into one of the empty booths that overlooks the parking lot.

"No customers inside after closing." I walk past him to hold open the front door.

He stands and walks quietly to the door. "I'll be in my car." He motions towards the almost empty lot at a sleek, black Mercedes C Class. "I'll drive you home."

"No." I shake my head slightly. "I'll be here for a bit. Maybe we can talk another day?"

"I'll be in my car," he repeats without emotion as he bolts into the rain.

I lock the door behind him and immediately reach for my

phone. I text Alexa telling her it's an emergency and I need her advice pronto. I get to work cleaning the counters and tables. I store all the perishables in the refrigerator in the back and prep everything that is needed for me when I arrive back for my usual brisk Monday morning shift. I glance at my phone and there's no response. "Dammit," I whisper under my breath. In a few minutes I'm going to be sitting in Hunter Reynold's car without a clue about what to do.

CHAPTER NINE

I PULL THE HEAVY GLASS DOOR SHUT AS I IMMEDIATELY FEEL the rain pelting down on me. The awning over the shop is doing very little to protect me from the downpour. I'm going to look like a pathetic drowned rat before I even get to his car.

I turn towards the lot and I almost run face first into his chest. He's raced over to get me, an umbrella above us. I smile at the sweet gesture as I allow him to guide me through the torrent and into the dry tranquility of his car.

"That's a lot of rain," he mumbles as he closes the car door behind him after helping me settle into my seat next to him.

"Yes," I offer. I feel my heart racing. Alexa's words taunting me to just go for it and sleep with Hunter are ringing in my ears. Maybe she's right. Looking at him now, with moisture pooling on his top lip, his hair disheveled and his skin glistening, I'm so tempted.

"What happened last night?" He doesn't waste any time jumping into the subject of the elephant in the room or in our case, the car.

"I'm not interested in a one night stand," I say the words calmly, trying to temper my racing pulse.

"Do you think that's what I want?" he asks. His eyebrow pops up in unison with the question.

"I think that's what you generally do." I want to be diplomatic but he was the one who showed up on my doorstep the other night looking for the number of a woman he just met a few hours earlier.

"Why would you think that?"

"You wanted Petra's number after the party." I gaze out the window, playing the next words I want to say over and over in my mind. They have to come out right. "I assume it was so you two could hook up."

"She's beautiful." His words bite. It's an obvious statement but one I don't need to hear.

"Exactly," I counter. "You do that, don't you? Have sex with one beautiful woman after another?"

"I try to get some sleep in between." He laughs.

I cringe. He didn't disagree with the statement. "That's not what my life is about," I say quietly.

"What is your life about?" He rests his hand on my knee and I flinch from the contact.

"School and work," I blurt out. "Those things are what I care about."

"You're on semester break right now." His hand traces a faint path along my knee.

I feel my breathing stall at his touch. "Why are you doing this? I'm not your type."

His hand drops to the seat. I can hear his breathing change. "What's my type?"

"Petra. Alexa. Someone beautiful. Not me." I look at his face. I want him to see that I'm serious. I know I'm not the type of woman he generally pursues.

"You're very beautiful." He meets my gaze and I see something within his eyes. "You're different."

"I don't want to be another conquest." I reach for the handle of the door. "Men like you don't pay attention to girls like me."

"What does that mean?" His eyes are glued to my hand. I jump slightly when I hear the unmistakable click of the car doors locking.

I try desperately to mask the panic I feel. "Please don't lock the doors," I whisper. "I don't even know you."

I catch my breath again when I hear the doors unlock.

"What do you want to know about me?" He pulls his hand away from my knee and leans back in his seat so he's almost facing me directly.

"Anything," I murmur. "I don't know anything about you."

"I'm twenty-six. I split my time between Boston and New York." He sighs before he continues, "I travel way more than I'd like for my job. I work too much."

I smile at the information. He's twenty-six. He's five years older than me. He seems so much older. Maybe I just feel that much younger than him because he's different than any other man I've ever been around. He's cultured, he's sophisticated and he's now showing me a side of him I didn't realize was there before.

"Tell me more about you." He lightly touches my hand.

I don't pull back. I adore his touch. I like the way it makes me feel inside. "You know a lot about me already." I lift the corner of my mouth in a sly smile. "I'm twenty-one. I go to work and school."

"That's it?" He cups his hand over mine now. "No exciting stories of your past to share."

I instinctively reach for my chest with my other hand. It's

a reflex response when I feel I'm exposing too much. My scar reminds me that I have to be protective of myself and of the person who gave me my life back. "Nothing really," I whisper.

"Why do I scare you?" His words are gentle. The tone of his voice controlled. "You were shaking last night when I wanted to kiss you."

I hold my breath for a second. "I've never been with anyone like you."

"Anyone like me?" he asks as he leans closer to me now.

"Yes." I stare at him, trying to pull some understanding from inside of him. "I'm not very experienced."

"You don't sleep with men you just meet, do you?" His breath traces a path across my cheek. I don't pull back this time. I won't. I can't. I don't want to.

I shake my head slightly. "I don't."

"Do you kiss men you just met?" His lips taunt me. They're now hovering so close to mine.

I don't respond. I can't find my voice. All I want is to feel. I lean in as his hand cradles my cheek and his finger caresses my skin. I want his kiss. I want to know what it's like to feel those soft, beautiful lips claim mine. I stare at his eyes as they gently close, the long lashes fluttering shut. I run my tongue along my lips just as his brush against mine. I'm lost in that moment. My hand grabs the back of his head, pulling his mouth into mine.

CHAPTER TEN

HIS KISS IS SLOW AND SENSUAL. HE RUNS HIS TONGUE ALONG my bottom lip before pulling it between his teeth. I open my mouth to take him in. I can taste his breath and feel his desire. He pulls me closer. His hand reaches behind me, pushing my back into him. I reach for his face with both my hands, cradling him. The soft stubble of the evening scrapes against my palms. As his tongue dances with mine I briefly flash to what it would feel like to have that stubble brush against my thigh and to feel this tongue at my core. If his kiss is any indication of his skill, I'd be lost in the depths of a pleasure I can't even imagine. This is what a prelude to ecstasy must feel like.

"Come home with me." He breathes the words into my mouth.

I want to. I want to so much. I pull back from the kiss. "I can't."

"We can just kiss." He smiles as he traces the outline of my top lip with his index finger. "I could kiss these beautiful lips all night."

I shiver at his touch. This is what my dreams have been made of since I knew what intimacy was. I've longed for a man just like this to desire me. I've wanted to be wanted. I've wanted a man to ache for my touch.

"I can't," I repeat. "I need to go home."

He scans my face. I know he's looking for some hint as to why I'm pulling back. I can't tell him. I don't want him to know about the scar.

"What is it?" he asks as he pulls me closer again. "Don't you want me?"

I almost laugh at the suggestion. Don't I want him? Does the man own a mirror? How could I not want him? How could any woman breathing not want this man inside of her?

"I told you." I pull back slightly. I can't think straight when I can feel his warm, delicious breath dancing over my skin. "I don't sleep with men I don't know."

"You know me now," he breathes. "I won't do anything you don't want me to do."

He's so tempting. I've never once thrown caution to the wind and followed my desires. What would happen if I did go home with him? What would he think of the scar?

"Why do you want me?" I ask, the words tumbling out quickly. "Why me? I'm not like Petra."

His eyes search my face. The silence in the car is deafening save for the rain bouncing off the roof. "That's why," he says in a muted tone. "You're not like Petra. You're not like anyone."

I want to tell him to take me home with him. I want the world to melt away so I can experience a man like this at least once in my life. I want the scar to disappear. I want my inhibitions to melt away. I want to be like Alexa. I just want him. All of him. Now.

I hang my head low staring at the black pants I'm wearing. "I'd like to go home."

I watch him from the corner of my eye. He moves with

slow hesitation. I hear the car's engine roar to a start. "Buckle up, Sadie." He reaches over me to grab the seat belt and pull it into place.

I clench my fists together on my lap. Damn my heart. Damn my life. I may have just fucked up the best thing that's ever happened in my dull, boring, and predictable existence.

"HE WALKED me to the door, kissed me on the nose and said goodnight." I cringe as I recount the events of last night to Alexa.

She takes a lazy drink of coffee from a small paper cup she just filled. "You're saying that he wanted to take you home so he could ravage your body all night and you actually said no?"

I nod. I can almost see the wheels turning in her brain. She's searching the air around us for just the right thing to say. It's not going to be pretty. In fact, it's going to sting. I brace myself for the onslaught.

"I get it," she blurts out before she turns to pour the remaining coffee from her cup down the drain in the kitchen. "I need to remake the pot this came from, it's disgusting."

"That's it?" I ask tightly. "You're not going to give me a lecture on why I should have slept with him?"

I watch as she reaches for a container of robust dark roast. She methodically fills the machine with water before placing the grounds in the filter. "That's it." She doesn't turn to look at me when she finally responds.

"Why not?" I push. This isn't Alexa at all. Typically, by now, she'd be reading me the riot act about missing out on life and being too self-conscious for my own good.

She turns abruptly so she's facing me directly. "You're old

enough to make your own decisions." She reaches to rest her arms on my shoulders, clasping her hands behind my neck. "You need to stop worrying so much about this..." her voice trails as she bows her head down motioning towards my chest. "It's part of you. Just a part. Don't let your life slip by because you can't see that."

I stare in stunned silence as she walks away towards the front of the bistro. "Just a part," I whisper as I run my hand down the front of my apron. Maybe she's right. Maybe I have to stop worrying so I can start living.

CHAPTER ELEVEN

"I'M LOOKING FOR SADIE LOCKWOOD." THE SOUND OF AN unfamiliar male voice makes me pop my head around the corner to see who is standing by the counter.

I'm greeted by the sight of a massive floral bouquet and two burly hands holding onto it. His entire face is obliterated by the fragrant arrangement.

"I'll take it." Alexa reaches across the counter to cradle the flowers in her arms. "Do you need me to sign anything?"

"Nope." He tosses back over his shoulder as he heads for the door. "We're all good."

"Sadie." She pushes the flowers into my hands. "They're from him. They have to be."

I smile as my heart races. My mother loves fresh flowers so there's always at least a few bouquets dotting the house but this is unlike anything I've ever seen. The mixture of exotic flowers is breathtaking. I place them down on the counter as I reach for the card.

"What does it say?" Alexa is hovering over my shoulder. I can feel her breath on my neck.

I don't want to be rude but this feels important and

special. "Let me look first?" I ask even though it's more of a declaration.

"Sure." I can sense the disappointment in her voice. "Let me know, okay?"

I nod as I scurry to the back room. I sit in the chair by the desk and quickly run my finger along the seam of the small envelope, tearing it open.

"*Dinner. Tonight at eight. Just one kiss. H.*"

I hold the card in my hands, staring at the words. This is it. This is my second chance with him.

"I can't stand the suspense." Alexa peeks around the corner at me. "What does it say?"

I lower my gaze to the card; pull in a deep breath and say, "I'm having dinner with him tonight. I need you to help me pick out a dress."

"That's my girl." She claps her hands together in giddy excitement. "At least one of us is getting laid tonight."

"Alexa?" Josephine's stern tone coming from the front of the bistro makes us both laugh out loud.

———

I OPEN the door and I'm instantly assaulted with how amazing he looks. He's wearing gray slacks and a white sweater. The fabric is so thin I can almost make out the toned definition of his chest and abdomen. His black hair is pushed back from his forehead revealing his chiseled features. His blue eyes sparkle in the soft setting light of the evening.

"You look beautiful, Sadie." He drinks me in and I stand proudly on display. Alexa helped me get ready. The white dress I'm wearing is short enough to show off my toned legs. My back is bare which makes up for the high neckline in the front. I left my hair down letting the natural curl course through it after I showered.

I smile softly. My heart is pounding in anticipation of what's to come. This feels like a real date and I haven't been on one of those for so long.

"Are we set?" he asks the question as he steps next to me, his hand caressing the soft skin of my back.

I push back into his touch. I want to savor every moment of this evening. I know his attention is likely fleeting. This is going to be an experience I'll remember for a long time and I don't want to waste a moment worrying about anything.

"Where are we going for dinner?" I follow his lead and take his hand as we step down the concrete steps and follow the path to the street.

"My place," he says casually as he opens the passenger door of his car.

I freeze in place. It wasn't supposed to happen this quickly. I thought we'd have dinner first. I thought I could down a few glasses of wine to help curb my inhibitions. "Your place?" The question sounds harsher than I intended.

"Is that a problem?" He motions for me to get into the car.

"No," I say bluntly. "I just assumed we'd be going to a restaurant."

"I eat out every night. I get sick of the noise and the rush." He scans my face as if he's searching for reassurance that he's made a good choice in me. "I'll order something in and we can eat at my place. It's quiet. We can talk."

I don't say anything as I carefully lower myself into the car. Maybe I should have given this more thought. Maybe I'm not ready for this after all.

CHAPTER TWELVE

"I DIDN'T KNOW ANYONE ALIVE COULD ENJOY SUSHI AS MUCH as me." He pushes his empty plate to the side of the table. "You have a great appetite for someone who doesn't even weigh one hundred pounds."

I laugh out loud at the suggestion. "I weigh more than a hundred pounds." I take another long sip from the wine glass he's already refilled once for me.

"Okay, one hundred and one pounds." He laughs and stands to clear the table. "You're very tiny. I'm not sure where all that food went."

I giggle as I watch him move towards the kitchen. His home is spacious, bright and beautifully decorated. It screams of personal style with eclectic artwork on the walls and a bookshelf dedicated primarily to vintage titles. I caught a few familiar names when I first arrived but I haven't had a chance to go back to drink in all that literary gold.

"Do you play?" I nod towards the baby grand piano that is nestled into a corner by a huge bay window.

"No." He laughs as he guides me towards it. "My mother plays. It's here for when she visits."

I sit down at the bench and run my fingers over the keys. "Where does she live?"

He settles in next to me now, his hand resting on my thigh. "New York."

I scan the keys before my eyes move upwards to the top of the piano. A small, but vibrant, bouquet of dyed roses sits in a curved vase. Next to it are several framed photographs.

"Thank you again for the beautiful flowers," I say as I search the pictures for his face. I settle on one of him when he was younger. He looks as though he's in his late teens. "Is that you?" I reach for the frame.

"That's me," he says huskily. "That's Jax." He points to the other man in the picture.

I pull the picture closer noting how similar Jax looks now to the boy staring back at me from the frame. "You two have been friends a long time." It's a statement, not a question.

"We have." He reaches to touch the edge of the frame but I don't relinquish my hold.

"Who is she?" I nod towards the woman in the center of the photograph. She's stunning. Her hair is a vibrant red, her eyes a molten blue. She's firmly got Hunter's hand grasped in her own.

"Jax's cousin." The tension on the frame is more apparent. He's trying to pull it out of my grasp.

"She's holding your hand." I note with a faint smile. I can sense from his reaction and his palpable desire to get the picture away from me that he's not that comfortable talking about her.

"We dated briefly." He yanks the picture from my grip now. "It was a long time ago."

"She's really beautiful," I offer. It's obvious that this woman meant something to him judging by his reaction. "Did you meet her through Jax?"

"I knew her first." He stares at the picture that is now in his lap.

"What's her name?" My curiosity combined with the wine is making it easier to ask questions I normally wouldn't.

"Coralie." His voice breaks as he says it. "Coral."

"That's so pretty." I push myself away from the piano seat. "I need to use the washroom."

"Down the hall." He points past the kitchen. "It's the first door on your right."

I walk swiftly towards the reprieve of the restroom. I can't believe that just happened. Why did I pick up that frame and ask so many questions? Why does a girl he dated when he was a teenager still cause that powerful of a reaction in him? Dammit. I wish I had brought my phone to the washroom with me so I could have texted Alexa.

I take my time glaring at my image in the mirror before I return back to where Hunter is. He's staring out the bay window. I run my eyes across the top of the piano and notice immediately that the picture we were just looking at is now nowhere in sight.

"I'm sorry," I mutter.

He turns slowly to look at me, a faint smile pulling at his lips. "Sorry for?"

"For asking about Coral?" I spit out.

He cringes as I say her name. "It was so long ago. It feels like a lifetime ago. I was a kid."

"It didn't end well, did it?" I want to show him that I'm mature enough to deal with a discussion about another woman. Obviously, there have been a lot of other women in his life.

He brings his palms to his face, cradling his head briefly. "You could say that."

"I'm sorry," I offer again.

"Enough with the sorry this and sorry that, sunshine," he says it so effortlessly. "Let's talk about you."

"Me?" I giggle as he reaches to pull me closer, his hands circling my waist.

"Who was your first love?" He kisses the tip of my nose as the question leaves his lips.

I want to ask why he picked that particular question. Coral must have been his first love or he wouldn't be thinking about it. He has to be over her by now. He couldn't have been more than fifteen or sixteen-years-old in that picture.

"That was Johnny McDunkin or McDougall. Something with a Mc." I laugh.

A slow smile spreads across his handsome face. "He was that forgettable?"

"We had a clandestine affair in a supply closet in middle school," I quip.

"You had a what?" He pulls me closer to him now. I can feel the outline of his body pressed against mine.

"We kissed and he touched my breast and then a teacher caught us." I snuggle my cheek into his chest. "It was all very scandalous."

"Sadie Lockwood," he whispers as he pulls my chin up so our eyes meet. "The woman with the sordid past."

I part my lips, pulling my tongue along the bottom. I close my eyes as I wait for his kiss.

CHAPTER THIRTEEN

I MOAN INTO HIS MOUTH AT THE INTENSITY OF THE KISS. HIS hand is on my back, guiding me. His other hand is caught in my hair, pulling it softly. I push my mouth roughly into his. This is what I came here for. This is what I've longed for since he walked into my parent's house at the benefit dinner. I've wanted to feel him, taste him and know what it's like to be desired by him.

I feel myself being lowered onto something soft. It's a couch. I wrap my arms around his neck, edging my teeth along his lips. He groans in response and I pull on his hair, pushing him further into my mouth. I want to taste all of him. I want him to feel how much I want this.

He brushes his tongue along my lips. First the top, then the bottom. I moan from the sensation. He plunges his tongue deeper, coaxing mine. I can feel his want. I'm so aroused already.

I almost scream when his hand touches my thigh. I can't stop this. I won't. I want to feel him. I pull on the hem of his shirt. He acquiesces and breaks our kiss to pull it over his head. I breathe in the sight of his chest. The muscles so defined, the strength so apparent.

"You're beautiful. So beautiful," he whispers before his lips bear down on mine again. He nips at them, pulling them gently between his teeth. "I'm so hard. Sadie, so hard."

I reach for his belt, but the sensation of his hand traveling steadily up my thigh freezes me in place. He's going to know how badly I want this when he touches my panties. When he feels how sopping wet from desire they already are he'll know that I crave him.

"Christ," he growls into my mouth as he runs his index finger along the silk fabric. "You're so wet."

I nod slowly then gasp when he pulls them down in one swift motion. He pushes them from my body and I feel instantly exposed.

"Fuck." He purrs into me as his finger runs the length of my smooth cleft. "So wet, so perfect."

I push my legs farther apart. I want him to touch all of me. I want him to see what he's doing to me. I reach for his face. I need to kiss him while he strokes my core.

He slides away, his kisses trailing down my neck. "I have to taste you. God, how I've craved this."

I grasp the pale fabric of the couch when I feel him drape my right leg over his shoulder. He's silent. I can feel his heavy breaths on my wetness. He's looking. He's seeing me so open and wanting. "You're the most beautiful thing I've ever seen."

I pull in a deep breath. I want to feel his tongue. I need to feel his lips drawing my pleasure from me. Desire overtakes me and I reach down to grasp his hair within my hand. "Please."

He doesn't waste another moment as his runs his tongue the length of my slick cleft. A moan escapes him and travels through my body. I shudder at the sensation. "Sadie," he groans my name into me as his tongue lashes my clit.

I'm so close already. I've never experienced anything like this before. Will only went down on me once and I didn't come. I haven't come with anyone before. Only by my own hand.

I cry out as the intense sensations of his tongue overtake my senses. "Please, "I whisper again. "Don't stop."

"Never," he purrs before pulling my swollen clitoris into his mouth. "I'll never stop."

I can feel heat course through my body as I reach the edge. I plunge both hands into his hair, pushing his mouth onto me. My core clenches as I feel the rush of the orgasm through my body. I moan loudly. I can't see. I can't feel anything but this pleasure. How could it feel like so much and so amazing at the same time?

He rests his head against my thigh as my hips settle back onto the couch. I'm spent. My body is glistening with the sweet moisture of sweat. I feel so alive. I feel so sensitive. I never knew an orgasm could be like that.

"That was…" my voice trails as I feel the slightest pressure on my clit.

"Just the beginning," he growls as he once again takes it between his teeth.

I cry out loudly. It's already too much. It's all on fire. Every part of me is on fire. "I can't." My words are barely audible. "It's too much."

"You're so fucking tight," he says hoarsely as one finger enters me. "Christ, I want to fuck you."

I reach to pull his finger deeper into me and let out a guttural growl as another slides in next to it. He's aggressive as he pushes into me. I don't back down. I rock myself against his hand. I feel another wave rush through me the instant his tongue finds my clit again.

"Oh, God," I cry out as I come again. This orgasm is even more intense than the last. I lash about beneath him trying to disengage my body from his but he bites at my clit, pulling it deftly between his lips, lapping up every last drop of my desire.

I close my eyes as the sensations wash through me. This is what it's like. This is what I've been missing. How could I ever stop wanting him?

CHAPTER FOURTEEN

"I don't know what to say." I lean forward trying to retrieve my panties from where they fell on the floor.

He scoops them up before I have a chance to touch them. "These are mine. I'm going to sleep with them." He pushes them into the pocket of his pants and I smile. I don't want to think about how many other women's panties he likely has hidden around his apartment. This moment is mine and I won't let any thoughts that ruin that intrude on me.

"I feel selfish," I whisper as I sit up and adjust the hem of my dress. I've never gone anywhere without panties before. I still feel so swollen and wet.

"Because I didn't come?" He pulls his sweater back over his head.

I nod in silence. I do feel selfish for that but I also feel a sense of relief. My dress is still on me. The scar is still a secret.

"I will." He kisses me lightly on the forehead. "I can't wait to fuck you."

"What happens after we do that?" I ask the question even though I know it sounds childish and territorial.

"What happens after we make love?" He pushes a strand of my hair behind my ear.

"Yes. Is this over then?" I gaze down as I ask the question.

"I hope not."

"You hope not?" I volley back at him. "You don't strike me as the type of man who does relationships." The moment the words leave my lips I think about the photograph. Maybe Coral was the only woman he was ever in a relationship with.

"I don't." He stands and walks towards the kitchen.

I sit up straight on the couch before reaching to put my shoes back on. I've offended him. He gave me the most pleasure I've ever experienced in my life and then I offended him. Smart, Sadie. You are so fucking smart.

"Here's some water." He hands me a bottle of chilled water. "You look like you could use it."

I smile as I push a few strands of hair that are sticking to my forehead aside. I take a long, heavy swallow of the water. It quenches my thirst but not my curiosity.

"Are we just going to sleep together?" I blurt the question out. Can I possibly sound more juvenile?

"What's going on, sunshine?" He reaches to take the bottle from my hand. "Where's your mind at?"

I pull in a measured breath. "I told you before that I don't really do the just sex thing very well."

"You want to be wined and dined and then fucked?" He takes a drink from the bottle and I marvel at the muscles in his neck. Is there any part of him that doesn't exude raw magnetism?

"I like things to be in order." I breathe out a heavy sigh as my eyes dart around the room. "Everything in my world has its place. I just want to know where my place is in your world."

He sips more of the water as he nods slowly at me. "I get it. You want us to define what this is so that there are no misunderstood expectations?"

"Yes." I adjust myself on the couch. "Or at least an expectation of what we want from one another."

"That's fair." He places the bottle down in his lap. "You smart girls like to plan everything, don't you?"

His comment, although playful, stings. It's the second time he's brought up my intelligence. I'm not sure if he views it as a positive thing or a negative thing.

"Will we see other people?" I throw the question at him. It seems like a good launching point.

"See other people?" he repeats it back as if he's mulling it over. "As in fuck other people? Are you asking if you can fuck other men while we're sleeping together?"

I wasn't asking that but his assumption is telling. "Sure," I counter. "Can I sleep with other guys while we're sleeping together?"

"No. Absolutely not." His voice is stern, there's no compromise in the tone.

"So you won't be sleeping with other women either?" I clench my hands together in anticipation of his answer.

"After that..." He motions to the couch. "I don't want anyone but you. How can I fuck anyone else when I've tasted you?"

I'm stunned by his bold response. I immediately feel the heat return between my thighs. He really wants me.

"I don't do long term." The words hit me like a bullet from the distance that I couldn't have seen coming. "I want you while I can have you."

I scan his face looking for any hint about how long that might be. "Until I go back to school?" I offer.

His face brightens as if I've given him a key to a locked door. "That works for me."

"So we're fuck buddies until September?" I want the words to sound light but they feel heavy and emotionally weighted when they leave my lips.

"You're mine for the summer." He leans in closer. "Don't let another man touch any of this."

I nod as I once again feel his soft lips engulf mine in a heated kiss.

CHAPTER FIFTEEN

"What I would give to have a man like that go down on me." Alexa fans herself in the lounge chair next to me.

"I didn't even know it could feel that good," I say, a broad smile covering my mouth.

"I told you he wouldn't care about the scar." She points to my chest. It's near one hundred degrees out and even though she's wearing a tiny, pink bikini, I've covered my one-piece suit with a t-shirt.

"I haven't told him about it yet," I grimace as I take a long sip of iced tea.

"What?" she barks as she swings her legs over the chair so she's sitting straight up. "You agreed to be his fuck toy for the next two months and you didn't show him the scar?"

"No." I hang my head. "My dress stayed on the other night and after that I just didn't think it was the time to talk about it."

"Sadie," she scolds me. "That's not fair."

"I know," I mumble. "I just wanted the feeling to last. I've never felt like that before."

"You need to tell him today." She reaches past me to pull

my smartphone off the grass. "Call him and tell him need to see him."

"He's out of town." I juggle my phone between my palms. "He's in Denver until tomorrow."

"Denver? You're not serious?" She bolts to her feet, running to her backpack to pull out her laptop. "He's going to get washed away."

I chuckle at how dramatic she is sometimes. "What are you talking about?"

"There's a downpour there." She flips open the cover of her computer and taps on a few buttons. "Look at this."

I take the computer from her hands and watch a news video detailing a massive rainstorm in Denver. There are power outages, threatened mudslides and cars floating down the middle of city streets.

"What the hell?" I shake my head not just at the frantic sight of the damage Mother Nature can do but also at the fact that Alexa knew more about a breaking news story than I did.

"He's probably going to be stranded there for days." She leans back on her chair with a sigh. "You should call him and make sure he's okay."

I hesitate at the idea. Hunter and I may have agreed to be lovers for the next eight weeks but we're not officially dating. I don't think it's my place to call him up in the middle of the day when he's away on business.

"Do it, Sadie." She nods at my phone. "Guys love it when we worry about them."

I stare at my phone before thumbing through my contact list to his number. "Give me a minute," I say to Alexa as I step off the chair and onto the grass. "I'm just going to call from inside."

"Sure thing," she says as she lies back down to soak in more rays.

I close the patio door behind me before I press the call button. I take in a heavy breath as I wait for him to answer.

"Hunter Reynolds," he says into the phone.

"Hey, it's me."

He doesn't respond right away. Instead I hear muted footsteps and the distinctive click of a door closing shut.

"Sunshine. What a surprise." His voice is barely more than a whisper now. I push the button to increase the volume of the call.

"Am I interrupting you?"

"I was just in a meeting." He doesn't offer more than that. "I'm happy you called. What do you need?"

He's rushing our call and I want to believe it's because he's in the middle of a consultation with a new restaurateur. My heart is telling me that's not it at all.

"I was hoping we could see each other tomorrow night if you're still coming back then." I don't want to sound needy but Alexa is right, I have to tell him about the scar before this goes any further.

"I'll be there." I can sense the smile on his face.

"Your flight is still a go? There isn't a weather delay?"

"Nope," he says quickly. "It's a beautiful day here."

My heart drops in my chest. "The sun is shining?" I ask the question carefully not wanting him to detect anything unusual in my voice.

"Not a cloud in the sky," he retorts. "I've got to get back to the meeting. I'll pick you up at eight tomorrow night."

"Sure," I say faintly before the line goes dead.

CHAPTER SIXTEEN

"I MISSED YOU." HE BRUSHES HIS LIPS AGAINST MINE.

I retreat quickly from the kiss as I pull the door closed behind me. "How was your trip?"

"Boring." He laughs as he takes my hand in his to walk towards his car.

"Your flight back was good?" My thoughts have been so scattered since our phone conversation yesterday that I don't know what to say. We're not in a relationship. We had sex once. I don't have a right to question him about Denver, do I? How can I possibly ask him what's going on when I haven't been completely candid with him either?

"Great. I slept most of the way so I'm full of energy." He runs his lips across my neck.

He wants to make love tonight. He wants to help me feel pleasure and all I can think about is who he was giving that same pleasure to last night.

"I need to tell you something." I pull back from his kiss. I can't think straight if he's so close to me. He looks so inviting, dressed in a grey suit and black dress shirt. I hadn't planned on the evening lasting long so my jeans and blue short sleeved sweater seem out of place.

"Let's go to my place and we can talk." He opens the door to his car and I silently slide into the passenger seat.

I wait for him to sit next to me before I speak again. "We can't make love tonight."

"We can't?" He reaches for my hand, cradling it in his before he brings it to his lips. "That's fine, sunshine."

I feel deflated as he drops my hand onto my lap. Of course he doesn't care if we make love. He fucked someone else last night in some unnamed city. He was likely with her when I called him. Why is this so upsetting to me? What did I expect from this? He owes me nothing. Nothing. As the car races away from the curb in front of my parent's home I wish that I had confided in Alexa about my call to him yesterday. Why had I pretended everything was good? She would have known what I should say to him.

He sings along to the radio as he pilots the car through the crowded streets of the city. "Do you want to pick up some dinner before we get to my place or should we order in?"

"I'm not hungry." I don't volunteer why.

"That works for me." His gaze doesn't break from the road. "We'll be at my place in five."

My heart is pounding. He has no idea what's about to happen. I don't know if I should bring up my scar first or the fact that I know he wasn't in Denver. Do I even have a right to mention Denver? Why did I agree to be his fuck buddy? My heart is already invested. I'm supposed to protect this heart at all costs.

I follow him silently from the garage into the lobby of his condo. He presses the call button for the elevator as he thumbs through his phone. "Did you work today?" The question surprises me.

"I had a day off today," I answer snappily

"Did you do something fun?" He drops the phone into his jacket pocket before his gaze meets mine.

"Not really." I shrug my shoulders. "I hung out with Alexa. That's all."

"That girl is a handful, isn't she?" He laughs as he places his hand on my back urging me into the elevator.

"She can be." I feel protective of my best friend. I don't need this man that I barely know to make judgment calls about her. He's in no position to do that.

"I'll get the door." He steps off the elevator before me and pushes the key to his door into the lock. I watch as he enters a security code into the panel on the wall before he turns the handle. "After you."

CHAPTER SEVENTEEN

I walk into the room and soak in the beauty once again. It's such an elegant space and I'm envious that he gets to live here alone. My home is usually the dorms but during breaks I always stay at my parents' house. I often don't feel like I belong anywhere.

"I bought you something while I was away." He throws his suit jacket over the back of the couch as he fumbles in his overnight bag. "You're going to love it."

I stand in silence watching him gleefully rummage through the bag. His hand darts back out with a rectangular box covered in silver paper in its clutches. He holds it out and I stand frozen staring at it.

"Open it." He pushes it at me and I reluctantly take it.

I rip the corner of the paper from its place revealing a grey box.

"You can use it when you go back to school." He's standing right next to me now. I can feel his eyes boring a hole through my hands willing me to open the box.

I do and I'm caught off guard by the sight of a beautiful silver pen. "It's so nice," I whisper.

"It's engraved with your name." He reaches to pull it from the box and his arm brushes against mine. I feel regret course through me. I wanted this to be uncomplicated. I wanted this to work, even if it was just for the summer.

"I can't accept this." I push it back at him. "You shouldn't have gotten this for me."

"Why?" I can see pain cover his expression. "I saw it in the hotel gift shop and I thought you'd like it."

"In the hotel gift shop in Denver?" I spit the question at him. I know it sounds sharp, but I don't care.

"Yes." He bows his head staring at the box and tattered paper in his hands.

"You weren't in Denver," I seethe. "You lied."

He pulls his gaze slowly up to meet mine. I can see the vein in his neck pulsing. The joy that was on his face when he picked me up is now veiled by something darker. He's angry. I've never seen him livid but I recognize it within his eyes.

"You didn't just call me a liar, did you?" He drops the box onto the hardwood floor and the pen bounces out. "Who do you think you are?"

"Nobody," I volley back.

"What does that mean?" His voice is vibrating. He's trying to calm it. I can hear it within the tone.

"I'm nobody to you." I push my finger against his unyielding chest. "You weren't in Denver. You lied for whatever reason to me about that."

"Why would I do that?" He pushes back against me, catching my hand within his.

"You already broke our agreement," I spit at him. "You went somewhere to fuck someone else."

"You're kidding?"

I pull my hand back and cross my arms on my chest. "I

don't care what you do or who you do it with," I lie. "I just don't want to waste my time being part of some booty posse."

"A booty posse?" He arches his brow. "What the hell is that?"

"You travel a lot." I stand my ground. "You must have a different woman in every city that you screw when you're there."

"You've got no right questioning what I do." He points his index finger directly at me. "This wasn't supposed to be serious. What's gotten into you?"

"Whatever," I shout at him as I take a step towards the door. "You told me I couldn't sleep with anyone else and then you hop on a plane to go fuck someone less than forty eight hours later."

"You're acting like a child." He steps in my path. "Go fuck someone else if you want to, Sadie. I don't give a shit."

His words sting. I knew that's how he felt but when I hear the words roll of his tongue, I wince in pain. "I can't. It's not like that for me."

"You keep saying that." His voice is louder now. His anger is coursing to the surface. "You sure as hell weren't a prude when you were sprawled out on my couch the other night letting me eat you."

I feel like he's punched me in the stomach. He has no idea who I am. He thinks I'm just like the others. He thinks I just have random sex like him.

"I'm not like you," I say tightly. "I don't do those things."

"What things?" he barks. "You don't fuck? You don't enjoy yourself?"

"I don't." I want to hold it together but I'm racing towards lashing out. "I can't."

"That's ridiculous." The chuckle that accompanies the words sets me over the edge.

"It's not." I bite my bottom lip to hold back the anger.

"Why then?" He leans back against the couch before he crosses his arms across his chest. "Why is Sadie Lockwood so different than the rest of the world?"

"This." I scream the word as I pull open the front of my sweater. The buttons scatter. The room is so deathly silent that I can hear them all bounce when they hit the floor.

My eyes catch his for a brief moment before I turn to leave. The hand over his mouth and the clear shock in his eyes say it all.

CHAPTER EIGHTEEN

"How's Dylan?" I sit on the edge of my mother's bed watching her unpack one of the many suitcases she took with her when she raced off to Europe several weeks ago to rescue my brother from whatever legal hole he'd fallen into this time.

""Dylan is Dylan," she sighs as she rolls her eyes. "Daddy is staying there for a few more weeks. I couldn't stand it. I had to get home."

The faint smile she throws my way suggests that she's back and happy to see me. I know that she's back and happy to be lunching with her friends tomorrow and having her nails done the day after. I've never been high on my mother's priority list.

"How did the benefit go?" She turns her back to me as she places her jewelry box on her nightstand. "There were no hiccups, were there?"

"It was fine," I answer. "The usual suspects were here and a couple of new faces."

"Like who?" She twirls around quickly. I realized at a

very early age that the ultimate bait to catch my mother's attention is gossip. The juicier the better in her eyes.

"Rob Archer has a new wife."

"What?" The question comes out with a shrill shriek. "What's she like?"

"Young and pretty." I shrug my shoulders. "I didn't talk to either of them."

"Who else?" She sits down next to me.

"There was a guy here I hadn't seen before." I pretend to search my mind for his name. "Hunter Reynolds was his name."

She stares at my face before she responds, "I've never heard of him. Who was he here with?"

"I don't remember her name." I try to pull back a mental image of the woman Hunter arrived with. "She was maybe in her early thirties, brunette, short hair."

"Was she wearing an emerald colored gown? An off the shoulder, gaudy thing?" She motions towards her shoulder as she purses her lips together as if she's just eaten a sour lemon.

I laugh when I realize she's spot on. "How did you know what she was wearing?"

"Judith handled all the alterations. She showed me the gowns on Skype."

I burst out laughing. I don't know if I'm more bothered by the fact that my mother was scoping out everyone's dresses from across the Atlantic or that she was using Skype at all. I'm just grateful she's never tried to talk to me on it.

"I think that fellow, Hunter, owns a restaurant with her husband." She's a never ending source of information today.

"He does consultations for restaurants," I correct her.

"That sounds right." She quips before she walks over to her suitcase and silently starts sorting through it again.

———

"ARE you doing the whole surprise party thing for your mom this year?" Alexa pulls the bright red polish across her toenail. "Because if you are, I want first dibs on the guest list."

"Why?" I realize that I haven't even thought about my mother's birthday yet and it's less than two weeks away now. "There's a hot guy who works for my dad. I thought I could invite him."

I shake my head to clear away all of the confusion I'm suddenly feeling. "What? Why on earth would a guy who works for your dad come to my mother's party?"

"Sadie," she pulls my name across her lips in a whine. "My dad and your dad play golf. My dad works with the hot guy so it only makes sense that I'd invite him."

"Whatever you want," I say only because I can't follow her train of thought for longer than a minute at this moment.

"Unless Dylan is back, then I'll just hook up with him." She closes the lid on the polish as she waves her wet toes in the air.

"You're disgusting." I pick through the dozens of bottles of polish she pulled from her washroom cabinet. "You can't sleep with him."

"Who says I haven't already?" She falls back onto her bed giggling uncontrollably.

I stick my fingers in my ears. "I can't hear you," I scream. "Stop talking."

She sits back up and yanks my finger free. "What are you getting the old hag anyway?"

I laugh at that description of my mother. She's spent a small fortune making certain she looks nothing like an old hag. I know she wouldn't appreciate Alexa's view of her.

"Remember that guy, Jax?" I search Alexa's face to see if it jogs her memory at all.

"How could I forget that?" She runs her finger down the front of her jeans. "I've thought about him a lot when I've… you know."

"Shut up." I laugh. "His girlfriend owns a jewelry store in New York. She does custom pieces. I thought we could take the train there one day and get my mom something. She loves jewelry."

"I love it." She jumps to her feet and bounces on the bed. "The two of us will take Manhattan by storm. Those men won't know what hit them."

I cock a brow at her. "We're going to buy a piece of jewelry and maybe have a nice dinner. Try to rein in your hormones."

"What color are you doing your nails?" She's off the bed now searching through her massive collection of polish. "New York screams red, don't you think?"

I nod as I watch her choose a bottle filled with bright red liquid.

CHAPTER NINETEEN

I WANT TO TALK. CALL ME.

I'd been staring at my phone for almost an hour. I hadn't expected to hear from Hunter again and now I'm gazing at his words sprawled across the screen of my smart phone.

If I call him I have to face the consequences of my actions. I have to own up to being petty and jealous about his trip. More than that, I have to face him after baring my scar. I hadn't wanted to be so dramatic. I never would have planned it that way. It happened though and now I had to decide whether opening that wound again was worth it.

I tentatively press his number and wait for it to ring.

"Sadie." He sighs softly. "You called."

"You asked me to," I counter.

"Are you busy tonight? I can hear the trepidation in his voice. It's not the same unyielding, strong tone I'm used to.

"No. Why?"

"Can I pick you up in an hour? I'd like to talk."

I glance at the clock on my nightstand. It will be ten by then. "Sure. I'll be ready," I say the words before I slide my thumb across the screen to end the call.

I shower quickly and pull on a blue sundress. The very top of my scar is visible but at this point I don't care. I pull my damp hair into a tight ponytail and glide on some mascara. I can't imagine this conversation is going to take longer than a few minutes. I don't want to put too much effort into how I look. The look on his face when I flashed him my chest told me everything I needed to know.

I wait impatiently on the porch for him to come down the street. I would have told my mother I was leaving but, like usual, she's out on an adventure. Maybe everyone was right after all. My own mother seemed to have more fun in life than I did. The only difference was none of them carried the gift of someone else's heart inside of them. None of them understood my insatiable drive to honor that person.

He stops the car abruptly before he hops out and takes wide strides to reach my spot on the porch. "Sadie," he whispers as he pulls me into his chest.

I'm taken back by the gesture and I instinctively want to melt into him. I resist. I know he's not good for me. I knew it when I first saw him the night of the benefit dinner. My better judgement just keeps hiding behind my desire.

"Let's go." He takes my hand and I feel it go limp. I can't grasp onto his but I allow him to lead me to the car. I feel numb. I'm so humiliated by what I've done. Why did I show him the most vulnerable parts of me? Why did I expose myself to him when I know he's only interested in one thing?

I slide into the car and wait for him to take his seat. "Hunter." I gaze down at my hands as I clasp them together. "I need to say something."

"We can talk at my place." He starts the car's engine. "It's private. We'll be more comfortable there."

I gaze out the window as I watch my parent's home fade into the distance.

———

"DO YOU WANT ANYTHING?" He pushes his suit coat from his shoulders and pulls off his tie. "I have wine, water, some juice I think."

"I'm fine." I watch as he unbuttons the top button of the navy blue dress shirt he's wearing. I'll never get over how handsome he is. I know I'll never meet another man who measures up to him in any way.

"I'm sorry it took me so long to call after…" His voice fades as he sits next to me. "I wasn't sure you wanted to talk to me again."

I pull my gaze up with a breathy sigh. "I'm sorry." I search for the right words. They were on the tip of my tongue all day. I knew exactly what I wanted to say to him and now that he's sitting next to me, I can't think straight.

"You have nothing to be sorry for." He gently reaches for my hand.

I don't pull back. "I shouldn't have said the things I said. What you do or don't do in Denver or anywhere else is none of my business."

"Sunshine." He inches closer to me on the couch. I feel my heart jump at the sound of his nickname for me. "When I'm working I'm typically holed up in a hotel that is opening a new restaurant. My whole focus has to be on that. I run into so many logistical problems that I can't even remember what day of the week it is, let alone what the weather is like."

I search his face for some semblance of the truth but he's stone faced. Maybe he was actually in Denver and I just jumped to the wrong conclusion. I shake the subject out of my mind.

"I wanted to tell you about the scar, about my heart." I

pull in a breath trying to hold back my billowing emotions. "It's so hard. People treat me differently when they know."

"You're so special." He leans his forehead against my hair. "That makes you even more special."

I don't want to cry but the softness in his voice and the tenderness in his words are pulling everything I've felt for the past few weeks to the surface.

"The scar makes you more beautiful to me." He moves his hand from mine to my chest. I flinch slightly at his touch. "It means you're a true gift."

I try to process his words. "It's ugly," I spit out.

"Never say that." He reaches to cradle my chin in his hand. "It's amazing. You're so amazing."

I want to kiss him. I want to fall back into that place of pure pleasure with him. I can't. I won't. I don't want to be hurt by him.

I close my eyes when I feel his lips brush against mine. Every fiber of my body is calling at me to pull back but I can't. I wrap my fingers through his hair as I let him glide his lips across mine. I'm so hungry for his touch. I've wanted him so much. I don't care if I'm one of many. I don't care if it's only until September. I need this. I deserve it. I want it.

He pushes the strap of my dress down as his lips kiss a trail to my neck. "You're so beautiful," he whispers into my skin.

I don't resist when he moves to the other strap and the dress starts to fall. I look down. My nipples are so hard. My breasts heaving under the heavy breaths from my body. The scar is there. It's on display.

He leans down and takes one of my nipples into his mouth. I moan at the sensation. His tongue traces an outline, pulling the hard bud between his teeth. It's a mix of pure pleasure and pain. I groan at the sensation. I whimper when I feel the cold air attack my nipple as he moves his mouth to the other. He claims it with his hand before pushing the tender flesh into his mouth. I claw at his shirt, wanting desperately to feel his skin against mine.

"You want this," he growls. "You want me, don't you?"

"So much," I say through a moan.

He scoops me up in one movement into his arms. His lips fall hard into mine as he walks down the hallway. "I'm going to show you how much I want you." His voice is low and rough.

He sets me down on the floor in a dimly lit bedroom. I sense my dress being pulled down. I don't move. I want to soak in every moment of this. I want to know what it's like to be taken by a man like this. Even if it's just for tonight. Even if all I get of him is this one moment.

I watch as he quickly undresses himself. My eyes run slowly down his body, taking in the muscles of his arms, his chest and his abdomen. I settle on his cock. It's thick, strong and hard. He wants me just as much as I want him.

He pushes me lightly back onto the bed before he slides my soaked panties down my legs. "I love how wet you get."

I ache to be touched. I almost whimper at the first whisper of his hand on my breast again. "I want this," I say. I don't care what I'm supposed to feel or want. I can't think. All I can do is ache for him.

"I have to taste you." He's on his knees at the edge of the bed, pulling my body towards him. "I've been craving this taste for days."

I push my back into the bed to raise my hips. I know the pleasure that is about to come; I want to drink in every second of it. I want to feel it in every corner of my body, of my mind and of my heart.

I gasp at the first touch of his tongue on my clitoris. Just seeing his cock has made me so aroused. I know it won't take much to throw me over the edge into complete and utter euphoria.

"I love the taste of you." He laps at me greedily, pulling my desire to the surface swiftly. I pull on his hair as I come hard. I scream. I can't hold back the emotions. It's too good. It's too much.

"You were so ready." He's hovering above me now. His lips fall into mine and I get my first taste of my own desire.

"I want..." I can't finish my thought. I feel his cock rub against my thigh. It's so heavy, so full. I've never been with a man like this.

"Fuck, Sadie. Fuck." He grabs my hair, pushing it from my forehead before he presses his lips against me. "I'm clean. Tell me you're clean and on the pill."

I nod. "I am," I say. I haven't been with anyone since Will. "Please," I beg. "Inside of me."

I push my hips off the bed, trying to coax his cock with my slick cleft. I want him to slide into me. I want to feel that now. I'm going to explode.

He moans as he enters me slowly. "You are so fucking tight." His breath is labored, his heart pounding against my chest.

I groan as he pushes deeper. It's so much. I move my hips trying to accommodate more of him. He feels so deep already.

"I can't control it," he hisses before he pushes himself onto his elbows and fully into me.

I cry out at the sharp burst of pain. "Hunter."

"Christ. Christ." He finds his rhythm as his lips skirt across mine. "I've waited forever for this," he whispers into my mouth. "Forever."

I hold onto his arms, pushing up with every thrust. The

pleasure is so deep within me. He grabs my hips pulling them up from the bed. I gasp at the sensation of his cock hitting me in my most sensitive spot. I can't hold back. I'm going to come.

"Oh god," I cry out as I find my release.

"Sadie," he growls as he pumps himself harder into me, emptying all his desire.

I lay still, unable to move. I never could have imagined it would be like that. That I'd feel so much so fiercely. That passion could touch so many parts of me. I'll never be the same again.

CHAPTER TWENTY

"Can we talk about this?" He runs his index finger down the full length of my scar.

I nod silently. We're on his bed. The sheets are a rumpled mess beneath us and his head is resting on my arm. I'm completely exposed, yet I feel utterly comfortable knowing his eyes are scanning my body.

"When did you get a transplant?" He peers up at me.

"I was eleven." I smile back at him. "I was sick for a very long time."

"What was wrong?" His gaze falls back to my chest.

"I was born with a defect in my heart." I glance down at his finger once again touching the scar. "I was very ill when I was little. I was in the hospital a lot."

"That's horrible." His voice is barely more than a whisper.

"It was." I nod. "I kept getting sicker and sicker so they put me on the transplant list."

He leans onto his elbow now so he's facing me. "Would you have died without it?" He nods towards my chest.

"Yes."

"How did you get it? Where did it come from?" I can hear genuine tenderness in his voice.

"I was in the hospital one night and my mother came running in and said they found a heart for me." I push back the memory of that night. I was terrified.

"Do you know whose heart it was?" he asks tentatively.

"No. They don't tell you." I offer back. "It's all confidential."

"So you have no idea?" He stops his finger's path so it's directly above my heart.

"I was able to write the family of my donor a letter," I say quietly. "That was really hard."

"A letter?" His breath brushes across my nipple.

"When I was fourteen I wrote them a letter thanking them for their gift and promising them I'd take care of my heart." My voice cracks slightly.

"That must have helped them." He wraps his arm around my waist.

"I hope so." I sigh. "They lost someone they loved. I don't know how much comfort my letter gave them. I never heard back."

"I'm sure it helped them after she died." He traces his finger back up my chest.

"Or he," I say. "I never knew if it was a man or woman's heart."

He only nods in response before he moves slightly to place his ear next to my chest.

"I'm so grate…"

"Shhh." His voice interrupts me. "This is a miracle."

I close my eyes as I lie perfectly still knowing he's listening to my heartbeat.

———

"I WANT TO CLARIFY SOMETHING." His voice startles me and I realize I've dozed off.

I look down. He's still resting his head against my chest. "What?" I ask sleepily.

"It's about us seeing other people." He slides up my body so his head is resting against mine. "I don't want to see anyone else."

"You don't have to do that," I offer. "We aren't going to define this, remember?"

"Maybe I want to." He traces his finger across my chin. "Maybe I want to be Sadie Lockwood's steady boyfriend."

I giggle at the suggestion. "You're not the relationship type, remember?"

"People change." He pulls his head up and cocks an eyebrow. "Don't you want to be my girlfriend?"

"You don't have to do this," I say the words even though my mind is racing at the thought of being in an actual relationship with him.

"I want to do this." He brushes his lips against mine. "I don't want you doubting me. I don't want anyone else. I just want you."

"Hunter," I whisper as I scan his eyes for a clue about what he's really thinking. "What changed?"

"I had no idea how special you were." He tenderly pushes a stray hair from my cheek. "I didn't know I could feel like this again. I can't let you go."

The word again *echoes* through me. I can't get lost in that. Right now, right at this moment, he wants me. I want him. I can't say no.

CHAPTER TWENTY-ONE

"I'M FLYING OUT TO SAN FRANCISCO IN THE MORNING BUT I'll be back by the end of the week." He pulls a few pair of socks from one of the drawers of his dresser to place in an overnight bag.

"You're leaving tomorrow?" I bolt upright. "I thought you could come to meet my mother."

He rolls his eyes at the words and then bursts out laughing. "You're taking me home to meet mom already? But we just started going steady."

I giggle. "I'm having a party for her next week. It's a birthday thing. Maybe you can come to that?"

"I'll be there." He leans down to kiss me. "I should finish packing. My flight leaves extra early."

"Should I go home?" I pull my legs over the side of the mattress causing the sheet to fall from my body.

He kneels in front of me. "Not yet."

I stare into his eyes. "I'm still scared. You know that?"

"I know that." He nods his head slightly. "I will do everything in my power to protect this." He places his hand on my chest.

I shiver at the touch. "Thank you."

"We're going to move this along as fast or as slow as you want to."

"None of this seems real to me." A faint smile floats across my mouth. "Men like you don't like girls like me."

"The first rule in being my girlfriend is you can never say that again." He places his finger against my lips.

"But…" I start to protest but he cocks a brow.

"I have a confession." He hangs his head in my lap. "I should have told you this from the start."

My breath stalls. I don't want this moment to be broken into pieces. Please don't let him tell me something that will destroy what I'm feeling.

"I didn't come back to your house to get Petra's number." There's a hint of a small smile at the corners of his mouth. "I came back because I wanted you."

"No." I shake my head. "You're just saying that."

"You came down the stairs with your hair pulled back and your bare feet and I wanted to kiss you so badly. I just wanted you so much." He runs his hand along my chin. "I could tell you weren't sure. I could tell it was too much."

"I wanted that. I wanted to believe it that night but you treated me like I was nothing but a pathetic, inexperienced girl."

"You're not a girl. You are a beautiful, amazing woman that any man in his right mind would want." There's a hint of frustration in his tone. "Stop selling yourself short. I fucked up that night."

"You don't understand." I look away. "People usually reject me because of it. Because of the scar."

"Any man who sees you as anything other than perfection is an idiot." He pulls me closer until his head is resting on my chest. "You are a treasure. You're my treasure now."

I hug him tightly. I can feel the weight in his words. He cares about me. My whole life I've been waiting for this.

———

"I CAN'T BELIEVE you're bailing on me." My jaw tightens. "Now I have to take the train all the way to Manhattan alone."

"I'm sorry." Alexa pushes more cup stoppers into the container that's sitting on the counter. "I forgot I had a date."

"Seriously?" I don't try to tone down my frustration. "We were going to leave in an hour, Alexa. Now what am I supposed to do?"

"Wait until next week," she flippantly says. "I can't go today."

"I don't have another day off before the party." I want her to come with me. I've never taken the train alone.

"Call your boyfriend," she calls over her shoulder as she slips off the apron and reaches for her purse.

"He left for San Francisco yesterday." I follow her into the backroom of the bistro. "I told you that this morning."

"Right." She taps her forehead. "I forgot.

I sigh heavily before reaching in my purse to pull out my phone. "The train leaves right away. I don't know what to do."

"You get in a cab and you go to South Station." She places her hands on my shoulders. "Then you get on that train and you go to New York."

"I can't," I murmur.

"You can." She pushes me towards the door. "Live a little, Sadie. Go on an adventure. What's the worst that can happen?"

I smile at her even though I'm completely exasperated with her. "It would be fun."

"Text me once you're there so I know you made it in one piece." She throws me a wink as I turn to leave.

———

I GLANCE at my phone as the train finally pulls into Penn Station three and a half hours later. I sent Hunter a text message an hour ago asking how his meetings were going and there's still no response. I play back the conversation we had about him becoming immersed in his work. I have to give him space to do what he needs to do while I spend the day shopping for the perfect gift for my mother.

I rush up the stairs and onto the street. The mood is different here. It's not the same as Boston at all. People are rushing, the air feels heavier and there's an excitement brewing around me. I haven't been to Manhattan in so long. Hunter told me he divides his time between here and Boston. I need to ask him if we can have a weekend getaway here before semester starts again.

I stroll down the sidewalk, breathing in the city. The traffic noise is deafening, there are people everywhere but it's vibrant and alive. It reflects exactly how I feel now. How Hunter has made me feel since he came into my life.

I watch a woman hail a cab on the corner and I follow suit. I want to get to the jewelry store before they close.

I read the address on the card to the driver and he nods in response. I hold onto the car's door handle as he whips the car around and speeds down the street.

I glare out the car window, watching in wonder as countless people walk down the streets. The buildings whip by us as we careen through the city. I've never had a driver's license and judging by the traffic here, I'm not sure I'd ever be qualified to drive a cab. I giggle to myself at the thought of it.

The driver pulls the car next to the curb on a beautiful tree lined street. I look at the meter and pull a few bills from my wallet.

"Thanks," he barks back at me as I exit the cab.

I stare at the building in front of me. This is it. This is Hunter's friend's jewelry store. I smile at the prospect of his reaction when he realizes I traveled all this way to get something from Jax's store to give to my mother.

I push the glass door open and the fragrance of fresh flowers wafts in the air. It's a clean space, beautifully decorated. Several people are milling about looking at the cases. I see a clerk helping a woman pick out a necklace and there's a blonde woman talking on the phone.

I walk up to one of the cabinets and soak in the pieces displayed in the case. They are unique, vibrant and exactly my mother's style. She's going to love anything I choose for her here but it has to be perfect. It has to be her.

"Can I help you?" The blonde has popped up beside me, the phone now in her hand.

"I'm here to pick a gift." I smile at her. She's lovely. She's pretty and petite.

"Is it for someone special?" She moves next to the display case, her eyes scanning the different necklaces in front of us.

"My mother," I offer. "It's her birthday next week."

"That's definitely a special occasion." Her smile is warm and infectious. "Were you looking for something in particular? A necklace, or maybe a bracelet? I have some really lovely earrings over here." She motions towards another case next to us.

I turn and run my eyes over the beautiful jewelry. I settle on a pair of striking sapphire earrings. "Those are breathtaking." I point to them.

"Let me get them." She walks behind the case, pulling a

key from her dress pocket. She clicks the key into the lock before sliding the glass door aside. "These are very special."

She hands them to me and I watch them flicker in the light. My mother loves sapphires. "They're beautiful. She'll adore them." I hand them back to her.

"These are actually the first two pieces I made in my studio upstairs." She delicately places them into a white box emblazoned with the name of the store on it. "They hold a very special place in my heart."

"My mom will treasure them." I fumble in my purse for my wallet. When I find it I pull it free. I open it and start the search for my credit card.

"I'm Ivy, by the way." She looks up as she drops the box into a small white bag.

"You're Ivy?" I feel instant excitement. "I met your boyfriend a few weeks ago."

"Jax." His name escapes her lips with a broad grin. "Where did you meet him?"

"In Boston." I pull my gaze down to my wallet again. I thumb through some stray receipts. I know I put my credit card in here this morning before I left home.

"When he was there visiting Hunter?"

I jump at the sound of his name. This is the first person, besides Jax, that knows Hunter. "Yes. I was having dinner with friends and he was at the same restaurant with Hunter."

"Wait." She stops and her eyes scroll slowly across my face. "Do you know Sadie?"

Hunter must have told them about me. He must have told Jax we were dating. "I'm Sadie," I say with a broad grin as I hand her my credit card.

"You're Sadie!" She almost leaps across the counter to hug me.

I return the embrace. I'm not sure why she's so excited to

meet me but she's being so kind and welcoming. "I am," I whisper.

I hear the door of the store open and she lets out a screech. "Thank god you're both back. This is her, isn't it? This is the girl you found in Boston. She's the one you've been looking for."

She whips me around and my eyes settle on Jax's stunned face. There's someone behind him.

"Ivy, stop." Jax takes a step towards us and I see Hunter. Hunter is here. He's in Manhattan. He's supposed to be in San Francisco.

"Why stop?" She's pulling on my shoulder. "She's here. It's Sadie."

I stare in stunned silence at Hunter. The look on his face is unmistakable. He's horrified. He looks as though he's about to turn around and run through the door.

"Hunter, say something," Ivy calls over to him. "She's standing right here. Is that any way to treat the girl that got Coral's heart?"

I feel my body heave forward.

Coral's heart.

It's Coral's heart.

Coral's heart is inside me.

PART TWO

CHAPTER ONE

"ARE YOU EVER GOING TO TELL ME WHAT HAPPENED IN NEW York?" Alexa throws a piece of popcorn in the air before expertly scooping it into her mouth with her tongue.

"Nothing happened," I lie. "How many times do I have to tell you that?" I know I sound impatient, but I don't care. I've been back from Manhattan for two days now and Alexa hasn't let up at all. Suggesting we watch a movie was my lame attempt at getting her to shut up for an hour and a half. Obviously, the plan backfired.

"Sadie." She turns on the couch so she's facing me directly. "You're a horrible liar. Tell me."

I press pause on the remote even though I have absolutely no idea what the movie is about. I only vaguely remember Alexa making some comment when it first started about her, Channing Tatum and a nude beach.

"I'm not dropping this." She puts the bowl of popcorn down on the table. "You came back without anything for your mom and you lost your credit card. That sounds nothing like you, Sadie. Nothing." She enunciates each syllable of the last word, pulling it tightly across her tongue.

"I lost my bearings." I reach to pick up a wayward piece of popcorn off the hardwood floor. "I couldn't find the jewelry store and I misplaced my credit card. End of story."

"Bullshit." She grabs my hand and squeezes it. "You were crying when you came by my place. I'm sorry I had a date. I should have just cancelled and stayed to listen to you."

I stare down at her hand wondering if I should just confess to her that Hunter's dead girlfriend is my heart donor. Or maybe I can skip that part and just tell her that Hunter lied about being in San Francisco. Who am I kidding? If I start telling her what happened, she's going to start asking questions that I don't know the answers to.

"I was just tired." I know it sounds pathetic and she's not going to buy it so I segue into her favorite topic. "How was that date?"

"Shitty." She picks the popcorn back up and rests the bowl in her lap. "He was an F and by F I don't mean a good fuck. I mean a flop as in…" She holds up her index finger and lets it fall over. "He had no wind in his tiny sail if you get my drift."

The disgusted expression on her face pulls a giggle out of me. I wish I was more like her. She's so direct and unyielding. She knows what she wants. If she would have been in my shoes in that jewelry store in Manhattan, everyone in the vicinity would have been in her line of fire. She would have demanded answers and got them. All I did when Ivy announced that I had Coral's heart was race out the door and into a taxi. I can't even remember going to the train station or the entire ride home.

"I get your drift." I smile hoping she'll keep ranting about her less-than-stellar date.

"He's not like your boyfriend." She munches on more of

the popcorn. "How come you're not hanging out with him tonight?"

I thought I had avoided all the land mines that she was throwing in my path but I was wrong. How the hell am I supposed to answer her question? I can't exactly tell her that the only reason Hunter was sleeping with me was because he knew I had Coral's heart inside of me. It's so twisted.

"That's over." I try to sound nonchalant but it comes out more pathetic than anything.

"What?" A piece of popcorn flies from her mouth and lands in her lap. "Since when?"

"It just wasn't going to work." I shrug. No shit, Sadie. How was it supposed to work? I knew that he'd never want me for me. I should have listened to my heart. Or Coral's heart. Whoever the fuck my heart belongs to.

"Stop with the bullshit already." She slams the bowl onto the table so hard pieces of popcorn scatter everywhere. "I'm your best friend. Spit it out."

"There's nothing to spit out." I drop to my knees to pick up the mess. "It was a short term thing. It's over now."

"Right." Sarcasm laces the word. "That's why he's called three times in the last hour and you've ignored every call."

I shake my head. I didn't think she'd notice any of the calls since my phone was set to vibrate. I want to tell her what happened. I need to tell someone but it's too raw. I can't.

"Just tell me what happened." She's on her knees too now, her eyes imploring me to tell her the truth.

"Nothing," I spit back. "Please just drop it already."

"Fine." I can hear the anger in her voice but I don't care. Right now all I want is for her to leave. I can't deal with her questions. I can't even deal with my own questions.

"Can we hang out another night?" I stand and pull up the waistband of my sweatpants. "I'm wiped. I need to sleep."

She pulls herself to her feet and arches her brow. "I'm not letting this go. You're a wreck. We'll talk about it tomorrow."

I don't respond. I can't. I don't know how to form the words to tell anyone that the man I'm crazy about, the man who gave me more pleasure than anyone ever has, only wanted me because his dead girlfriend's heart is beating in my chest.

———

"WHAT DO you know about my heart donor?" The question is blunt and it's ripe with emotion but I try to pepper that with a smile.

My mother doesn't flinch. "Not much. Why?"

I stare at her reflection in the oversized mirror watching her painstakingly apply her make up. "I'm curious."

"That was a lifetime ago, Sadie." She purses her lips together as she applies a generous coating of mascara to her false eyelashes. Her beauty is fading and it's obvious that she believes that with more make up no one will be the wiser.

"Not to me," I counter. "I've been thinking about my donor a lot lately."

"You should focus on the here and now. School's starting again soon." It's her usual comeback. Anytime I ask about anything other than her, she throws school back at me.

"Not for another six weeks," I spit back.

"How's work?" she casually tosses the question into the air.

"Fine, Mother." I sigh. "Tell me what you know about my donor."

She locks eyes with me in the mirror and I swear I hear her curse softly. Her refusal to talk about my heart has always been a sticking point with us but I'm not letting her slink out of the room without a full confession about what she knows.

"Tell me," I repeat this time with a slight hint of anger edging the words.

"It was a girl." She spins around in her chair to face me. "A teenager. She died in a car accident."

The words feel like an assault. She knew this all along and never shared it with me. "What was her name?"

"That I don't know." She twirls a tube of lipstick between her fingers. "All I know is she was a little older than you and was in a horrible wreck. A bunch of kids were in a car and she was thrown through the windshield when it crashed."

"How do you know that?"

"Daddy heard two nurses talking about it that night." The way she turns the chair back around signals she wants the conversation to be over.

"And you never bothered to find out who she was?" I shoot her a pleading look. I can't understand why she didn't pursue it.

"Why would I have done that?" She traces the bright crimson lipstick around her mouth, blotting her lips with a tissue.

"I lived because she died," I almost scream the words at her. "Didn't you want to talk to her parents at least?"

"What would I have said?" She tightens her gaze so she's glaring at me. "Thank you for letting my daughter live? I'm sorry yours died?"

I close my eyes. She was a daughter. Coral was someone's daughter. She was Hunter's girlfriend and people loved her. The Pandora's Box that Hunter opened was in my hands now. I needed answers and there was only one person who could give them to me.

CHAPTER TWO

I suck in a deep breath as I catch a glimpse of him through the window of the restaurant. I can do this. I just have to avoid his eyes directly and I can't look at his face; at his gorgeous, beautiful face. I glance down at my phone. I don't want to be staring at him as he approaches the table. I have to temper my emotions. I need to stop thinking about what we did in his bed.

"Sadie," he whispers as he sits across from me. "I'm so glad you texted me."

I dart my eyes up and my breath hitches. He's so handsome. He hasn't shaved in a couple of days. The grey suit he's wearing fits him perfectly. It's no wonder several women's heads turned when he sat down.

"I brought this." He places the small white bag from the jewelry shop on the table between us. "Your credit card is inside with the earrings."

I nod. It was thoughtful but it's a small gesture. What about the fact that he forget to mention that I was his dead girlfriend's heart recipient? "Thank you," I say as I rummage through my body for any slight spark of strength that might be there. Why did I think I could do this? How am I supposed to get through this conversation?

"You must have a lot of questions." His voice is deep, rich and tender. "Are you sure you want to talk about this here? We can go back to my place."

My body trembles at the mention of his place. That's where I gave myself to him. That's where I let go and felt safe. I can't go back there to discuss this. "Here is fine." I don't offer anything more. I don't want to be alone with him. I can't right now.

"It's a nice restaurant. I've never been." He scans the room before his eyes settle back on my face. "Are you hungry?"

The casualness of the question irks me. How can I be hungry when I feel so utterly disconnected from my own body? How am I supposed to deal with the fact that I slept with the boyfriend of my heart donor? How do you want a sandwich when you have to process all of that? "Sure," I lie.

"Where do you want me to start?" he asks quietly.

"When did you know I was her recipient?" I can't bring myself to say Coral's name.

"Seven years ago." He exhales audibly. "When you sent the letter to her family. I..." he stops speaking when a waitress appears next to him.

"What can I get you?" She doesn't acknowledge my presence. Her gaze is locked on Hunter. I can't blame her. I sit in silence staring at the seductive way she leans in closer to him to tell him the daily lunch specials. Her breasts are practically tickling his nose.

"Sadie, what would you like?" He shifts back in his chair.

"A salad," I say without thought.

"I'll have the same." He doesn't move his eyes from my face. "Bring two sparkling waters too."

"What kind of salad?" She's leaning into him again. "There's garden, crab, a strawberry chicken, cobb..."

"The first one," I interrupt.

She shoots me an angered look before she pulls her chest across Hunter's shoulder when she reaches for our unopened menus. "I'll be right back," she literally whispers into his ear.

I watch her walk away, a slight wiggle in her hips. So many women must come on to him. Why did I think he actually wanted me? Why was I such an idiot?

"Where was I?" He sounds anxious.

"You were telling me that you knew about the letter I sent." I bite back the urge to raise my voice. He let me go on about the letter in our post love making embrace. He already knew about it.

"You signed the letter with your full name," he says hoarsely.

"I remember."

He shifts slightly as the waitress places two glasses of sparkling water on the table. "I've known your name since then."

"Why did you come looking for me now?" I spit out. I can't believe he's known about me for so long. I'm painstakingly aware that the waitress is hovering near our table, listening to our conversation.

"I didn't." He rests his forearms on the table before clasping his hands together. "I always wondered about you but I didn't seek you out."

The words sting but I pull in a heavy breath to hold my composure. "So you just ended up at my mother's fundraiser?" The question is edged with sarcasm but I don't care. He's been withholding information since that night.

"No. An associate was invited and he couldn't go. His wife was going and when they mentioned the last name I realized it was your family." He shoves his hands through his hair. "I was awestruck when I saw you. You weren't what I was expecting."

The comment catches me off guard. I won't let him charm me into abandoning my need to know how I ended up in his life and in his bed. "There's no way in hell that you ended up at my house out of pure coincidence. To suggest that's the case is really insulting, Hunter."

He shrugs his shoulders and throws his gaze past me. He's searching for an explanation. I can see it within his eyes.

"The truth. Just tell me the goddamned truth." I know my voice is slightly raised. I can tell by the reaction of the couple seated next to us. "How did you end up in my house that night?"

His posture tightens and I see the vein in his neck pulse. He's getting agitated. "Not here. You can't suggest a public place and then interrogate me."

"I can do whatever the fuck I want." I push my chair back from the table. "I never asked to be part of your sick, twisted game."

"Don't go." His tone is both pleading and demanding. "Don't walk out of here."

"He's all yours." I push the waitress out of my way. I don't turn back around. Hunter Reynolds can go fuck himself or that waitress. I don't care anymore.

CHAPTER THREE

"You're actually wearing that to my mother's birthday party?" I gawk at the red mini dress Alexa has squeezed herself into. "You can't be serious."

"Deadly serious." She flips her long, blond hair onto her shoulders. "I look hot, right?"

She does. How can I disagree with her? "Of course, but maybe you could save that dress for another occasion, like when you decide to turn in your teaching career to become a cheap call girl."

She pretends to pout but she can't hold back a giggle. "That means it's newsworthy."

"Newsworthy?" I raise an eyebrow. "What?"

"My date is a junior reporter for that college cable channel." She smiles.

"I thought your date was some guy who works for your dad."

"He was a C." She doesn't expand on her critique of him and I'm grateful. I'm really not in any mood to hear about her recent conquests since I'm still feeling the piercing bite of humiliation over sleeping with Hunter.

"I should go downstairs and check on the caterers." I run my hand over the belt of my dress. It's plain, black and covers my scar. It's comfortable, practical and makes me invisible. It's perfect.

"You should do something with your hair." She reaches to grab hold of the high ponytail I've pulled my hair into. "Let me help you curl it."

"No." I shoo her hand away with a quick flick of my wrist. "It's fine like this."

"You've gone back inside yourself." She glares at me. "Tell me what happened."

"I can't." I hear the slight crack in my voice.

"Just talk to me," she whines. "You'll feel better if you do."

She's right. I know she is. I want to confess everything to her. I want her to help me deal with all of this but I can't. I can't let anyone know that Hunter only wanted me because of Coral's heart. That's a secret I'll take to my grave.

"The guests will be here soon." I walk past her to the door of my bedroom. "I need to go downstairs."

"You better hurry." She's already occupied with her own reflection in the mirror again. "Or the hag is going to flip her lid."

I smile softly at her nickname for my mother. "I'll see you downstairs."

———

"THIS ISN'T the wine I wanted." My mother wrinkles her nose as she takes a heavy sip from the goblet in her hand. "Who approved this?"

"I did." I sigh. I knew this evening wasn't going to be

easy. My mother is notoriously picky. She'll criticize anything and everything she can.

She turns her back to me and hands the glass to a passing waiter. "Get a bottle from the cellar. Anything in there is better than this."

Her tone is sharp and I roll my eyes at her insistent need to be difficult. I turn to walk away. Maybe if I hid in my room for a few hours no one would notice.

"It's nice to meet you, Hunter." My mother's voice lifts above the hum of the room. She didn't say that. She couldn't have. I'm so fixated on him that I'm now hearing things.

"I'm a friend of your daughter's." There's no mistaking that tone. It's him. He's here.

I dart back around and I'm greeted with the sight of him towering over my mother's head. He peers at me, his eyebrow cocked. I shake my head trying to register what's happening. This can't be real. He can't be standing here in a sleek tailored navy suit kissing my mother's hand.

"We're not friends," I blurt out before wincing at my own choice of words.

"Technically we're…"

"Nothing." I move to stand between them. "We are nothing."

"Stop being so rude, Sadie." My mother's hand hovers just above my shoulder as if she wants to give the impression she's touching me. She never touches me.

"I'm not being rude." I stare at Hunter with my back still turned to her. "I didn't invite him."

"I brought the gift Sadie picked up for you." He dangles the gift bag from Whispers of Grace in front of her.

She snatches it greedily from his grasp. "How thoughtful of you to bring me a gift."

"It's from your daughter, not me." He corrects her in an

even tone but she's ignorant of anything but the prize that awaits her inside the bag.

"These are spectacular." She turns the box into the light so the sapphire earrings sparkle. "How did you know sapphires are my favorite gem?"

"I didn't." I can hear the exasperation in his voice. "Sadie got these for you."

"I'm going to put them on right now. Don't you move an inch." She pats him on the chest and trots off towards the staircase.

"Why are you here?" I ask as I lift my eyes to his face.

"You forgot the gift at the restaurant." He reaches in his suit jacket and pulls out my credit card. "You forgot this too."

I snatch it swiftly from his grasp. "You can leave now," I seethe. I don't want him here. I don't want to be near him. I can't be.

"I just got here." He expertly scoops a wine glass from a tray being carried by a waiter. "We have a lot to talk about."

"We don't." I sigh. "You lied when we met. You lied in the restaurant the other day. Hell, you even lied about being in San Francisco. Is Hunter Reynolds even your real name?"

He chokes on the mouthful of wine he's just taken. I stand in silence watching his body heave with heavy coughs. I stand stoic hoping he'll believe my unemotional reaction is real.

"You need to let me explain." His voice is a tender whisper. I can tell he's still trying to catch his breath. "I..."

"Why?" I cut him off. "So you can lie to me again and again."

"I'm not going to lie to you." He moves closer and I catch the hint of his cologne.

I take a step back. He's like a drug. I can't be anywhere near him. I don't trust my resolve even after everything that's happened. "If I want answers, I'll find Coral's family myself."

"No." His gaze darkens slightly. "I'll answer your questions."

"I don't trust you," I snap. "See yourself out."

I tense as I feel him grab my elbow. "I'm not leaving until we talk."

"Hunter." My mother is back and in full display mode. "Come. Let's toast my birthday."

His eyes search mine for an escape route but I just smirk as I tug my arm from his grasp and slip into the crowd.

CHAPTER FOUR

"They're going to cut the cake soon. Don't you want to come back down?" Alexa runs her hand softly over my forehead. "You're not fevered. Are you sure you're not just hiding from the hag." She laughs and clenches her teeth.

"She's in one of her moods." I roll over on my bed. I hate looking directly at her when I'm being dishonest. "She won't even notice I'm not there."

I feel the bed shift under her weight as she sits. "I saw him, Sadie." She tenderly strokes the back of my hair. "I saw Hunter."

"He was just dropping something off." I meter my tone so she won't suspect I'm breaking into a million pieces. "He's gone."

"Sooner or later you have to tell me what went down between you two."

"Later, okay?" I turn back slightly to look and her as I pull a weak grin across my lips. "Much later."

"Okay." She leans down and softly kisses my forehead. "I'll go down and lead the masses in singing to the old witch."

I can't help but laugh as she tosses me a wide smile when

she leaves the room. Just as I settle my head into my pillow the unmistakable click of the door opening jars me. "What did you forget?"

"Sadie." His voice startles me and I'm jerked to a sitting position.

"Get out." I jump to my feet, tumbling forward as I do.

He catches me before I hit the floor. "Slow down," he says gently. "I need to talk to you. I can't leave until I explain a few things."

"You shouldn't be in my room." I feel lightheaded. He's here. He's in my room. A few days ago I'd imagined that exact scenario but he was sprawled out naked on my bed while I gave him the same pleasure he's given me. I shake my head to try and chase away the images.

"Five minutes." He motions for me to sit on the bed. "Just five minutes."

I need to tell him to go to hell but the pleading look on his face is tempting. It's only five minutes. Even though my better judgement is screaming at me to tell him to fuck off, my heart won't let me say the words. I just nod.

"It wasn't all about Coral," he says softly. Hearing her name on his lips tears through me. She's no longer a fleeting teenage crush. She's a part of me now.

"Most of it was." I know the words will bite him.

"It might have started out that way." His voice cracks before he continues, "But none of what's happened between us is about her."

"How can you say that?" I snap. "It's all been about her."

He squats in front of the bed. His face is so close to mine now. I can see the moisture beading at the top of his lip. His lips are so elegantly shaped. They're so soft. I have to stop looking at him.

"Coral was a part of my life when I was a teenager,

Sadie." He rests both his hands on either side of me on the bed. "I'm twenty-six now. She's a very distant part of my past."

"She's not." I shake my head for added effect. "You came here that night because of Coral."

"I came here for you, not Coral," he whispers. "I wanted to see you."

"It was a private fundraiser." I point out. "How did you even get invited?"

He bows his head silently for a moment. I know he's searching for something to say. "I've known about your mother's charity since I first learned your name. I've been contributing anonymously for years now. I just called her administrative assistant and asked for an invite."

"And he just took your word for it that you were the anonymous donor?" I had heard my mother speak about large contributions that were coming in without any names attached. That can't really be him, can it?

"I gave him the numbers." He shrugs his shoulders.

"So why now?" I give him the benefit of the doubt. I can check with Chris, my mother's assistant tomorrow to confirm Hunter's story. "Why suddenly come out of the woodwork now?"

"I don't know." He exhales. "I guess part of me just wanted to see you in the flesh. I wanted to talk to you."

"So why not tell me who you were?" I press. "Why not just tell me about Coral?"

"I was scared," he says curtly before gazing down. "I was scared about how you'd react."

I'm suddenly aware of how close he is to me. His left hand has been grazing the side of my thigh while he's talked. I haven't pulled away. I haven't tried to break free of the prison he's built around me with his body.

"If I would have just told you I knew your donor, I was worried you'd want nothing to do with me." He's looking at me now.

"So you just didn't mention it?" I bite my lip to push back the tears I know are approaching. "Her heart is inside of me." I pull my hand to my chest. "I'm alive because of her."

"I couldn't tell you." He reaches to cup my cheek with his right hand. "You're so beautiful. I just wanted you so much."

I pull back and his hand lingers in the air before falling to the bed. I can't read anything in his expression. I can't tell if he's being genuine or trying to seduce me with his charm again.

"What about San Francisco?" I ask through clenched teeth. Maybe if I try a different approach, his unyielding resolve will crack.

He scowls. "I can explain that. You jumped to the wrong conclusion."

I ball my hands together into fists. He's pushing the onus for this back onto me. How dare he? He said clearly he was going to San Francisco and then he was standing in the middle of a store in Manhattan. There is no mistaking the deceit in that. "Explain then."

"I flew to San Francisco the morning after we were together." He traces his finger over the blanket. "Something urgent came up in New York and I went there to put out a fire. I was booked on a flight back to San Francisco the evening I saw you there."

"What came up?" I ask coldly. I don't believe him for a second.

"Just work stuff." He doesn't offer anything more.

"Work stuff," I repeat. "That clarifies everything, doesn't it?" The facetious tone in my voice is more than noticeable. He recoils slightly at the words.

"I wasn't doing anything sinister." I swear he's smirking at me.

I pull my gaze from him to the clock sitting on my bedside table. "Your five minutes is up. You need to go."

"I'm not leaving." He shifts both his hands slightly so they're barely touching my outer thighs.

I try to pull myself up from the bed but I have no room. He's completely blocking me. "Move. I want you to go."

"Do you remember when I made love to you, Sadie?" The question slides off his lips and buries itself within me instantly. My body reacts. It's betraying me.

"I don't want to talk about that." I push against him again and his chest is so unyielding. It's too strong. It's too much.

"I've never wanted a woman more than you." He's leaning closer now. I can feel his breath whispering across my cheek. "I think about you every second of every day."

"Don't." I hang my head down. I can't look at him. I can't think about that night. In spite of everything, I've imagined feeling his hands on me again. I've imagined the depth of the pleasure when I came under his tongue and when I felt him filling me.

"You can't deny you wanted me." His lips are grazing my neck. Why aren't I moving? Why haven't I pushed my way past him?

I don't respond. If he knew how wet I was becoming from his very presence, he'd know that my body still longed for his. He'd know that I wanted to push down all my doubts and just let him take me right here.

"You still want me." He traces his lips down my neck and I shudder under the touch. "You want me to fuck you now."

I do. Please. I want that. I want him to push me down. I want him to pull my dress from me. I want him to bury his face between my legs.

"I want you to leave." I find the will to pull back from his lips. "I don't want you," I lie.

"You don't want me to go anywhere." His hand is pulling on my ponytail. My hair tumbles over my shoulders. "You want me to make you come until you scream my name."

"You lied to me," I mumble. "It was all a lie."

"No." He brushes his lips over mine. "This was never a lie."

I feel the weight of his kiss and I pull my hands instantly to his hair. I weave my fingers into it, pulling him harder into my mouth. His hands are on my back. The faint pull of the zipper at the back of my dress gives way to a burst of cool air as my skin is exposed. He's going to fuck me. Right here, now. He's going to make me come. I crave him. I'm so addicted to him.

"Sunshine. I need to taste you," he breathes into my mouth as the dress slips from my shoulders. A chill courses through me and I shudder.

He glides his tongue down my neck. I glance down and watch him trace a line with his kisses down my scar. My scar. The scar. Coral's heart.

"No." I jump back. "No. Stop." I push on him so hard he falls backwards onto the floor.

"Sadie. Please." He jumps to his feet. "Don't push me away. I need you."

"I can't do this." I feel the bite of tears at the corner of my eyes. "I can't want you. Everything is a lie. Go."

He moves to sit next to me and I bolt to my feet pulling my open dress to cover my chest. I point to the door of my bedroom as I cover my mouth quieting a sob.

CHAPTER FIVE

"Wait." Alexa grabs both my shoulders in her hands. "You're telling me that his girlfriend's heart is inside your body?"

I nod. It's taken every ounce of strength I have to confess everything to Alexa. "Coral. It's Coral's heart."

"So he tracked you down and then what?" The confused look on her face speaks volumes. "Decided to fuck you in memory of her? I don't get it."

I wince at her words. It's brutally direct but it resonates through me. It's exactly the same thing I've thought about for days. "I have no idea why he did it."

"You don't want to know?" She eases herself back onto the couch. "You didn't ask him why?"

"He never gives me a straight answer." I pull on a thread that is hanging from the bottom of my sundress. "He just said he wanted to meet me and he was worried I'd react badly to him knowing my donor."

"That kind of makes sense." She purses her lips together tightly. "It is a little freaky that he used to date a girl who had the same heart inside of her."

I smile slightly at the irony of her words. It's true. It's more than a little freaky. "It's too bizarre. I just need to forget about him."

I reach for the remote to turn on the television. I invited Alexa over for a movie and my sudden need to admit everything to her has sidelined that.

"We're not forgetting anything." She jerks the remote from my hand. "You need to get more answers. We need them."

"We?" I laugh. "We don't need any answers from him." I wave my hand in the space between us. "It's my heart now. I get to make the decisions about what we need to know."

"You can't just drop this." Her tone is insistent and wearing on me.

"I can and I am." I push back. I don't need Alexa to tell me what to do. I decided last night after I ushered Hunter out of my bed and my life that I wanted nothing to do with him anymore. Any lingering curiosity I've had about my heart donor had been satiated when I saw Coral's picture and learned how she died. I just wanted to refocus on what was important to me. School and work was all I really needed.

"I know that look," she says it offhandedly. "You're turning back into boring Sadie."

"Boring Sadie?" I arch a brow. "What does that mean?"

"That means that you're going to pull back inside your shell again."

"It's not like that," I scoff. "I'm just being realistic. I have responsibilities. I need to focus on those."

"You have questions." She reaches to squeeze my hand. "Now is your chance to get answers. Go talk to him. Don't let him lie to you anymore."

I stare at her face. I see the persistence in her eyes. She's right. I do have questions. I have loads of questions and Hunter Reynolds is going to answer them.

———

"I WOULD HAVE PICKED YOU UP," he says as he opens the door of his apartment.

"I was fine." I step past him and hear the door close behind me. "I just took a taxi."

He motions towards the couch. "I was glad you called." He smiles thinly.

I don't reciprocate. I don't want to leave here without some solid answers. I'm tired of him pushing the truth aside. I want to know his true intentions. "I just need some clarification," I whisper dryly. "It's all been a lot for me to absorb."

He nods. I expect him to sit down next to me but he doesn't. My eyes follow him as he moves towards a desk and pulls a large book from it. As he nears the couch I realize it's a leather bound photo album.

"Hunter," I say his name not knowing what to say next. He must sense my trepidation. He has to know this is hard for me.

"Let me talk." His tone is reassuring and gentle. "I've been an asshole. I've handled all of this in the worst possible way."

I smile slightly at his words. He's right. He has been an asshole. He has been lying to me since we met.

He sits down next to me. I don't move when I feel his thigh resting against mine. I vowed that I wouldn't get too close to him but I don't want to recoil and risk losing his vulnerability. I feel as though he's ready to finally confess to me what's really going on.

He opens the photo album slowly and I'm greeted with the vibrant face of a young redheaded girl. It's Coral. She can't be more than six or seven-years-old in the photograph.

"Coral's mother gave me this after she died." His hands are trembling as he speaks. "I don't look at it anymore. I keep it close to remember her though."

I watch in silence as he turns the page and my breath catches. There beneath the hazy page protector is the letter. The letter I'd written to my donor family so many years ago. I hesitantly reach for the album. "May I see?"

He hands it to me and I rest it in my lap. I pull my head down to study the paper. The handwriting is so clean and perfect. I remember sitting at the desk in my room for hours working with tireless care to get it to look flawless. I must have rewritten it more than fifty times. I start to read the words and my emotions flood to the surface. I watch as a single tear falls onto the page. Before I can wipe it away, Hunter's large hand scoops it up.

"Her mom gave me the letter." He pulls the album back so it's resting on his knees. "I cherish that letter."

My gaze moves to his face. His eyes are moist too. It's the most exposed I've ever seen him. "I wrote it so long ago," I whisper.

"I didn't know I'd feel what I feel for you." He snaps the book shut sharply. "It's not about Coral."

I glare at the book. I want to see more. I want to know more about her. I need to know who she was. What her life was like.

"It is about her." I sigh heavily. "You wouldn't have come to look for me if I didn't have her heart."

"That part is true." He acknowledges with a quick nod. "Everything else is about you. What I feel now has nothing to do with Coral."

"What do you feel?" I snap. "I need to know."
"Like you're my destiny."

CHAPTER SIX

THEY'RE THE WORDS THAT FAIRY TALES ARE MADE OF. I'M HIS destiny. He said it. I heard it leave his lips. I see it in his eyes.

"I can't explain it." He reaches to cover my hand with his. "I've never felt like this before."

"You did with Coral," I shoot back. I know that he must have loved her. If he didn't, he wouldn't be cradling that book of memories so carefully in his lap.

"Coral was great." His face brightens as he says her name. "We were kids though. It was a crush."

"I think it was more than that," I counter. "She's obviously still a big part of your life." I nod towards the album.

He reaches forward to place it on the coffee table. "It's very complicated."

"Explain it." I challenge.

"We were in a lot of the same classes at school." He lifts his head to look directly at me. "She had this mess of red hair. She was cocky and brutally honest and I was a teenage boy."

I smile at the thought of Hunter as a teenager. I wonder if he was as beautifully reckless then as he is now. If he took what he wanted with the same virile force that he does today.

"We dated as kids that age do. You know..." his voice trails and I realize he's waiting for me to acknowledge the statement.

"I haven't dated much." I blush. "I'm not sure I know."

"We went to the movies and hung out with friends." His eyes are searching mine for some understanding. It's so long ago. I don't want him to tell me she was his first. I can't shoulder that knowledge. I don't want my heart to belong to his first lover.

"We kissed and held hands. We didn't do anything else."

I breathe in a heavy sigh of relief at the admission. "Yes," I whisper. "I understand."

"It was volatile and we argued. Teenagers are unpredictable." He laughs. "We broke up and got back together so many times I lost track."

I smile at the statement. I've seen brief flashes of his anger and I can imagine how that would blend with an equally temperamental redhead.

"I spent so much time at her house that I became part of her family. They helped me a lot after she died."

"What's her family like?" I ask boldly. Ever since I found out I had Coral's heart I keep flashing to her parents.

"Her mom is amazing." A wide smile takes over his face. "She's great."

I take comfort in the words. "What about her dad?"

"He died a few years ago." His gaze falls past me into the air behind me. "He had a weak heart. It didn't last long after we lost Coral."

We. The word is bittersweet. He lost Coral too. Even if they weren't as close as I thought they were. He cared deeply for her. Obviously many people did.

"Did she have siblings?"

"Two." He shifts slightly so there's more distance between us. "A brother and a sister."

"I have a brother too," I offer. "He's a jerk."

He smiles. "Coral's is too."

"What about her sister?" I've always secretly longed for a sister. Alexa is like a sister to me but it's still not quite the same as growing up beside another girl.

"Christina." He sucks in a heavy, throaty breath. "She's a year younger than Coral was."

"What's she like?"

"She's spoiled," he says tightly. "Pretentious and expectant."

"I take it you don't get along," I joke.

"We do." He closes his eyes as he pulls the knot of his tie looser. "She's just difficult sometimes. Often, very difficult."

"Do you still see them all regularly?" I ask already knowing the answer to the question. His friendship with Jax, Coral's cousin, is evidence enough of his bond to her family.

"Fairly regularly." He offers nothing beyond that.

"I'd like to meet them." I shove my hair back behind my ear. "I think I should meet them."

I feel his body tense next to mine. "No. That won't work." His tone is dismissive and terse.

"Why not?" I raise my voice slightly. "You wanted to meet me. They probably do too."

"Coral's death was devastating to all of them." He pulls his fist across his thigh. "You'd just be opening up old wounds."

The comment hurts. I have a part of someone they love inside of me. How could they not want to meet me as much as I wanted to meet them?

"You haven't told them about me, have you?" I shoot back. "Is Jax her only relative who knows about me?"

"That's how it has to be." He's unyielding. This is obviously not a subject that's up for discussion.

"Don't you think they should decide?" His unwavering stance is annoying. I want to meet them. I want them to see what I'm doing with her heart. I want them to know the life I'm building.

"I don't discuss her with them anymore." I can see the vein in his neck throbbing.

"What? Why not?"

"I killed her, Sadie." He says through clenched teeth. "I killed Coral."

CHAPTER SEVEN

IT'S AS THOUGH THE WORDS FLOAT THROUGH THE AIR. I CAN'T grasp them. I can't get my hands around them or my brain to absorb them. My mother said Coral died in a car accident. He didn't kill her. He couldn't have killed her.

His head is resting in his hands. I can see his measured, heavy breaths. I don't know what to say. I can't speak.

"I was driving." The emotion in his voice is thick and transparent. "I was driving the car."

"It was an accident." I reach to touch his back and he flinches. "My mother said it was an accident."

He nods his head slowly. "There was a truck. It came out of nowhere. I didn't stop in time."

"You didn't kill her," I whisper softly as I rest my head against his. "It was an accident."

His eyes dart up and meet mine. His gaze is heavy, dark and intense. I see a flash of something obscure. "It was my fault. I was careless."

"Accidents happen, Hunter." I run my hand down his back. I want to comfort him. Despite the past few days I want to cradle him in my arms and help take his pain away.

"I only had my driver's license a few weeks." He takes in a heavy breath to quiet the tremor in his voice. "She wasn't wearing a seat belt. She was sitting next me."

I move my hand to his shoulder, pulling him in closer to me. "You couldn't have known."

"I was looking at her. She was laughing. I didn't see the truck." His face is wet with tears. "It was over in an instant."

I reach for his hand and grab hold of it. I want to shield him from this pain. I can see how it's worn on him for so long.

"We were both okay but Coral." His body shakes with sobs. "She wasn't there. She went through the windshield."

My breath catches in my chest. I can feel my heart pounding. Coral's heart. The heart she lost that day. "I'm so sorry," I whisper.

He stands abruptly, pushing my hands from his body. "She was just there. Her body was there. Coral wasn't there."

"It must have been horrible," I mutter.

"Horrible?" he snaps at me. "Horrible? It was fucking disgusting, Sadie. So much blood. Her eyes vacant and empty. Christina in the back seat screaming. I'll never forget the smell, the sounds. I'll never forget."

I sit silently. I know why he searched for me now. He feels responsible for her death. He wanted to make sure I was taking care of the only thing left of her. "I think I should go." I start to stand.

He crumples to the floor next to the couch. "I'm not a monster. Don't go."

I fall to my knees. I can't walk away. I can't leave him like this. He's bared so much. He's given me so much today. How can I abandon him?

"Hunter, let me help you." I pull myself onto his lap so I'm facing him. "Let me take the pain."

He greedily pulls my body into his. The sobs coursing through him reverberate through me. "Don't leave me. I need you."

I reach to cradle his face in my hands. I search his eyes. All I see is deep regret and pain. "I'm not going," I whisper.

———

"THANK YOU, SUNSHINE." He breathes into my neck. He's been silent for more than thirty minutes just allowing me to hold him.

"Thank you for sharing so much." I shift my head from his chest so I can stare into his eyes again. The darkness is gone. Something has loosened within him.

He pushes a stray hair from my forehead. "It's so hard to talk about."

"I'll always listen," I offer. I move my body slightly suddenly aware of his growing hardness beneath me.

"You're an angel." He grazes my forehead with his lips, pulling my hips down into his lap.

"I'm just your friend. I'm not an angel."

"You're more than my friend," he purrs softly. "I can't be this close to you, Sadie and not want things."

"We can't do that anymore." I move to pull back but it's with little effort. Feeling his erection has made me desire him all over again.

"We can and we will." His lips trace a path across my cheek.

"No," I say breathlessly. There's no substantial meaning in the word and he knows it. The faint wetness of my panties on his lap is giving my desire away.

"You want me now." His hand drops to his lap; it's mere

inches from my core. "You can have me. Anytime. Anywhere you want."

I pull myself across his groin. He's so hard. So ready. All I have to do is reach down and undo his pants.

"Use me," he whispers. "You want me."

I pull back so I'm staring into his eyes. I see my desire there. He wants me just as much as I want him. I can feel how badly he needs me. Hunger courses through me. I have to feel that again. I have to come under his touch again.

His lips seal over mine as he lets out a low moan. He pulls my bottom lip between his teeth, biting it softly, sucking at it. I groan as I reach for his belt. I fumble with it before I feel his hands take over. He loosens it quickly and the smooth sound of his zipper lowering follows. He pulls his cock free and I tremble at the sight of it. It's so large, so perfect, so ready for me.

"You want me to fuck you, don't you?" He breathes into my mouth.

I nod quickly. "Please," I whimper. "Please, Hunter."

He pushes my panties to the side as he slides his cock along my slick cleft. I'm so wet. So ready to take him inside of me again.

"I can't get enough of you." He growls as he slowly pushes himself into me.

I move to take more of him in, leaning forward against the couch. He's so big. It's painful. So painful and so perfectly blissful.

"Fuck me, sunshine." He nips at my neck. "Fuck me now."

I move my body slowly against his, finding my rhythm. His hands are pushing on my hips, coaxing me to move faster. I do. "Oh, please," I moan through a heavy breath. "This is so good."

"This is yours." He pumps his hips up and into me. Pulling me down harder with each thrust. "Fuck me hard. Use me."

I move faster, allowing my body's natural desire to take over. I throw my head back as I grasp onto his shoulders. "Fuck, yes," I whisper. The brazen sound of my own voice is so foreign to me. I don't do this. I don't fuck men like him. Men like him. There's only one man like him.

"Christ." He's bucking wildly now, his cock plunging into me so deeply. An animalistic growl courses through him and into me.

I push harder, taking all of him. I'm so close. "It's too good," I scream. "Please, don't stop."

"I'll never stop wanting you." He groans as he empties himself into me as I rush over the edge into an intense orgasm. "I can't."

CHAPTER EIGHT

"So you fucked and made up?" Alexa giggles as she fills a cream container. "Was it as amazing as last time?"

"Better." I smile. "Raw or something. It was mind blowing."

"It was weird though, right?" She places the cream down as she screws the lid back onto the container. "One minute you're talking about his dead girlfriend and the next he's fucking your brains out."

I wince at the words. "Alexa."

"Bad choice," she sighs. "So you're just going to drop all the questions and crawl back into bed with him?"

"No," I offer weakly. I'm not, am I? Last night was a start but I want more answers. I want to know more about what's happened in his life since the accident.

"When are you seeing him again?" She picks up an apron and pulls it over her uniform.

I follow suit and pin my nametag on the front of mine. "We didn't discuss it. After we had sex, he drove me home."

"What did he say? What did you talk about on the way back to your place?"

I didn't want that question to come up. "Nothing, "I say offhandedly hoping she'll let it drop.

"What do you mean? The weather? Sports? What?"

"I mean nothing, Alexa. He didn't say anything until he kissed me on the cheek on my parent's doorstep and said goodnight." I shove the words out quickly.

"You don't think that's a problem?" She rests her hands on my shoulder, pushing my hair back so my nametag is visible. "He fucked you and then just took you home like that."

"It was an emotional night." I turn away. She's right. I've thought of nothing else since he left me standing by the front door. When he came everything changed. He quickly helped me compose myself, pulled his pants up and took me home. The only word he said was a weak *goodnight*.

"Don't let him fuck you around." She taps me on the shoulder. "You're too good for that."

"I won't." I smile at the flash of protectiveness.

———

"WHEN'S YOUR BREAK?" His voice pushes through the dim lull of the crowded bistro. I turn to see him standing next to the counter. He's striking in a dark navy suit, and white shirt.

"At noon," I call back as I try in vain to finish taking an order. How am I supposed to concentrate on anything when he's standing there looking like he just jumped off the pages of GQ?

He glances swiftly at the watch on his wrist. "I'll wait."

"It's an hour away, Hunter." I smile as I take the cash the woman ordering offers to me. "You don't have to wait."

"I'm waiting," he says curtly before walking to the back of the line.

"He's so fucking hot I can't breathe." Alexa's voice trails along my neck. "Does he bark orders to you like that when he's inside of you?"

I turn quickly and throw my hand over her mouth. "Be quiet. He'll hear you."

"Christ, he's delicious. Just look at him." She twirls me back around and I stare down the line of waiting customers until my eyes reach him. He's staring at his phone. The grace with which he stands only adds to his height. He's imposing and strong and many of the women in line are twisting their necks back to catch a glimpse of him. Of the man who told me last night that I was his destiny.

"Take over for me." I push myself away from the counter. "I'm going to the back to count cups."

"You're so lame." She pushes me aside. "I'll take his order and I'll deliver it, if you get my drift."

I shake my head with laughter as I take one last fleeting glimpse of him before walking to the back room. I need some air and I need to get my head back out of the clouds before I talk to him again.

CHAPTER NINE

"LAST NIGHT WAS REALLY HARD FOR ME." HIS DEEP VOICE fills the space in his small car. We're parked in a corner of the parking lot. "I've never shared the stuff about her with anyone before."

"Coral," I say her name softly. I don't want to shy away from that or from her impact in both of our lives.

He nods. "It's not something I like to talk about."

"I understand."

"I just want to make it clear that what we have isn't about her." His chest expands as he takes a very deep breath. "I've never felt this way about anyone."

I don't know how to respond. I want to believe in his words. I want to embrace this but there are still so many unanswered questions.

"I'm so wary of this." I just say it. I don't know how to temper it or the things I'm feeling.

"Of me?" He arches a brow. "Are you wary of me, Sadie?"

I nod. "Of you, of my own feelings, of everything about Coral." I hate that I ended that with her name. I am worried that his interest in me stems from some morbid curiosity about Coral's heart. I can't shake that.

"I want you to understand something right now." There's a stern undertone in his voice. "Something you really need to get."

"What?"

"I may have met you because you had Coral's heart but everything after that point was because of you." He tilts my chin up with his index finger. "You."

"You're like a stranger to me." I know the words will sting but I don't know how to quiet my fears. "You swoop into my life and then suddenly you're this guy who used to love the woman whose heart I have. Do you see the problem with that?"

"I never loved Coral." He corrects me. "Never."

"Have you loved anyone?" I spit the question out even though it's misplaced in the moment.

I can tell from his stunned expression that he didn't see it coming. I didn't see it leaving my mouth either but it's out there now. It's floating in the deafening silence of the car.

"Once, I thought I loved a woman." He looks directly into my eyes. "I was wrong."

"Was it serious?" I press. I need to know everything I can about him. He makes me feel things that leave me open and exposed. I can't keep wondering who he is and what's on his agenda.

"There was an engagement." His choice of words isn't lost on me. He didn't say he *was engaged*. He said there *was an engagement*. There's a distance there. I can feel it.

"You were engaged? When?"

"It doesn't matter, Sadie." He expertly skirts the question as he moves his hand towards my lips. "All that matters is in this car, right now."

I pull back from his touch and disappointment courses through his eyes. "No. There's more than just us."

"What?" he asks as he leans closer to me. "What happened last night was magical. I've never wanted anything as much as you. Why can't you just accept that?"

I want to melt into his words and his arms. I want so desperately to kiss him. Nothing in this world feels as wonderful as when his lips glide over mine. Nothing except when he's inside of me. I can't think straight when he's talking like this.

"Please, Hunter." I reach to grab his hand and clasp it in mine. "Please just be honest with me."

He drops his gaze to my lap. I can sense the deflation in his stance. He's leaning forward now. "I am," he whispers.

"Do you want me because I have Coral's heart?" My heart aches in my chest as I ask the question. I want so much for him to say no. I want him to want me for me.

"I'm falling in love with you, Sadie Lockwood." He turns to look at me. "It scares the hell out of me but I can't stop it."

"Please don't say things that aren't true," I murmur. I'm falling in love with you too I want to scream back but my better judgement has a rein on that. I can't do it, yet.

He tenderly grabs my face with both hands. "You are it for me. This is it. I can't stop what I'm feeling."

I close my eyes in utter helplessness as his words rush through me and his lips crush mine.

CHAPTER TEN

"MOM SAYS YOU HAVE A BOYFRIEND." MY FATHER TAPS ME on the forehead. "Are you and Will back on?"

I grimace at the mention of my ex. He couldn't hold a candle to Hunter. "No. It's someone new."

He tosses me a quizzed look. "What's his name?"

"Hunter," I reply. "He's older."

"How much older?" I watch as he stands straight up and his hands jump to his hips.

"Not much. Twenty-six."

"Does he have a job?" My father furrows his brow before sitting back down. "What are his intentions?"

I laugh at the questions. "He does have a job and his intentions are good." I bite my lip at the last part of my response. I think his intentions are good. I need to trust him. If I don't I'm going to drive myself crazy.

"When do I get to meet this fellow of yours?" He takes a long sip of the coffee sitting in front of him. I waited as long as I could last night to greet him when he got home from the airport, but I was too wiped. Getting up early to have break-fast with him is the next best thing.

"This week?" I suggest with slight trepidation. I haven't discussed my father with Hunter. Maybe I shouldn't be rushing us into something when I'm not even sure where we stand.

"Make a reservation at a nice restaurant and invite him along." My father doesn't glance up from the newspaper.

"Any preference?" I ask knowing he's very choosy about where he'll spend his money. I've been privy to enough of his inconsiderate ramblings at wait staff in restaurants.

"Anywhere you like is fine with me." He pats my hand before his gaze drops back to the business section.

"Daddy, I need to ask something?" I instantly feel a huge pit form in my stomach. This is one subject both of my parents aren't fond of. I need to know though. Any small bit of information will help.

"Sure." He finally places the newspaper down. "What's up?"

I study his face before I respond. He's so handsome. The grey on his temples only accentuating his strong features. My father has weathered so many storms with my brother and me. I hate to do this to him but I can't keep wondering what he knows.

"It's about my heart donor," I whisper the words without my voice cracking. "Mom said you overheard some nurses talking that night."

"Sadie," he spits my name out quickly before he takes in a sharp breath. "That was so long ago. It's a part of your past now."

"It's always a part of me." I pat my hand against my chest. "I just want to know about her."

"Your mother told you it was a young woman?" he asks with surprise.

"She said that you heard she'd been in a bad car accident?" The question sounds genuine even though I already know the answer. Maybe I just need confirmation from my dad.

"It was tragic." His voice tightens. "She wasn't buckled in and the boy who was driving was reckless. They hit a truck. I remember hearing she flew onto the road."

I wince at the words. It's the same story Hunter told me only this time the words are edged with displeasure and disgust.

"Her brain died and her parents decided to donate her organs."

"So other people got her organs too?" I feel my heart beating harder at the realization that others may have parts of Coral too.

"I think so." He studies my face carefully. "I don't know the specifics. All I know and care about is that her heart saved my little girl."

"Did anyone tell you her name?" I don't want to know that. Why am I asking?

"Nope." My father shakes his head before picking opening the newspaper. "All I know is that the accident happened somewhere on Long Island and she was airlifted to the hospital."

I stare at his hands. They're trembling. The vibrations are coursing through the paper causing it to flutter above the table.

"Thanks, Dad." I kiss his cheek as I rise from the table.

"Sweetie?" he calls after me as I reach the doorway of the dining room. "Don't forget to invite your young man to dinner. I need to meet him."

CHAPTER ELEVEN

"How do you feel about parents?" I take a small sip of the wine Hunter poured for me when I arrived at his place.

"My own or generally?" He raises his brow and smirks. "If it's my own, they drive me nuts."

My response is stalled when I realize he's never spoken of them. "You don't talk about them."

"I've got nothing to say about them." He pushes the words back at me and I instantly recognize it was a way to avoid the subject.

"Are you estranged from them?" It's a stupid question but I don't want the conversation to end before I know more.

"No." He pulls the word tightly across his lips. "I just don't want to discuss them."

I hate when he throws a wall up. This is part of who he is and if he can't talk about his own family, where does that leave us?

I take a bigger swallow of the wine to curb my racing pulse. "The reason I'm asking is my father is in town and he'd like to meet you."

"Your father is back?" He shifts on the couch until he's facing me directly. "You didn't tell me he was coming back."

"We don't talk a lot about everyday things," I murmur. We don't. Our last conversation in his car ended with us kissing for ten minutes before I had to race back to work.

"How's your mother handling his return?" The question is ripe with sarcasm. "She seems a bit adventurous."

"I guess." I feel slightly offended by his insulations about my mother. She may not be the greatest parent but she'd always stayed committed to my dad, or it seemed that way to me.

"Do you like living there with them?"

I'm not sure how to answer. I wasn't expecting him to ask me about that. "It's okay. I only do it on breaks."

"When I was your age I had my own place." His tone is clipped.

"When you were my age?" I parrot back. "That was such a long time ago, Mr. Reynolds. Did they even have heat and water in houses back then?"

He kisses my nose as he chuckles. "You know what I mean. Don't you feel stifled there?"

"Not really." I shrug my shoulders. "They don't even really know I'm there. It's convenient and soon I'll move back to the dorms."

"I wanted to talk to you about that." He tenderly reaches to push my hair behind my ear. "Have you thought about getting an apartment off campus?"

I consider the question. I have thought about it a lot. Not because I need the extra space but it would be amazing to have my own place. Somewhere that I can truly call home. "I've thought about it at times. Why?"

"I don't think your bunkmate is going to appreciate

watching us make love in the dorm." He runs his tongue over his bottom lip and I stare at it mesmerized.

"We're going to make love when I'm back at school?" I cringe as I ask the question. We haven't discussed the scope of our relationship since I found out about Coral. "I mean… I… I wasn't sure if this was a temporary thing still or not," I stammer.

"I don't want that." He shifts his body closer to mine and the soft scent of his skin is my reward. "I want to be with you. I want us to see each other as much as we can for as long as we can."

He didn't say forever. Why would he? I study his face for some hint. What does as long as we can mean? "As long as we can," I whisper under my breath.

"I want to move this at a pace you're comfortable with." His lips graze across my cheek and I tremble inside. My body aches for his touch.

"Can't we just come here when we want to…to…you know?" I struggle with the words.

"When you want to fuck me, sunshine?" His tongue slides across my neck. "When you need to feel my tongue on you or my cock in you?"

My breath quickens at the mention of his body. "Yes."

"Like now?" he growls into my ear. "Like you want me to fuck you now?"

I reach for his head and pull his lips into mine. I can't resist him. It's impossible. The moment he touches me or says those things to me, my body is on fire. I wait for him to touch me and he's focused on my face. His hands are caressing my cheeks, his tongue tasting my mouth. I pull on his shirt, fumbling with all of the buttons. His hands drop and I sense him removing his cuff links before he makes quick work of the buttons and the shirt slides off his shoulders.

"Touch me," he commands as he places my hands gently on his chest.

I'm in awe of the muscles and the sharp tone to them. He's so chiseled and hard. Every part of him screams pure and raw masculinity. I trace my hands down his stomach until they rest on his belt. He kisses me again and I'm grateful for the gentle reprieve. I've never touched a man like that. I've never brought a man pleasure with my hands or my mouth.

"You're everything to me, Sadie." He pulls back from the kiss to undo his belt. "Everything."

"I've never." I feel embarrassment slide through me. I can't tell him this. He's so experienced. He'll be so disappointed.

"Only when you're ready." He slides his pants to the floor followed by his boxer briefs.

I stop and look down at him. I soak in the beauty of his cock. It's so perfect. Everything about him is so well defined.

"I want to." I slide my hand over the tip, marveling at how smooth the head is. I can barely wrap my hand around him. I want to taste him. I want it now.

I push the coffee table back with my foot before I drop to my knees.

"Fuck." He pulls in a tight breath as I circle the head with my tongue. "Christ. Sadie."

I can feel his hands wrapped in my hair, pulling it, guiding me towards him. I open my lips and run my tongue over him once more before taking him in. The wide crest flows into my mouth and I moan at the sensation. He groans loudly in response.

"Like that, sunshine." He's coaxing me as I run my hand down the length, pulling it back up as I slide him effortlessly across my lips. I can't take him all the way in. There's too much. He's so big. I just want him to feel the same pleasure he's given me so many times.

I wrap my other hand around him too, pumping him faster as I suck harder. His hands push me down and pull me up as his hips follow the rhythm. I stop and suck hard on the head, pulling it softly between my teeth. My reward is a heavy groan. "You're so good. This is so good." His voice is so low, so filled with desire.

I take him farther into my mouth as I increase the rhythm again. My jaw aches. My knees hurt but I can't stop. I want to taste him. I want him to give himself to me.

"I'm so close," he whispers breathlessly. "Stop. I'm going to come."

I push my head down as he pulls on my hair. The sting resonates through me. I shake my head and moan in protest.

"Oh, fuck." He pulls the words from deep within as his hips buck off the couch and I feel the first hot burst of him hit the back of my throat. His hands clench the sides of my face as he jerks in my mouth. More and more of him is filling me. I take it all in. This is what it's like. This is what I always want to give him.

CHAPTER TWELVE

"YOU NEVER ANSWERED MY QUESTION." I SMILE AT HIM across his small dining table.

"Is it who just blew my world apart?" He winks before he takes another bite of his sandwich. "The answer is you."

I look down at the food on my plate. I'm not hungry. I still have to bring up the subject of meeting my father to him.

"The question wasn't about that stuff." I grin broadly.

"That stuff?" He cocks a brow. "You're the sweetest thing in the world. Do you know that?"

I wince at the compliment. "I'm not sweet."

"You are." He reaches across the table to push my sandwich closer. "You're sweet and amazing and one-of-a-kind."

I ignore the subtle suggestion that I eat the delicious looking turkey sandwich he made for me. I suggested we eat out but he was resistant. Maybe he liked restaurants as much as my dad did. I breathe heavily as I get ready to launch into the conversation I've been avoiding all night.

"The answer to the question is that sometimes someone else stays here and I don't want us to have to rely on this as our only place to be alone."

I sit in stunned silence. I meant the question about how he felt about parents. He obviously was still focused on where we would be fucking once I went back to school.

"Like a roommate?" I quickly scan the room realizing that everything in the place screams Hunter. I can't imagine anyone else staying here besides him.

"You could say that." He darts his gaze away from me. "I just think it would be better if you had your own place and we could hang out there."

"I'll think about it," I say without really meaning it. I'm still stuck back where he said someone else stays here.

"Is it Jax?" I offer up the name of the only person I know who visits him in Boston.

"Just a friend," he shoots back without any further details.

"Is it a woman?"

I instantly see a shift in his expression. It darkens and he silently stares at me as he chews and swallows the food in his mouth. I watch as he pulls the linen napkin curtly across his mouth before folding it and putting it next to the plate. "You need to stop this," he snaps.

"Stop what?" I fire back. "Stop asking questions."

"You think I'm going to jump into someone else's bed whenever I get the chance," he scowls. "You don't trust me at all."

"I wonder why." I push back from the table. "You never answer my questions directly, Hunter."

"That's bullshit." He stands and picks up his empty plate before throwing me a disappointed look. "I've answered all of your questions."

"Does a woman come here to stay?" I enunciate every syllable of the question, pulling the words tightly across my lips. "Answer the question."

"This is going nowhere if you're going to be jealous. A lot of women pay attention to me, Sadie."

I scoff at the words. Did he actually just say something that utterly narcissistic to me? "What the hell does that mean?" I chuckle. "So now you're so stunningly attractive that women can't stay away from you?"

"I know what I look like. I know what I have to offer." He turns and walks out of the room, plate in hand. I hear the sudden crash of it hitting something and smashing.

"I'm leaving," I call in the direction he's gone. "I won't be back."

"You're not leaving." He's in the doorway, his hands resting on the frame. He's imposing and strong and right now the expression on his face is bordering on intimidating.

"You can't tell me what to do." I shake my head. How did we go from the people on the couch an hour ago to this?

"I don't want anyone else." He throws his head back and I see the veins in his neck. "I can't want anyone else. Don't you see that?"

"I see someone who will never be direct with me." I shrug my shoulders as I reach for the purse I dropped on the floor when I got there. "I see a man who is always hiding behind faint truths and small white lies."

"That's not who I am." He lunges towards me, grabbing my shoulders with his hands. I almost tumble backwards from the force of his touch. "I've never been this open with anyone."

I don't know how to comprehend that. This is open to him? Not answering a simple question is open? "This isn't open, Hunter."

"What does that mean?" His tone is icy. It's reflected in his blue eyes.

"You can't be like this when you're in a relationship..."

"What?" he interrupts me. "What do you know about relationships, Sadie? You've never been in one."

I take in a heavy breath to temper the sharp edge of his words. He's right. What do I know? I've never been in a relationship.

"I didn't mean that." He's pulling my limp body into his chest. "Christ, Sadie. Please. I didn't mean it."

I push back with all the strength I can pull from within me. "You're right. I've never been in a relationship. If this is what it's like. I don't want to be."

"Don't go." He's tugging frantically at my arms as I pull away.

"I can't stay." I pull free and turn to walk out.

CHAPTER THIRTEEN

"YOU KNOW MORE ABOUT MEDICINE THAN I DO," ALEXA SAYS as she takes a bite of her pizza. "My best guess is that he's bipolar."

I almost choke at the suggestion. I try to swallow the pizza I'm chewing on before my laughter causes it to fly out of my mouth. "He's not bipolar. He's a liar."

"Why do you keep sleeping with him?" She picks at the mushrooms on her slice, pushing them to the edge of the plate. "There are so many cocks in the ocean. I'll find you another one just as nice."

I push my head back to roar with laughter. "I needed that."

"It's true." She winks as she takes a sip of soda. "Why do you think I like swimming so much?"

"You're on fire tonight." I chuckle. "Seriously, he's got way too much going on for me. It's like a police interrogation every time I ask him anything. I feel like he's on the verge of asking for a lawyer when I ask him simple questions."

"Maybe he's in witness protection." She pulls her brows together. "I saw something like this on an episode of Law and

Order SVU. The guy wasn't who he said he was and he did a lot of messed up shit."

I stare at her wondering exactly how her mind strings all these random thoughts together into such semi-coherent thoughts. "Maybe I'm just being too overly cautious."

"You're not married to the guy." She points her finger at me. "You're fucking him. Don't make it more serious than it is. Just enjoy it."

I purse my lips together as I consider her words. Maybe she's right. Maybe I need to lighten up. He did tell me everything about Coral and he seems honest about his feelings for me. Maybe I do need to just embrace it for what it is and push my doubts aside.

———

I'M DOWNSTAIRS. **Please let me up.**

I stare at my words on my phone's screen. It's been over five minutes since I sent that text and I've gotten no reply. It's eleven o'clock on a Tuesday night. I thought he'd be here. I assumed he'd be at home.

I was in the shower. I'll be right down.

I feel a lump in my throat at his reply. My mind automatically jumps to the conclusion that he's not alone. Why else would he be showering this late and why didn't he just buzz me up?

The elevator chimes its arrival and I turn to see him step off. His black hair is still damp and pushed back from his face. The blue sweater he's wearing brings his eyes to life. They are so brilliantly blue. I run my eyes down his jeans before they settle on his black dress shoes. How does anyone look so amazing right after they shower?

"Are you hungry?" He pulls me into a quick embrace. It's

as if the heated conversation we had in his dining room a few days ago never happened.

"Not really." I glance up into his eyes." I was just hoping we could talk about something."

"We will." He brushes his lips against the tip of my nose as his arm encircles my waist. "I haven't eaten yet. Let's go."

I follow his lead in silence. I came here to tell him that I was going to push my petty jealousy aside because I just wanted to enjoy every moment I could with him. Now, we're going out late at night to a restaurant. He hates restaurants and he loves having me in his apartment. How can I talk to him about not being jealous when it's all I can feel in this moment?

"Why can't we stay here?" I ask as he presses the elevator's call button. "Is your roommate here?"

His shoulders heave forward and I know he's disappointed by the question. "No, Sadie."

I turn my gaze down as I cross my arms on my chest. "Okay," I whisper.

"Every time we try and talk upstairs I end up ravishing you." A grin pulls on the corner of his lips. "I want that now too, but what happened the other day can't happen again. I want to talk in a neutral place and I want some food."

He has an answer for everything. Why is it so hard for me to believe him? I want to follow Alexa's advice and just take what I can from this. I have to do that. If I don't, I'm going to lose any time I have with him.

"Thai food?" I push myself into his chest.

"You are hungry, sunshine." He reaches for my hand, as the elevator swings open in the lobby. "Thai food it is."

CHAPTER FOURTEEN

"I HAVE A GIFT FOR YOU." HE FINALLY MOVES HIS HAND FROM my thigh. He rested it there when we sat down at the table of a small, dimly lit restaurant. "Something I think it's important that you have."

"Is it the pen?" I ask expectantly. I've felt badly about it since the day he offered it to me and I threw it in his face.

"That's on your desk in your room at home." He smirks. "I put it there when I was snooping in your room the night of your mom's party."

"You were in my room before I got back up there?" I try to remember if anything seemed out of place. "How did you know it was my room?"

He blushes. It's the first time I've seen a pale pink tint rush over his face. "This is humiliating."

"You found my vibrator?" I grimace.

He throws his head back with gleeful laughter. "You have a vibrator?" The words are barely audible through the chuckles.

I scrunch my nose and nod my head quickly. "Now who is humiliated?"

"That wasn't it but you'll have to show me that and more importantly what you do with that." He winks at me.

"We'll see about that." I move the food around on my plate. "How did you know it was my room?"

He reaches between his legs to pull the wooden chair across the floor so his knees are touching mine. I don't hesitate when he brushes his soft lips against mine. I moan at the sensation of his tongue dueling with mine.

"You're the only woman who can make me hard with a kiss," he whispers into my mouth. "Only you."

I smile at the words. I want to be the only woman. That's what I want most. It's the only thing I truly want.

"I got on the bed and smelled your pillow. I breathed it in. I imagined being there with you." He lightly brushes his lips against mine again. "I could have stayed there forever."

Emotions course through me. I can't speak. I just nod slowly holding my hand to his cheek.

"The gift." He pulls back slightly and reaches into his pocket. "Close your eyes."

I hesitate. I'm so witless when I'm around him. He has the power to make me forget everything. He's doing that now.

"Close them." He reaches to lightly kiss my left eyebrow.

I close them and feel his hand opening mine. Something metal is there. It's a set of keys. My eyes pop open.

"These are keys to my place." He pulls my hand in a fist to cover the key fob. "They're for you."

I search his face for anything he can offer. "Why?"

"I don't want there to be any doubt." He brings my hand to his lips and kisses it.

"You don't have to do this." My hand pops open. "I don't want to push you into anything."

"I can't lose you, Sadie," he whispers as he presses his face into my neck. "I'll do whatever it takes to keep you."

———

"DID you make plans for me to meet your young man?" My father is standing in the doorway of my bedroom, leaning against the frame. "I'm anxious to meet him."

"Not yet." I turn to look at him. I thought I could bring the subject up last night after dinner but Hunter insisted on driving me home. The lingering doubt about someone being with him was quieted by the gift of the keys but I still had questions I knew he'd likely not answer.

"What about tonight?" He walks into the room and picks up the keys Hunter gave me that I threw onto my desk.

"I'll call and see if he's free." I scroll through my phone.

"What are these?" My father dangles the key fob in his hand.

"Just keys," I offer. He'll flip if I tell him that the keys are for Hunter's place.

He studies them as if they hold a clue to another wonder of the world. "Do you have your own place? These look like apartment keys."

"Just extra keys a friend gave me." I stand and scoop them out of his hand. "I've been thinking about getting a place though."

"You don't want to live in the dorms?" His eyes trailed the keys and they're focused on my hand now.

"I'd like more privacy." I sit on the edge of the bed. "Maybe I can get a small apartment close to campus."

"Have you talked to your mother about this?" He raises his gaze to my face. "You know how she feels about you living alone."

"I'm alone most of the summer when I'm here."

"The staff is always here," he says. He has no clue that when I'm here by myself I send them all away.

"I'm old enough to live alone. Alexa does." I sound like a petulant child. I don't care. I want my life to finally be my own life. Now that I know about Coral I don't feel as though I'm living my life for someone else. I want to live it for me.

"That girl is not a good example of anything, Sadie." He shakes his head and rolls his eyes.

"She's my best friend," I say curtly. "I'm going to start looking for a place next week."

"Let me know how much you need." He throws the words in my direction as he walks out of the room.

"I'm doing this myself," I call after him. "I don't need your help."

CHAPTER FIFTEEN

"HE'S LATE." MY FATHER GLANCES DOWN AT HIS WRISTWATCH for what feels like the thirtieth time since we sat down at our table.

"He'll be here soon," I whisper while tapping out another text message to Hunter on my phone.

Please get here soon. My dad is flipping out.

"Who picked this place?" He brings the glass of scotch to his lips. "It's a bit too trendy for my taste."

My mother ignores our conversation, her gaze planted on a table where three men in their thirties are toasting with a rich burgundy.

"I picked it," I answer. It's a new place and I wanted to experience it with Hunter. Seeing how he rarely wants to eat out, dragging him here with my parents seemed like the ultimate trick to get him through the door.

"What's it called again?" My father throws his gaze around the room as if a neon sign is going to be flashing the name in his direction.

"Meteor." I sigh. It's now almost an hour past the time

Hunter was supposed to meet us. I glare at the entrance willing him to walk through it.

I'm startled when my phone chimes signalling a new text.

I'm stuck in a meeting, sunshine. I can't leave. Give my regrets to your folks. H.

I feel my blood pressure rising as I read the words over and over again. He's not coming. He promised me earlier on the phone he'd be here. He even said in a text ninety minutes ago that he was on his way. The moment I texted him the name of the restaurant he fell silent. He had to have known his meeting might run late. Why didn't he tell me there was a chance he couldn't come?

"He's not coming, is he?" My father is already on his feet, his wallet in his hand.

I shake my head silently from side-to-side. Humiliation is pulling my voice within.

"We're leaving. We'll eat at that steakhouse by the court-house. Let's go." He throws a few bills on the table as he barks at my mother.

"This was such a waste of time." My mother's gaze is still entranced by the trio of businessmen in the corner. "Are you coming or not?"

I pull myself from the chair feeling as though my feet weigh a ton. How could he do this to me? It was a simple request? It was just one meal. All I wanted was a few hours to show my father what an amazing man I'd met.

———

"CAN you cover my shift on Saturday?" Alexa yanks hard on my ponytail causing my neck to snap back.

"Ouch," I scream at her. "Easy on the hair." I rub my hand

over the back of my head. "You almost gave me whiplash, jerk."

"Sorry." She scrunches her lips together. "Can you do it?"

"Sure," I answer. I wasn't going to have plans. I hadn't heard from Hunter since he stood me up last night and I wasn't sure I wanted to hear from him anytime soon.

As if on cue he's standing at the counter. Sunglasses are covering his brilliant blue irises. His suit is dark, almost black and with his current stance he looks like a cross between a secret service agent and a hit man.

"Can I get you something?" Alexa pipes up and a wide smile pulls on her lips. "Coffee? Tea? Maybe me?"

"I'm here to see her." He motions over her head in my direction. "Sadie, take a break."

"You're him?" Alexa seems startled when she realizes it's Hunter beneath the dark glasses. "You look different."

He ignores her comment and pulls the glasses from his face. "Sadie, can you take a break?"

"I can't." I shrug my shoulders as I continue to restock the cup stoppers. "We're swamped today."

He cocks a brow as he circles his head around the almost empty bistro. "Take a break. This is important."

"Go." Alexa pushes on me. "Just go."

I throw her a steely gaze. Why doesn't she have my back on this? I told her on the way to work that Hunter stood me up and now she's practically throwing me into his arms.

"Five minutes," I warn as I take off my apron and follow him to a table near the front window.

"You're pissed about last night, aren't you?" He questions as I lower myself into the chair opposite him.

I scan his face, noting how tired he looks. "You stood me up. It was an important night for me and you just didn't bother to come."

"It's not like that." He reaches across the table with both hands to grab mine but I'm too quick and I retreat.

"What's it like then?" I challenge. "You said you'd be there and then suddenly you were too busy."

"Sometimes my clients aren't flexible." He leans back in his chair. I can tell I've bruised his enormous ego by not falling into his hands the moment he reached for me.

"What restaurant are you working on now?" I know the question reeks of distrust but I don't care. I want answers.

"It's in the early planning stages. They haven't named it yet." He looks past my head to the counter behind us.

"So what was the emergency?" I lean back now too. "If it's so early that it doesn't even have a name why did you have to stay?"

"It's more complicated than that, Sadie." I can hear the whispered tone of exasperation in his voice. "You wouldn't understand."

"Don't insult me." I cross my arms over my chest. "You didn't have the balls to come meet my dad and so you bailed at the last minute."

The thin smile that sweeps over his perfect lips doesn't go unnoticed by me. "You've seen them, Sadie. You're not questioning their size, are you?"

I can't help but smile back. "Don't do that. Don't talk about sex when I'm mad at you."

"Let me take you into the back room and I'll make you come so hard you won't ever be mad at me again."

I laugh at the remark. "I'm right, aren't I? You didn't want to meet him."

"I panicked," he admits. "I've never met the dad of a woman I'm dating before except for..." his voice trails.

"Except for Coral," I whisper.

He nods his head. "I'll make it up to you. We can plan another dinner with him."

"It's not that important," I skirt the truth. "We'll just see how this goes. I need to get back to work." I stand and walk back towards the counter, the weight of Coral's connection to him once again pushing on my shoulders.

CHAPTER SIXTEEN

"HE'S NEVER GOING TO GET OVER HER. I'M RIGHT ABOUT that. Don't you think?" I open another of the doors in Alexa's kitchen looking for the spices.

"I don't know about that." She points to the cabinet above the stove. "You're kind of a reminder of her."

I can't turn back around to face her after the remark. The same thought keeps coursing through my mind. I'm the ulti-mate reminder of the girl who died when he was next to her. How does a person get past that?

"Should I end it now?" I ask in barely more than a whisper as I sort through the spices looking for something to season the salmon fillets I brought with me.

"No." I hear her rush up behind me. "You can make him forget her. You just have to lighten up."

"You don't know what it's like." I spin back around so I'm looking at her. "You can't know what it feels like that have her heart inside of me and to know that he's probably thinking about that every time he sees me."

"Maybe he sees you." She cups her hand over my cheek.

"Maybe you're already making him forget her and that's hard for him."

"I don't know what you mean." I turn back towards the cabinets so I can begin a hunt for olive oil.

"Think about it." She reaches past me to retrieve the bottle of white wine she opened when I arrived. "You said he hasn't had a lot of serious relationships, right?"

"He's alluded to that," I sigh. "And I guess the fact that he only ever met Coral's dad says something about how casual his other relationships have been."

"I think Hunter is falling in love with you," she doesn't hesitate as she says the words. "I think you're making him forget Coral and since he thinks he's responsible for her death he's having trouble with that."

"You mean he feels guilty if he finally finds happiness?" I can feel my pulse racing at the mere suggestion that he's falling in love with me.

She nods as she refills her wine glass. "You're the one woman who is making him let go of all of that."

"I hope so." I exhale sharply as I turn back around to season the fish. "Nothing would make me happier."

———

ARE YOU DECENT? ***I'm coming over.***

I wait with baited breath for him to reply to my text. I'm sitting in a taxi in front of his building.

Turn around and see for yourself.

I crane my neck around to look behind me and I see him standing directly on the sidewalk in front of the building. He walks swiftly to the taxi's door as I push it open. I fumble in my purse for my wallet but before I can retrieve it he's pulling some bills out of the pocket of his suit's jacket. "Have a good night," he calls over the seat to the driver as he hands him the cash.

"How did you know I was in the taxi?" I sigh as he brushes his lips across my cheek.

"I can sense when you're close." He cocks a brow as he bends lower to kiss my lips. "It's my Sadie sense working."

I raise my brows in response. He's so charming, it's no wonder I keep feeling the pull back to him.

"Did you bring your keys?" He holds out his hand and I feel a tinge of disappointment race through me. I don't want him to take them back. Maybe he's pissed after the way I dismissed him at the bistro the other day.

"I did." I let them fall into his palm.

"Mine are somewhere in my bag." He motions to the laptop bag he has strung over his shoulder. "I'll just borrow yours until we're inside."

I smile at the suggestion that the keys still belong to me. I follow him silently to the elevator and wait patiently as he scrolls through his phone after pressing the call button.

He reaches around to lazily run his hand down my back as we wait for the lift to arrive. I lean in closer to him, wanting to melt into his body. His hand moves lower, skirting the top of my jeans before he dips a finger just inside the waistband.

The bell signaling the elevator's arrival startles him and he jumps a touch. I giggle in response and he throws me a playful frown. I want it always to be like this. Even in utter silence I can feel the connection between us.

He drops his bag to the floor as the elevator door's slide closed and pulls me into a heated kiss. I'm taken back by the strength of his touch but I let him claim me. He pushes me against the wall, his knee separating my legs. "Do you know what I've thought about all day?" he growls into my ear.

"What?" I can barely find the breath to say the word.

"Tasting you. Being inside your tight little body. Fucking you, Sadie."

I moan at how brazen his words are. I can feel how erect he already is.

The elevator jolts to a stop and he pulls away just as abruptly as he grabbed me. I whine at the loss of his embrace and that brings a sly grin to his mouth. "Get in my apartment. Now." He guides me into the hallway.

I don't make it through the threshold of the door before I feel his hands on my waist. He scoops me up into his arms. I hear my purse hit the floor with a dull thud as he kicks his shoes off in route to his bedroom.

I'm thrown onto the bed. There are no words spoken. There doesn't need to be. His lips find mine again and he's aggressive with his kiss. He's biting my lips, nibbling at my tongue. His hands are pulling my clothes from my body. I feel my jeans being pulled down and my panties ripped off. He fumbles with the tie on my wrap around shirt. I reach down to help but he pushes my hands away, his lips never leaving mine. I hear the shirt's fabric as he pulls it apart. He's ripping it, clawing at my skin. He's an animal. An animal hungry for anything he can take.

I didn't know it could be like this. My eyes flutter open and I'm startled by the sight of his brilliant eyes boring into me. He's kissing me feverishly all the while he's staring at me. Deep guttural groans are pouring from him. He's fully clothed. I'm completely naked and I've never felt so comfortable in my entire life.

Suddenly his lips are gone and he's pushing me onto my back. I feel his hair grazing my breasts and my stomach before his lips glide over my slick cleft. "My Sadie is always ready for me," he purrs into my wetness.

I moan at the first delicate touch of his tongue against

my clit. He's not going to be gentle. I can tell it's going to be different this time. He pushes his mouth onto me, sucking my folds between his teeth. He grates them across my clit and I almost scream. I pull his hair with my hands, wanting him to take me to the edge, needing to come like this.

"Please, Hunter," I beg. "Please."

"Please what?" He stops and I push my hips into him. "Say it. Tell me what you want."

"Lick me." I moan loudly. "Lick me until I come."

He grants my wish and buries his face between my legs. His hands push my thighs farther apart. I'm spread so far open. I'm so exposed.

"I'm so close," I scream. "So close.

He licks harder. My clit is so raw, so sensitive. I race towards an orgasm. This isn't like before. It's already so intense. I dig my fingernails into his scalp. "No. Oh god, no," I cry out as my entire body shakes from the pleasure. I come hard, withering beneath his lips.

He licks me gently as I float back into my body. I shiver at the touch. I'm too sensitive. Everything is so much right now.

I watch silently as he stands. His eyes are locked on mine. He doesn't say anything as he quickly pulls his shirt off, buttons scattering everywhere. His pants follow suit and he stands, stroking his thick, heavy cock as he stares at me.

I motion for him to come closer and he pulls himself over me. I feel his cock pressing against my leg. I want it so much. I want him so much.

"I can't ever stop this." He moans as he runs his lips over mine again. "I can't let you go."

I scream out as he pushes himself into me in one fluid motion. He runs his lips over my forehead as he fucks me hard. He's not gentle this time. His desire is consuming him. I can feel it. I work to keep up to his rhythm.

"Look at me." he commands. "Sadie."

My eyes flash open and lock with his. I can barely keep them that way. The pleasure is so deep. The ache of him inside of me is so consuming.

"Sadie," he repeats my name again followed by a deep moan. "I can't be away from you."

I stare into his eyes as he fucks me hard. "No. Please, "I whisper back.

"Your body is mine." He moans so loudly it bounces off the walls.

I'm so close to coming again. I feel my body start to heat through. "Hunter." I glide my hands down his back to cup his ass and push him deeper into me. "I'm coming."

He throws his head back as he jerks within me. His body is shaking with the strength of the orgasm.

I close my eyes and hold my breath as I feel the pleasure overtake me too.

CHAPTER SEVENTEEN

"THAT WAS DIFFERENT," I SAY AS I GLIDE MY HAND ACROSS his smooth chest.

His body rumbles as he laughs. "That was fucking amazing."

I giggle in response as I look up at his face. "It was so amazing."

"What got into you?" I reach up to kiss him lightly on the chin. "You were a man on a mission."

He pulls me by my arms so my face is resting against his. "I have to go away again and I can't stand the thought of leaving you."

Disappointment washes over me. "Where to now?" I ask. It doesn't matter where he's going. What matters is that he isn't going to be here with me.

"New York," he says without any hesitation. "I have a soft launch there the day after tomorrow and I can't miss it."

"That's when a restaurant tries out their menu on a few people?" I want him to know that I'm interested in what he does.

"Impressive, Ms. Lockwood." He taps me on the tip of my nose. "Did you see that on the Food Network?"

"You're a fucking riot." I try to keep a straight face but a smile takes over. "I read about restaurant openings online."

"To learn more about what I do?"

"Yes." I blush. My inexperience in the real world is humiliating sometimes and I don't want him to see me as inexperienced anymore. "Maybe sometime I can come along for one."

"I'd love that." He traces a path across my forehead with his finger. "I hate being away from you."

"When will you come back?" I don't know how to hide the hint of desperation in my voice.

"Three days. I'll only be gone three days."

"They'll be the longest three days of my life," I whisper into his chest.

———

"CAN I BORROW A SHIRT?" I hold the remnants of my torn shirt in my hand. "Mine got ruined somehow."

He smiles as he reaches behind him to pull a dress shirt from a chair. "Wear this one. I wore it today." He pulls it around my shoulders.

"It smells just like you." I breathe in the intoxicating mixture of his cologne and his natural scent that has settled into the fabric.

"Now it will smell like us both." He carefully buttons each of the buttons.

"It's perfect. Thank you. "I giggle as I toss the sleeves playfully around. My hands are hidden beneath the length of the fabric.

"You have tiny arms." He smiles. "Let me fix that."

I relish in his touch as he carefully folds each of the arms of the shirt up until they're settled on my forearms.

"It looks better on you than it does on me."

"That's not possible."

"You're beautiful." He takes my hand guiding me to the edge of the bed. "I'll take you home in a minute. I want to talk about something first." His tone is serious now.

"What is it?" I ask even though I'm not sure I want to know the answer.

"I wish I could hide away in a room with you forever." His beautiful lips are so close to mine.

"That would be heaven," I whisper.

The fingers of his left hand pull at the collar of the shirt he just put on me. "I can't though. I have to go do this trip but I need you to understand that I'd much rather spend that time with you. Here or anywhere."

"I do understand." I nod slightly. "I wish you could stay here too."

"The moment I'm back I'll pick you up and we'll spend the entire day together if you're not working."

I smile at the promise. I'll make sure I'm not working that day. I can't wait to be back in his arms again. "Maybe we could..." I let the words trail from my mouth as I kiss his lips softly. "Maybe you could help me look for a place of my own and then I could give you one of my keys."

"I'd love nothing more." His mouth curves into a soft smile. "I'm going to miss you so much."

"I'll miss you too." I shiver as I lean into him.

"You're cold." He pulls away from to retrieve the suit coat he pushed off his shoulders before we made love. He wraps it tenderly around my body. "Wear this. Let's get you home."

I smile at how loving he's being with me. "Can I have my key back?"

"It's in the pocket." He gestures to the jacket. "Keep it until I'm back. I like the idea of you wearing my stuff."

CHAPTER EIGHTEEN

"So all is good on the Hunter front?" Alexa is looking through my dresser drawers. "Where's that pink t-shirt you bought last month? I want to borrow it."

I point to a pile of clothes on the chair by my desk. "Somewhere in that mess and you can have it. Once you wear it, it's going to be stretched out." I motion to her chest.

She grins as she reaches to pick up Hunter's suit jacket from the top of the messily stacked clothes. "Since when do you wear men's business suits?"

"That's Hunter's. He gave it to me the other night. I was cold."

"This is premium." She slips it over her shoulders. "Not only is he a great fuck, he has good taste in clothes."

I laugh as I join her at the desk. I start rifling through the pile of clothes trying to find the pink t-shirt that she's suddenly claimed as her own.

"Seriously, this is gorgeous." She runs her hands over the fabric of the jacket. "This suit costs a lot of money. I can't afford anything nice on a teacher's salary. Maybe I need to go into the restaurant consultation business too."

I laugh at the suggestion of her switching careers at this point. The reason she wanted to be a teacher in the first place was for all the vacation time.

"He left his keys in here." She whips the keys he gave me out from one of the pockets. "He should have noticed by now that he didn't have these."

"They're mine." I beam. "He gave me keys to his place."

"Shut. The. Fuck. Up," she says slowly. "You have keys to his apartment. You can come and go as you please?"

"I guess." I realize when I answer that Hunter and I never defined any rules for when I can go over there. "He didn't say otherwise."

"This is way more serious than you've been letting on." She sits next to me. "You're practically living with him."

"I'm not," I scoff. "It's just keys."

"What's this?" She pulls a white piece of paper from the inside pocket. "He's full of surprises. Is it a love note?"

I reach to grab it from her grasp but she's too quick. She scrambles over the bed as she pulls the note open. I watch as she scans the paper and then throws it on the bed. "It's nothing. Something about an appointment."

I pick it up and instantly recognize Hunter's handwriting. It's the same curved letters that were on the card when he sent me flowers. It's scrawled recklessly but I can make out tomorrow's date and a Manhattan address.

"This must be the new restaurant opening that he had to go to New York for." I stare at the paper finding some brief thrill in touching something Hunter held in his hand.

"We should go." Alexa blurts out as she slides the suit jacket off her shoulders.

"What?" I shoot back. "You're kidding."

"Why?" She smiles brightly as she pulls the pink t-shirt from the pile of clothes. "You told me he said he wanted you to go to a soft launch with him one day. What better chance are you going to get?"

I feel excitement run through me at the suggestion. "Do you think he'd be pissed if we just showed up?"

"He'd be thrilled that you surprised him." She pulls the white t-shirt she's wearing over her head, revealing her bright red bra.

"I don't know, Alexa." I'm wary of the idea. The sharp chime of my phone breaks our conversation.

"He's hot for you. He'd want to see you if he could." She pulls the pink shirt over her head and it hugs her curves like a glove. I instantly regret buying it when I see how much better it looks on her than on me.

I glance down at my phone.

I miss you so much. I wish you were here. H

"He misses me," I whisper.

"That's our sign." She scoops her purse off the bed and reaches for the doorknob. "We're taking the train into Manhattan tomorrow to surprise your boyfriend."

CHAPTER NINETEEN

"Do you think he'll be excited to see me?" I pull the belt on my blue dress tight around my waist. I peer at myself in the mirror. This is the first time I've gone anywhere since the transplant with so much of my scar on display.

"He's going to ravage you on the spot." She motions for me to zip up the sleek red dress she brought with her. "With any luck he'll have a friend who is as hot as him. I need to get laid."

I laugh out loud. "If things go well maybe you'll be back here alone with a guy tonight."

"Count on it." She traces a tube of pink lipstick around her mouth. "I'm ready to paint the town red or pink or whatever."

"Thanks for suggesting we do this." I settle onto the edge of the bed as I watch her play with her hair in the mirror.

"You need to do more of this." She turns to look at me. "He's helped you a lot."

"What do you mean?"

"He's made you trust yourself more." She piles her hair on

top of her head before she turns to each side to survey how it looks.

"I'm not sure I understand that." I look down at my lap. "I've always trusted myself."

"He's helped you believe that it's okay to have fun. He helped you trust that people don't care about the scar as much as you think they do."

I nod. "I guess that's true."

"Do you think we should pin my hair up or should I wear it down?" She lets her hair fall back down around her shoulders.

I instantly pull her hand to my straightened dark hair. This is the first time in a long time that I haven't wished I looked exactly like Alexa. Maybe she's right. Maybe he has helped me trust in myself more. I trust that I'm enough now.

"Let's pin it up." I reach to grab her overnight bag where she's stored all of her hair accessories. "Your neck is so beautiful. You should show it off."

She reaches to grab my hand. "You're beautiful too. You believe that now, don't you?"

"I do." I squeeze her hand as I smile at her reflection in the mirror.

————

"THIS IS THE PLACE," Alexa shouts through the barrier at the cab driver as he pulls the car to a sudden halt next to the curb.

"You're sure?" I glance out the window into the street and I don't see anything even remotely notable. I pull a few bills from my purse and hand them to the driver. My heart is beating so hard I can hear it in my ears.

"It's the address that he wrote down." Alexa squints at the note that Hunter left in his suit jacket. "It's a restaurant so this has to be it."

She pulls me towards the bank of windows and we both peer in. It's full and I can't imagine how we're going to weave our way through that crowd. People are laughing and as I scan the faces I don't see Hunter's anywhere. Maybe this was a mistake after all. Maybe we should just turn around and go back to Boston.

"Mr. Reynolds invited us." Alexa has snuck over to the door and she's talking to an attractive man stationed there. I listen intently as she tells him she's single and asks what he's doing after the party. The fact that he now has her phone in his hand suggests she's already collected her first number of the night. It's impressive considering the fact that we haven't even gotten inside the building yet.

"Sadie, let's go." She motions for me to follow her and I hesitate briefly before I step towards the entrance. I won't turn back now. Once Hunter sees me, I can't control his reaction. I just want so desperately for him to be as excited to see me, as I am to see him.

We're greeted with the smell of delicious food and a warm ambiance. The restaurant is decorated in the same tones and warmth as Axel, back in Boston. I smile as I think back to Hunter taking me home that night and asking if I wanted to kiss him.

"This is so much like Axel," I whisper into Alexa's ear, hoping she'll hear me above the noise in the room.

"It's called Axel NY," she calls back towards me. "Did you know he was working on this?"

I shake my head even though her gaze is cast forward and she can't see my reaction. Why wouldn't he have mentioned this was one of his projects when he saw me at the Boston location?

"Let's grab a drink." She grabs tightly to my hand and weaves her way through the crowd to the bar. "Two of those," she yells to the bartender and I shudder at the thought of what she's just ordered for us. I don't let go of her hand as I search the room for Hunter. I still don't see him within the crowd.

"I haven't noticed either of you lovely ladies in here before." A blond man grabs my arm and I recoil at his touch. He's older than us. Closer to Hunter's age I'd guess. Why would we have been here before tonight? It's the soft launch.

"We're just in town visiting." Alexa spins back around so she's practically touching his nose.

I tune out their conversation as I reach into my purse to fish for my phone. After checking for any messages from Hunter, I contemplate sending him a text telling him I'm here. I don't want to ruin the surprise though. I didn't come all this way to miss the reaction on his face when he sees me in the crowd.

"Alexa, I'm…" my voice trails as I realize she's no longer standing next to me. Panic rushes through me. There are so many people in the room. It's so noisy and I'm alone. I wish I could find Hunter. I need to ask someone where he is.

I push my way away from the bar towards one of the open windows near the street. I pause when I see a flash of red hair in the crowd. I recognize the hue. That's the same red hair that Coral had in the picture.

I maneuver my way towards her and I'm rewarded with the silhouette of a woman near the window. She turns to face me and I instantly can see the distinctive curve of her nose. This has to be Christina. She must be Coral's sister. It would make sense that she'd be here. Hunter is like family to her family.

"Excuse me," I say quietly hoping she'll turn. She stands silent, her gaze cast to the street.

"Miss." I tap her on the shoulder and it causes her to jump.

"Yes?" Her voice is lovely. She's regal. The deep blue dress she's wearing highlights the color of her eyes.

"I'm looking for someone." I try to level my voice. This has to be the woman Hunter told me about. She knew and loved Coral.

"Who might that be?" The way she pulls her gaze over my body suggests she doesn't think I measure up to her. He did say she was pretentious. He was right.

"Hunter Reynolds."

She raises her left brow before she laughs. "You're not one of those, are you?"

"One of what?" I try to hold onto my composure. Hunter wasn't kidding when he said she was difficult. I haven't been speaking to her for more than a minute and I can already feel her displeasure in my disturbing her.

She inhales sharply. "One of those people who still calls him by that wretched nickname. He hasn't been Hunter since high school. "

"Nickname," I whisper. Hunter is his nickname?

"Do you know where he is? He's handling the launch of the restaurant, isn't he?"

"This restaurant?" She furrows her brow in confusion. "We've been open for months."

"This isn't a launch party?" I scan the room searching desperately for any sign of Hunter. Maybe that note in his pocket had nothing to do with his job. Maybe I've stumbled into a private party for Coral's family.

"What's your name?" she asks without any reservation in her tone.

"Sadie."

"You're Sadie? The Sadie?" Her voice is louder now and I can see people turning to look at us through the corner of my eye.

"Sadie Lockwood," I offer.

Her gaze falls from my face to my chest. Her eyes are glued to the top of my scar. "He brought you here for me, didn't he?" She pulls her hand to cover her mouth. "Are you the surprise he promised me?"

I can't understand what she's saying. "Am I what surprise?"

"My engagement present." She reaches to touch my chest and I pull back sharply. I look behind me for Alexa. I want to go. I can't do this. I don't understand what's going on.

"You have Coral's heart." Her voice cracks as she says her sister's name.

"You're Christina, aren't you?" I ask even though I already know the answer.

"He told you about me?" She smiles brightly.

I can only nod in agreement. I feel as though I've stepped into an alternative universe.

"You *are* my present." She pulls me into a tight embrace. "Zander promised us he'd find you before the wedding and he brought you to our engagement party. Wait until my mother sees you."

The light above us catches on her diamond ring, just as she gasps loudly. "Zander, you're finally here..."

She rushes towards the doorway and I take the reprieve from her to once again scan the room behind me. I have to find Alexa. I need to leave before Hunter gets here.

"Zander, you don't know what this means to me." Christina's voice rises above the low hum of the room. "I love you so much. It's so perfect you brought her here."

My eyes leave the crowd as I turn to look at her once again. My gaze slowly snakes up her back to settle on her head. She's embracing a man tightly. My legs give out as his eyes lock on mine. It's Hunter. Her Zander, the man she's marrying, is my Hunter.

PART THREE

CHAPTER ONE

"SADIE." ALEXA'S VOICE DRIFTS INTO MY EAR AS IF I'M IN some sort of transparent bubble. I can barely hear it, but it feels as though it's vibrating through my body. "Sadie, what the hell is going on?"

I turn to grab hold of her. She'll steady me. She's my anchor. She'll know what to do.

"Is that Hunter with that redhead?" she's whispering now. "Why is she clinging to him like that? Go over there and tell her to get her hands off of him."

"She's Christina," I say as if that's going to somehow make Alexa shut up. She has no idea who Christina is. Until five minutes ago she was just Coral's sister. Now, she's Hunter's fiancé. No, wait; she's Zander's fiancé. How could he be marrying someone else? He said I was his destiny.

"I don't give a fuck who she is. Tell her to back off or I will." She's pulling away from me and I can't let her go. I cling to her arm, clawing at the fabric of her dress, trying desperately to get her to stay here, beside me. I'll fall over if she walks away.

"Sadie?" There's another voice next to me. It's low and

unfamiliar. It's so soft but the fraught emotion within it is unmistakable.

I turn slowly. My heart already knows who it is. "I'm Sadie," I say in a broken hush.

She's even more petite than I am. Her hands are trembling. I stare at them. I can't bring myself to look at her face. I know that within it I'm going to see all the pain that has washed over her since that day so many years ago. The day when Coral's heart became mine.

"Sadie," her voice breaks as she speaks my name again. "I'm..." the words trail.

I raise my eyes slowly and I realize in that instant that the air is silent. No one is moving. Alexa is next to me, now holding tightly to my hand.

"You're Coral's mom." I look at her face. It's weathered. The fine lines around her eyes are clear signs of her age but there's more there. I sense the sadness as soon as her gaze catches mine.

She nods silently and her eyes drop to my chest. I pull my hand up to cover the scar. I suddenly feel as though my heart is on display. In this room, it's not my heart anymore. It's Coral's heart.

"I'm sorry," I say to her as I squeeze Alexa's hand willing her to understand that I need to leave. I have to get out of this restaurant. I feel as though the walls are closing in on me so rapidly that soon I'll be buried beneath all of the raw emotion that is permeating the air.

"Sadie, let's go." Alexa takes my cue and guides me softly to the right in the direction of the door.

I can't move. Coral's mom has pulled me into a tight embrace. I close my eyes as I feel her sobs radiate through me. How can I walk away? How can I leave this woman standing here alone? I can't control my own emotions anymore. I feel a tear stream down my cheek.

"This isn't the place or the time." A man's voice, deep and comforting breaks through the heavy cloak of stunned silence that is drifting through the room.

My eyes pop open and his blue eyes lock with mine. He's older than me, his brown hair a soft mess of curls around his handsome face.

"Mother, let her go." He gently grasps the arms of Coral's mom and pries them from my shoulders.

"This is her, Clive," she whispers through her tears. "She's here for us."

"She's overwhelmed, Mother." He pulls his mother's head into his chest, cradling it as she cries. "I don't think she was expecting all of this." The way he raises his eyebrow as he looks at me suggests he's asking me a question.

I shake my head slowly from side-to-side. How could I have ever expected any of this? How did I even end up here? I'm in the middle of a room filled with people who loved Coral. Everything was so perfect just an hour ago when we were standing outside the front door of the restaurant.

"Mother, Zander brought her here for me," Christina's voice is next to me again and I instinctively melt into Alexa.

"Christina, stop." Hunter is so close now too. I can't look at him. "I didn't. It's not like that."

"We have to go," Alexa's voice cracks. Her arm is cradling my waist, pulling me towards the entrance of the restaurant. I glance up and look at the door. That's my salvation. I have to get through it. I have to walk out of here.

"I'll see you out," Hunter says as I feel his hand sweep across my elbow. I yank it away violently as a rush of emotions course through me.

"No." Clive tenderly pushes his mother towards Christina. "I'm seeing her out." His tone is authoritative and calm.

I don't look at anyone but Alexa. I can see the utter confusion in her face. She can't comprehend what's happening. How could she when I can't? I want to go. I want to go to the train station and go back to Boston.

"Sadie." Hunter is behind me. The mere sound of his voice is making me nauseous. How could he make love to me and be engaged to her? How could he have lied to me? How could he be marrying Coral's sister? We talked about Coral so much and he never said anything.

"Leave her alone," Alexa seethes.

I hear sobs. They have to be coming from Coral's mother. I've imagined meeting her for more than a decade but not like this. Never like this.

I turn around abruptly to face her. I sense Hunter to my left and Christina to my right. My eyes are locked on Coral's mom. "Ma'am," I mutter. "I have to go but..." But, what? How can I tell her that I'm thankful that her daughter lost her life so mine could be saved?

"I'll give you her phone number, Sadie." Clive's voice calls from behind me. "You can call when you feel it's time."

I nod as I reach to embrace Coral's mom. "I will call," I whisper into her ear. "I will call."

CHAPTER TWO

"I can't believe he's marrying someone else." Alexa
runs her hand over my forehead as we lay together on one of
the beds in our hotel room. "How did you know her name?"

I briefly glance up at her face. She's still wearing all the
makeup she had on when we left our room hours ago.
"Hunter told me about her," I wince as I say his name. Ever
since Christina scolded me for calling him that I've been
struggling to view him as Zander. That's who he is though.
He's Zander to all of them.

"He told you he was marrying that bitch?" She bolts to
her knees. "Why didn't you tell me he was getting married?"

"No." I roll over so I don't have to face her expression
once I explain about Christina. "She's Coral's sister. He's
marrying her sister. I had no idea."

She reaches for my arm in an effort to pull me back over.
"Sadie. You're telling me that he's marrying the sister of the
dead girl he used to date?"

I pull in a heavy breath. I know she needs answers but I'm
so tired and spent. Talking about this is only adding salt to the

open and gaping wound that is my heart. "I don't know." I bite my lip to hold in a sob. "I don't know what's going on."

"I'm sorry." I feel the bed shift as she lies back down and pulls her arm over me. "Let's not talk about him anymore."

I nod at the welcome break in the conversation. I can't wrap my mind around the fact that Hunter is marrying someone else, let alone Coral's sister. "Thanks," I mutter as I close my eyes in the hope that sleep will envelop me quickly and chase away the night's events even if it's just for a few hours.

"Let's talk about Clive." She pulls in a breathy sigh. "He didn't have to ride all the way back here in the taxi with us but he did."

My eyes jar open. Is she seriously talking about him right now? "Alexa, I'm really tired."

"He's hot." She giggles into my back. "Do you think he was interested in me?"

I'm more than mildly annoyed that she's actually talking about how hot she thinks Coral's older brother is right when I'm trying desperately to forget the last few hours ever happened.

"He put his number in my phone in the taxi." I motion to the desk where I dropped my phone when we got back to the room less than an hour ago. "Call him and ask him yourself."

I turn over to watch her spring from the bed and scoop up my phone. Her expression instantly shifts as she slides her thumb across the screen. "There are fourteen missed calls."

"From Hunter?" I ask, not because I don't already know the answer but because I want to stall this conversation while I absorb the idea of talking to him again. I set my phone to silent in the taxi after we left the restaurant when he called the first time.

"Twelve from him." Her eyes don't leave the phone. "Two from your dad."

As much as I know I should call my dad to see what he wants, I can't do it. He'll hear the pain in my voice and as soon as I say Hunter's name everything else will pour out. I'm ashamed that I slept with someone who is engaged to another woman. My parents would be distraught if they ever found out.

"I'll call my dad in the morning." I turn back over to close my eyes. "I have to sleep. I can't think anymore."

———

"CLIVE IS WAITING downstairs in the lobby for you," Alexa says as I emerge from the washroom, my hair still wrapped in a towel. I must have spent the past forty-five minutes in the shower. The warm water was only a gentle reprieve from the realities that I have to face, beginning today.

"He's what?" I feel instant panic tear through me.

"He's downstairs." She swings her legs over the side of her bed. I marvel at how great she looks even when she first wakes up.

"Why?" I quickly towel dry my hair before I start searching through my purse for a hairbrush. "How do you know this?"

"I texted him as you when you fell asleep." The words tumble out of her so quickly that I'm not sure I heard her.

"You texted him pretending to be me?" I stop and turn to look right at her. "Tell me that's a joke."

"I did it so I could tell him how great I was." She shrugs her shoulders.

"So you pretended to be me to get him to want you and now I have to go meet him?" I tap the brush in the air as I try to make sense of the words. "I don't want to meet him. You go."

"No can do." She brushes past me. "He wants to talk about Coral. You have to go."

"I don't want to talk about her." I feel a pit forming in my stomach. "Why would you do this to me?" I shoot the words out. I can't believe she's put me in this position all because she wants to get laid.

"He misses her a lot." She reaches for my phone and shoves it into my hand. "Read his texts. He needs this."

I glare at her before dropping my gaze to my phone. I rifle through the countless text messages that Alexa exchanged with him. My heart drops as I read his responses. It's obvious he's in pain and misses his little sister.

"I'll go." I walk back into the washroom to blow dry my hair.

"You're an angel." She winks at me as she surveys the room service menu.

"I hate you," I call back before slamming the door behind me.

CHAPTER THREE

"You looked really overwhelmed last night." Clive stands as I approach the small table he's sitting at. He's dressed in a three-piece suit and he looks as stunning today as he did last night.

"I was." I smile awkwardly as I sit down before he does the same.

I watch as his eyes drop to my chest. I'm wearing a sweater that completely covers the scar. I can't display it anymore. It feels so private. I feel so vulnerable and betrayed.

"Zander didn't bring you there as a surprise, did he?" He cocks an eyebrow as he waits expectantly for me to answer.

I pull in a heavy breath at the sound of his name. Zander. How am I going to get used to that? He's Hunter to me. "No," I offer in response.

"How did you know about the party?" He leans forward, resting his elbow on the table.

"I knew there was a party. I just thought it was the opening of a restaurant that Hunter, or, Zander was helping with," I grimace at the fumble of his name.

"One of his restaurants?"

"One of the ones that he's been consulting on," I push back. I didn't come to talk about him. I came based on the tone of the text messages that Clive had written last night. I felt I could help him deal with the pain of losing Coral. Now it's all turned into an inquisition about Hunter.

"He owns Axel. You know that right?" he snaps.

His words hit me like a sharp slap across the face. I feel as though I'm a sitting duck and he's the hunter with the rifle. In this case, the ammunition is the truth and it's hitting me square in the face.

"The one in Boston too?" I ask sheepishly.

He nods. "He didn't tell you that?"

I shake my head slightly. He didn't tell me anything. I don't even know him and I shared so much of myself with him.

"What's going on with the two of you?" There's a dark edge to his voice.

"Nothing," I whisper. "Nothing."

"He told you he was Coral's boyfriend, right?" He leans back in his chair and I feel as though the room suddenly has more air.

"Yes and that I had her heart." I instinctively look down at my chest.

"Did he tell you my sister and mother wanted desperately to meet you?" His arms are crossed. I can sense that he's shifting into an offensive mode. Maybe he knows that something is going on with me and Hunter.

"He told me about them." I sit up and stare directly at him. "He told me about you too. He said you were an asshole."

He laughs and I see something shift in his eyes. "He's the asshole," he counters.

"I won't argue with you." I smile.

He cocks a brow and a sly grin runs over his lips. "My mother wants to see you. She called me twice already today asking me to arrange it."

"I want to see her too." I give him a brisk nod. "I have to go back to Boston today. I can come back in a week or two." I mean it but right now I can't even imagine seeing Coral's mother.

"I can bring her to you," he offers. "She'd like to talk to your parents if they're open for that."

I exhale sharply. I haven't even considered the thought of my parents meeting Coral's family. "I'll need to talk to them first."

He runs his index finger over his lips as he takes in my reply. "Just let me know when the time is right."

I move to push myself back from the table. As much as I wanted to help him by talking about Coral's heart, I need to get back to the room so Alexa and I can make it to the train station on time. "I have to go."

"He didn't say a word about you to any of us." He stands at the same moment I do. "Nothing. We didn't realize he'd found you."

"He's full of secrets," I whisper before I turn and walk away.

CHAPTER FOUR

"WE NEED TO TALK."

I jump at the sound of his voice behind me as I lock the heavy door of the bistro. I should have taken Alexa up on her offer of a ride home but I wanted to walk to clear my head. Now, after avoiding him for days, I'm finally going to have to face Hunter face-to-face.

"Zander," I pull the name across my lips slowly. "Leave me the fuck alone."

"Don't call me that." He grabs my shoulder.

I pull back harshly as I twist my body so I'm facing him. I don't look up. I can't. I don't want to face him after realizing how easily he played on my emotions. "That's your name," I spit back.

"Look at me, Sadie." He takes a step towards me and I retreat so my back is pressed against the door.

I pull my gaze up so I'm staring directly into his face. "Why?" I seethe. "Why are you even here? Shouldn't you be with your fiancé?"

He doesn't flinch at the words. He doesn't move an inch.

His gaze darkens as he runs his eyes over my face. "I need to explain."

I laugh at the suggestion. "You can't possibly explain everything." I try to push past him but his stance is resolute.

"I can and I will." He sighs and shoves a hand through his hair. I use the opportunity to quickly escape. "You're not leaving." I feel his hand grab my elbow just as I take a step towards the parking lot.

"Let go of me, Zander," I say his name again. It's giving me the emotional distance I need to keep myself in one piece.

"Never." He pulls me into his chest with both hands. "I will never let you go."

I stand silent for a moment soaking in the words. When he said that to me last week it offered an oasis of comfort and desire. I got lost in the words. I was so lost in him.

I twist abruptly until I'm free of his grasp. "It's not your choice." I turn and face him.

"Sadie, stop this," he pleads. "Come to my place. Let me explain."

"You've got to be kidding." I'm startled by his bold suggestion. Does he not understand that I'm never going back there? "We're done," I state boldly. "Done."

"No." He's shaking his head wildly back and forth. "Don't say that."

"You are marrying someone else," I scream. "You're engaged to her and you fucked me. That's disgusting."

"I don't want to marry her." His hands are trembling. "I want to be with you."

"You're unbelievable." I take a step back to gain distance. I can't listen to him telling me he wants to be with me. He doesn't mean it. He can't mean it. She's wearing his ring.

"Please," he begs. "Give me an hour to explain. One hour."

"No." I turn to walk away. "You're a liar. I don't want to hear it."

"I can't lose you." I hear him calling after me as I run through the parking lot towards the street. Once I'm certain he can't see me, I crumble to the grass and let out a deep, guttural cry.

———

"I WANT TO GO VISIT DYLAN." I try to sound convincing. I doubt my father is going to buy into this. He knows that whenever my older brother and I are in the same room, the air is filled with tension and resentment.

"Since when?" He drops the newspaper he's reading so his eyes are peering over it. "Maria, get me another coffee, please."

Maria throws me a sympathetic look. After running my speech about how much I missed Dylan past her in the kitchen a few minutes ago, she warned me that my father would have more doubts about my sincerity than she did.

"I thought it would be good to go see him before school starts again." I sit across the table from him hoping he'll just agree so I can go upstairs to pack.

"What are you running away from?" He places the paper on the table, pulls off his reading glasses and stares directly at me.

"Nothing," I spit back a bit too eagerly.

"Last week you and your friend hopped a train to New York." There's no discernable emotion in his voice.

"You make it sound like we stowed away on a freight train." I laugh awkwardly. "We wanted to go explore the city."

"No." He leans forward and lowers his voice. "You wanted to go see a man."

"It doesn't matter anymore," I say fiercely. I refuse to tell my father about what happened. I don't want to confess that I was sleeping with a man who was engaged to someone else. I still have to broach the subject of my parent's meeting Coral's mom.

"It does." His tone is insistent. I'm regretting ever bringing up the subject of running off to see my brother.

"It's over, dad." I stand to leave the room. "It's not worth talking about."

"You were seeing Zander Reynolds, weren't you?"

I fall back into my chair. How did my father know that? How does he know his name? "How?" I manage to whisper.

"I warned him to stay away from you." He slams his clenched fist into the table. "I told him there would be hell to pay if he went anywhere near you."

I shake my head hoping to escape the horror of the moment. My father knows Hunter? He's spoken to him?

"You know him?" I suck in a trembling breath. This can't be real. We can't be having this conversation.

"He's been trying to talk to you for years. Years, Sadie." He bolts from his chair and walks towards me. "He wanted to use you to relieve him of all the guilt he felt over her death."

"Wait," I bark at him. "You knew about Coral. You lied." I stand and point my finger directly at him. "I asked how much you knew about my donor and you lied."

"It was better that way." His tone is dismissive and terse. "You're too emotional for your own good."

The words bite. He's lied too. Every day since I got Coral's heart has been filled with lies.

CHAPTER FIVE

"Hunter," I whisper his name as he steps over the threshold into his apartment.

He jumps at the sound and the overnight bag in his hand falls to the floor with a dull, empty thud. He stares at me as if he's trying to register what I'm doing in his home.

"I used this." I point to the key I placed on top of the piano. "I wanted to return it and talk to you."

"How long have you been here?" He slides his suit jacket off.

"I'm not sure." I shrug my shoulders. "Hours, I guess."

"I'm sorry I wasn't here." He moves towards me. "I should have been here."

"Don't be silly," I say as I walk to the bank of windows so I can distance myself from him. "You have a life in New York." I know the words will sting but I don't care. He can't grasp all the pain he's caused me.

He pulls in a heavy sigh and sits on the piano bench facing me. "I deserve that."

"I deserve the truth," I counter. "I don't expect it from

you. I really don't but there is something I need to understand."

"What's that?" He rests his elbows on his knees as he cradles his face in his hands. "Whatever it is, I'll help you understand."

"When did you meet my father?" My voice cracks even though I rehearsed the question countless times before he arrived.

His head shoots up and his eyes catch mine. I can see the shock in them but it's still only a fraction of what I felt when I was hit with the realization that he was marrying Coral's sister.

"How do you know about that?" He clears his throat. "Who told you I know him?"

"It's the reason you didn't come to dinner that night, isn't it?" I toss the words carelessly at him. Ever since my father said Hunter's name I've been replaying that night in my mind. It's no wonder he backed out at the last minute. How could he have come to that restaurant and faced my father after he was warned to stay away from me?

He nods. "I couldn't. He hates me."

"I can't believe you know each other." I reach to the edge of the piano to steady my balance. "You're both such good liars."

"Stop that," he hisses. "You haven't let me explain. Don't put me in the same category as your father before you know my side."

"Your side?" I glare at him. "What's your side? That you somehow forgot to tell me that you were getting married? That you actually own the restaurants you pretend to be helping with? Clive said you were an asshole and I have to agree with him."

"What?" He pulls the word through his clenched teeth. "When did you talk to Clive?"

"That's none of your business." I exhale harshly. "Who I talk to about you or anything else is no longer your business."

"He hates me," he snaps back. "They all hate me."

"Hardly." I laugh as I reach for my purse on the piano. "You're marrying one of them."

"You're not leaving until we settle this." He jumps to his feet and steals my purse from my grasp.

I cross my arms across my chest. "Hunter, I don't want to settle anything. You're a liar and a cheat. That's all I need to know."

"I am an asshole. Clive was right about that," he says in a rush. "I'm an asshole for letting things with Christina get as far as they have."

"You mean asking her to marry you?" I almost laugh at the audacity of the words. "You realize you're not making any sense, right?"

"It's complicated, Sadie." His jaw tightens. "I don't love her."

My heart jumps at his announcement but any joy is brief and fleeting. He's marrying her. I saw the ring. I saw her rush into his arms. I was at their engagement party.

"Then end it," I push back.

"I can't." His shoulders tense and he heaves his head forward. "I can't."

"Then we have nothing left to say to each other." I pull my purse from his grasp and march towards the door.

"I love you, not her," he says as I put my hand on the doorknob. "Only you, Sadie."

I shake my head as I step through and listen to the door slam closed behind me.

CHAPTER SIX

"HE TOLD YOU HE LOVED YOU?" THE GIDDINESS IN ALEXA'S
voice is both misplaced and unnerving.

I pull both my eyebrows up in mock surprise. "This isn't a
cause for celebration."

"Why not?" She genuinely seems shocked.

"He's marrying someone else." I lean forward as if my
stance is going to help her to absorb the words. "Did you
forget that part?"

"He won't marry her if he's in love with you." She turns to
refill a napkin holder. "He's going to end it with her, rush in
here and sweep you off your feet."

"If we were part of a scripted reality show that would
happen." I smooth my hands over my apron. "He said he can't
end the engagement."

"He actually said that to you?" She turns so quickly that
she knocks the napkin holder onto the floor.

I wait for her to bend down to retrieve it but she stands
stoically staring at me. I sigh before I kneel to pick up the
holder and all the wayward napkins that are now strewn
everywhere. "He said it."

"Leave that alone." I feel her grab the top of my apron trying to pull me to my feet. "This is an emergency."

"What is?" I glance up at her. "That Hunter is a cheating bastard who has no intention of leaving her for me? How can you be surprised by that?"

"Stand up," she barks. "Now, Sadie."

I pull as many of the napkins into my hands as I can. "Why are we debating this?" I stand and look directly at her. "Why bother?"

"You think he's not breaking up with her because she's better than you." It's a statement, not a question and it irks me.

I train my gaze over her head. I can't look her in the eyes when I respond or she'll see right through my thinly veiled attempt to be strong. "He's marrying her. That's what he said. End of discussion."

"Why did he say he loved you then?" I hear the irritation in her tone. I know she wants me to fight for him but what is there to fight for? A man who repeatedly lied to me? A man who apparently thought it was okay to fuck me while he was planning a wedding with someone else?

"I don't care, Alexa." I turn to straighten the napkins on the counter. "I have to forget about him. I have to."

She wraps her arm around my waist, pulling me into a tight embrace. "You can't. You love him too."

"I'M GOING to meet the mother of my heart donor tomorrow." I throw the words out casually as if I'm announcing that I have an appointment to get a manicure.

Both my mother and Maria turn in unison. "You're going to what?" My mother drops the apple she's been peeling onto the counter. It starts to roll before Maria scoops it up in her hand.

"I'm going to have dinner with Coral's mother," I say the words proudly.

"Coral?" she asks tightly. "Who is that?"

"It's the name of my heart donor." I tap my foot in frustration. "Please don't act like you don't know her name."

"Don't take that tone with me." She drops the paring knife she's holding onto a plate. "I don't know her name. I've never known her name."

Her reply jars me. How could she have not known? My father knew who Coral was. He even knew Hunter.

"Dad knew," I spit back. "You're telling me you had no clue."

"Your father knew?" she asks, her voice trembling slightly.

"Yes." I don't move from my spot near the kitchen's entrance. "He knew all about Coral and how she died."

"For how long?" She pulls her hands into her lap to hide the fact that they're shaking.

"I don't know." I suddenly feel a pang of guilt for throwing this at her in the middle of a Tuesday afternoon. I thought she knew. I thought she and my father had agreed to hide the truth from me.

She bows her head towards her lap. "Why didn't he tell me?" she mumbles in barely more than a whisper.

"Do you want to come with me?" I know the timing is horrific. She just found out that my father had knowledge of my heart donor and now I'm asking her to face the mother of that woman in a little more than thirty six hours.

Her eyes dart up and lock with mine. I see a faint hint of sadness wash over them. "I can't. I can't, Sadie."

CHAPTER SEVEN

"I'M SO GLAD YOU CAME, SADIE." CHRISTINA GREETS ME AS I walk through the door of Axel NY. When I spoke to Clive on the phone and he suggested the restaurant as the destination for my dinner with his mother and sister, I almost hung up on him. Finding the strength to board the train and travel back to Manhattan, and this place in particular, wasn't an easy task.

I don't look at her. I can't. This is the woman who is going to marry Hunter. She's going to have a life with him. All I had were a few fleeting weeks when I believed he could actually be my destiny.

"My mother is over there." She points to a small table tucked away in a corner near the back of the room. "She's so excited."

I nod silently as I follow Christina across the crowded space. I breathe a small sigh of relief when I realize that the table is only set for three. Hunter won't be here.

"You were never properly introduced." Christina stops as we near the table. "This is my mother, Faye Parker."

The petite woman stands and reaches to embrace me. I pull her into my chest knowing that this is just the first moment in an evening that is going to be filled with deep and difficult emotions.

As she pulls back I'm instantly aware that she's staring at my chest. I chose a black dress that completely covers my scar for tonight. I didn't want the constant reminder of her daughter's heart to overshadow our time together.

"Do you always cover it up?" She motions to my chest.

I'm staggered by the boldness of her question. "Normally, yes."

"Are you ashamed of it?" She sits next to Christina.

I lower myself into a chair opposite them. "Not at all." I know my voice is trembling. I had imagined the evening in my mind all afternoon as I rode the train into the city. This particular scenario, of Coral's mother launching, without any small talk, into a conversation about her daughter's heart, wasn't what I anticipated at all.

"You're a very lucky young lady." She takes a heavy swallow from a glass of red wine. "If it wasn't for us you'd be dead."

I cringe at her words. How dare she? How does she expect me to respond to that? For a brief moment I wish I had asked Alexa to come with me. "Excuse me?" I ask hoping that by some small and unexpected miracle I misheard her cold and insensitive words.

"If my Coral hadn't died that night, you wouldn't have made it." The words spill out of her with very little discernable emotion.

I move my gaze from her face to Christina's and I'm instantly struck by how gleeful she looks. She's nodding in agreement. I feel as though I've stepped into a lion's den and I'm their bait.

"I would have stayed on the donor list until another heart was available," I whisper.

"Your dad said you were on the list for months."

Christina's mention of my father so casually bites into me. I silently wonder how long he's been in contact with them. He knew I was meeting them tonight, why didn't he warn me they were vultures who would instantly be circling my heart?

"I was sick for a long time," I offer. I feel vulnerable and exposed. Sharing details of my illness with them feels like too much. It's obvious, by the first five minutes of our time together, that who I am matters little to them. It's Coral's heart to them.

"Now you're fine because of my daughter." Faye empties her wine glass in one quick gulp and I watch silently as Christina reaches over to refill it without any prompt.

"I'm very grateful." I try to sit up straighter.

"You should be," Christina spits back. "If Zander hadn't killed her, you'd be the one in the ground."

The words are so bitter. I don't respond. I stare into her face. He's marrying her. He's choosing her over me. This spiteful, mean woman is going to walk down the aisle and he's going to promise to love her forever.

"I'm sorry I'm late." As if on cue, I feel his hand lightly brush my shoulder as his voice greets me from behind.

"That's typical for you, Zander," Christina snaps. "Sit down. We were just getting started."

CHAPTER EIGHT

"WHAT DID I MISS?" HE LOWERS HIMSELF INTO THE CHAIR next to me. I watch Christina's face as he sits. They don't acknowledge one another at all.

"We were just telling her how grateful she should be to us." Faye motions for a waiter. "You took so long to get here, Zander. I think my blood sugar is dropping. We need to order."

I clench my fist on my lap at her mention of my need to be grateful yet again.

"Sadie is very grateful," he offers as he reaches to fill both of our glasses with wine. "We've talked about Coral a lot."

"Why didn't you tell me that you found her?" Christina hisses in a hushed tone as her gaze is locked on him. "How long ago did you talk to her?"

"Not long." He nods at the waiter as he finally approaches.

I order and sit in stunned silence watching the three of them casually order their dinners. I can smell Hunter's cologne. The table is tucked into such a small, cramped space that his leg is pressed against mine. I know I should pull it away but it's offering me comfort and a sense of stability right now. As much as I know that Hunter has lied to me, the cruelty that these two women have exhibited is disorienting me to the point that I'm unsure whether I can even make it through dinner.

"When Zander?" Christina asks as soon as the waiter takes his leave.

"When what?" He swallows half of the wine in his glass in one swift movement. I stare at his hand as he lowers the glass to the table. That hand. It's the hand that cradled my face, and held mine and brought me so much pleasure.

"When did you find her?" She enunciates each word in between clenched teeth.

"Recently," he offers. "How was the train? Did you get in on time?" He shifts his entire body so he's facing me directly.

I look into his eyes knowing that if I don't temper what I'm feeling for him, both of these women are going to realize that there's more to Hunter and my friendship than a shared interest in Coral's heart.

"Zander." Christina exhales loudly. "Don't ignore me. Answer the question."

"I did." He loosens his tie, never once shifting his gaze from my face. "Did you travel alone or is Alexa in Manhattan too?"

"Who the fuck is Alexa?" Christina slaps her hand against the table. "Stop talking to her. I'm sitting right here."

"She's Sadie's friend." His voice is calm and controlled. I stare into his eyes and I see a veil of darkness there. His body is there, next to me, leaning into mine but his mind is somewhere else.

"No," I whisper. "I'm here alone."

"Is she old enough to travel alone?" Faye asks flatly. "She's a teenager, isn't it?"

"She's older than that," Christina blurts out. "I heard she goes to college."

"She's a student at Harvard." Hunter's hand brushes against my leg and I flinch. "She's studying to be a doctor."

I pull my eyes around the table, stopping to study each of their faces. I feel as though I'm invisible to these two women. The way they're carrying on a conversation as if I'm not present is disheartening. I had such high hopes for this evening and they've all crumpled into a messy heap.

"She goes to Harvard?" Small droplets of wine shoot from Christina's mouth onto the stark white tablecloth.

Hunter finally turns to look at her. "Control yourself, Christina."

The blush that rushes over her face isn't from embarrassment. The rage in her eyes is unmistakable. "Don't humiliate me. You'll regret it."

The threat sits in the air with a heavy silence. I glance at Hunter and I see him roll his eyes in exasperation.

"I wanted to do something substantial with my life," I spit the words out hoping that they'll shift the conversation to a brighter place. If I can just make it through this dinner, I'll be free from having to see any of these people again.

"With Coral's life you mean." Faye reaches across the table to tap my hand. "It's Coral's life."

"No." I lean back to gain distance and hopefully some perspective. "It's my life."

"Sadie. You would be dead if it weren't for my daughter." The muted chuckle that accompanies her words bites into me. She truly only sees me as a vessel for Coral's heart.

"That's enough." Hunter pulls my hand into his under the table. I know I should pull away but I can't. I'm so close to falling apart.

"What's enough?" Faye's eyes bore into him. "What? We wouldn't even be here if it wasn't for you."

"I didn't find her so you could treat her like this." He squeezes my hand.

"That's not what I meant." She flippantly waves her hand in the air. "We wouldn't be here if you hadn't killed my precious Coral."

CHAPTER NINE

THERE ARE NO WORDS AS THE WAITER SETS EACH PLATE DOWN on the table with a flourish. He explains in pointed detail what each dish contains. The smell of the food should be making my mouth water but al I feel is a deep and penetrating sense of nausea.

No one speaks as they each eat in silence. I move the salad I ordered around on my plate, never once bringing the fork to my mouth. How could she speak to him like that? How could she blatantly accuse him of killing Coral right in front of me? She said it so effortlessly. It flowed off her tongue as if she's said it countless times before. Maybe she had. Maybe that's all he's heard for the last ten years.

"He didn't kill Coral." I drop my fork onto the plate and the sound echoes through the silence hovering over our cramped space.

They look up in unison. I can't look at Hunter. I can't pull my eyes away from Faye's face.

"You don't know what happened that night." Christina jumps in. "You weren't there."

"You think he killed her too?" I snap. "You think he killed your sister?"

"Why the hell are you defending him?" She pushes her plate away from her as if she's readying herself for a fistfight. "Who are you to stick your nose in our business?"

"You don't seriously believe he intentionally killed her, do you?" I push back. I can't believe that they've spent most of our time together, pointing their fingers at Hunter over an accident that happened more than a decade ago.

"What do you know about it?" Christina takes a long drink from her wine glass and my eyes settle on her massive engagement ring.

I pull in a deep breath, trying to calm my pounding heart. "I know that Coral died in a tragic car accident. An accident," I say the last word slowly as if I'm hoping she'll magically comprehend the meaning of it.

"If he had been paying attention that night, Coral would be here," Faye's voice cracks. "He killed her."

I bite my lip trying to temper my emotions. It's as if these two women are stuck on the side of the road next to the smoldering remnants of Hunter's car. They haven't moved past that point in time emotionally. Why did Hunter tell me Faye was amazing? She's amazingly cruel; maybe that's what he meant.

"It was an accident," I repeat.

"You're saying that to make yourself feel better. That's your guilt talking." The calmness in Christina's voice is jarring.

"My guilt?" I raise my brows. "What guilt?"

"The guilt you have to live with every day." She pulls in a heavy breath. "The guilt of knowing that my beautiful sister died and that you're alive because of that."

"I don't have any guilt," I say defensively. "It was an accident. Accidents happen."

Hunter shifts in his seat so his leg is pressing harder into mine now. I'm finding strength in his touch even though I can't bring myself to look at him.

"You should feel guilty every time you take a breath," Faye seethes as she points her finger at me. "My baby is dead. You should be dead and not her."

I feel as though my lungs collapse at the contempt in her words. I can't speak. I look down at my lap.

"That's disgusting." Hunter's voice carries over my head. "Don't talk to her like that."

"Why not?" Christina spits back. "You're just as guilty as her. You killed my sister and she stole her heart away."

"Shut up," he bites out. "Shut the hell up."

"Don't you dare tell me to shut up," she snaps harshly.

"You two are getting married?" I push my hands against the table to make room so I can rise out of my chair. Why is Hunter marrying this bitch? Why would he choose to build a life with her? She's so vindictive and cruel.

"What kind of question is that?" Christina pulls herself to her feet. "You don't know anything about us."

"I know you're all stuck in the past." I sigh as I grab my purse. "I'd say it was lovely to see you but that would be a lie. I'll take care of Coral's heart. Which..." I lean down so my face is mere inches from Faye's. "Is my heart now."

I stare down at Hunter's face silently before I turn and walk away.

CHAPTER TEN

"THAT SOUNDS LIKE A CIRCUS." ALEXA'S VOICE HAS BEEN THE comfort I craved since I got back to my hotel room. I called her to check the train schedule to see if there was any way I could escape the hell that was Manhattan tonight but I was going to have to tough it out until the morning. No good seemed to come from my being in New York.

"It was surreal." I realize it's an understatement but there are no words to describe the sheer hell that I endured at Axel.

A soft knock at the door invades the quiet solace of the room.

"I have to go. My dinner is here." I perch the phone between my shoulder and my ear as I reach for the white plush robe in the closet. I'd pulled all my clothes off the moment I got back in the room before jumping in the shower. Unfortunately, the hot water had done little to wash away the bitter taste of my time with Coral's mom and sister.

"Weren't you just out for dinner?" Alexa's smile carries through in her words.

"Bitter resentment steals my appetite away." I laugh. "I'll call you before bed."

The knock is more persistent now and I pull the towel off my head and shake my hair out before I swing open the door.

My breath stalls. Hunter is standing in the doorway. One arm is leaning casually against the door frame while his hand stops in mid-air just about to knock again.

"How did you find me?" I stand my ground. I can't let him into my room. I just want to forget that this night ever happened and I can't do that if I have to spend another moment looking at him.

"I followed you." He pushes past me to enter the room. I don't resist. I know I should but I can't.

"What?" I turn around, the open door still resting in my hand.

I jump at the sound of a steward behind me announcing that he's brought my room service order up. I motion for him to leave the tray on the desk as I sign the receipt with shaking hands.

Hunter casually walks over and removes the steel lid from the plate. "You must be starving," he says as he pops one of the fries into his mouth. "A tiny thing like you is going to finish this entire burger?"

I purse my lips at the mention of how diminutive he thinks I am. He may tower over me, but after that ridiculous evening at the restaurant I've realized that his outer presence is only a thin façade. The man underneath the brawn is weak and emotionally porous. -

"Why are you here?" I perch myself on the very edge of the bed, pulling the robe tighter around me. I should excuse myself and throw on some clothes but I just want him to answer the question so I can get this over with as soon as possible.

"I wanted to apologize for them." He rolls the padded chair that is near the desk so it's facing me directly. He casually unbuttons his suit jacket before he sits down, his knees almost touching mine.

"So you followed me here?" I shift slightly to gain some distance. He's so imposing and being this close to him is already melting my resolve.

He nods. "I waited in the lobby for almost an hour." He taps his finger lightly on my knee. "I didn't know if you'd want to see me."

"What about your fiancée?" I ask harshly knowing that the question will bite him.

"Don't call her that."

"That's who she is." I move again, this time shifting my entire body over. "By the way you have excellent taste in engagement rings."

He moves the chair so he's closer to me. "I didn't choose it. She did."

A brief moment of joy courses through me. Why should it matter to me who picked it out? It's not about the ring. He's still marrying her. He's still going to spend his life with that bitch.

"When's the wedding?" I know it sounds childish but I've wanted an answer to that question since the night I stumbled into their engagement party.

"I don't want to marry her."

"How long have you been engaged?" I spit out the question with a vile tone in my voice.

"Weeks. Not long," he answers abruptly.

"Long enough," I mutter under my breath.

He traces a path over my knee. I pull back harshly.

"Don't touch me," I say quietly. "You never should have touched me."

There's a moment of silence before he speaks. "You're all I've ever wanted."

"You're marrying her." I push his hand away. "You shouldn't be here."

"I can't be anywhere else." He reaches to grab both of my hands. "You are where I belong."

CHAPTER ELEVEN

"YOU REALIZE THAT MAKES NO SENSE, RIGHT?" I TRY TO PULL my hands free of his grasp but he's too strong.

"None of this makes sense," he counters. "None of it."

"We're on the same page then." I tense. "You need to go. Let's just end this and walk away from each other. Please." My voice is pleading. I can't keep looking at him. I can't keep imagining what it would feel like if I was wearing that ring. I can't keep wanting him even though I know he's a two faced liar and a cheat.

"You were fifteen the first time I saw you," he says hoarsely. "You were coming out of a movie theatre with a boy."

I'm speechless. Fifteen? Six years ago?

"I saw him reach for your hand but you pulled it away." A small smile pulls at the corner of his lips. "You were shy. He looked heartbroken."

That was so long ago that I can't even recall who he's talking about. It was before Will. It was before I dated.

"I sat in the balcony at your high school graduation." His fingers brush against mine and I'm too stunned to pull away.

"No," I whisper. He's a liar. He's saying those things to make me weak.

"You were the valedictorian. Your speech was amazing. I don't think there was a dry eye in the house."

He's making that up. He read somewhere that I was the valedictorian. He couldn't have been there.

"I choked up myself when you mentioned the brevity of life and second chances. I knew you were referring to your heart." His voice cracks.

My breath stalls. I remember that as if it was yesterday. The speech had been deeply emotional for me. It was so difficult to share with my classmates the promise of what tomorrow would be for all of us while I was living with someone else's heart inside my body.

"Then your first day at Harvard." He scans my face before he reaches in his pocket to pull out his smartphone. "I have a picture of that."

I recoil. I feel as if I'm being assaulted. "You don't," I mutter. "You can't."

He hands me the phone and I peer down. I'm there, in a pair of jeans and a pink sweater. My hair piled on my hair in a messy bun. The shot is from the side but I'm clearly walking towards the front doors of one of the buildings on campus. I pull my index finger to the screen and scroll through the images. There's one of me and Alexa. The Christmas decorations and our oversized winter jackets suggest it's winter. I'm smiling as she stands in a long line in what appears to be a shopping mall. Another is of me and Dylan at our parent's country house. He's getting behind the wheel of his car while I stand and watch him. I drop the phone in my lap. My hands are desperately shaking. There are so many images. So many years captured in photographs.

I vaguely realize that he's dropped to his knees. "I've loved you forever."

I don't protest when he rests his head in my lap. "I don't understand," I say weakly. I can't understand. He's been there, in my life, for so long.

"I first came to find you when you sent the letter." He pulls his head up so he's looking at me. "I watched outside your parent's house until you came out."

"Years ago?" I ask.

"You were fifteen. I was twenty-one." He stresses the numbers. "I went to Boston every Saturday on the train for years and years."

"You didn't." I stare at his face. How do I know he's telling me the truth?

"I took the early train there and the late train back," he pauses briefly. "When I was completely impatient from not seeing your face for an entire week, I'd book a flight on Friday night and stay in a hotel near your parent's home."

"You didn't talk to me." I'm sobbing now. The realization that he'd been so close for so many years is washing through me.

"I couldn't." He lowers his head and pulls in a deep breath. "Your father had me arrested."

"When?" The thought that this had gone on without my knowledge chills me. Why hadn't my father told me about Hunter?

"A few years ago." He pulls himself up so he's sitting next to me now. "I was at the airport, waiting for arrivals. You'd been in Europe with your mother for three weeks. I couldn't breathe anymore. I missed seeing your beautiful face so I was there waiting for you to appear."

I pull my hands to my face, covering my eyes in an effort to push my mind back to that day. "No, Hunter. No." I turn to look at him, my hand reaching to grab his suit jacket. "There was a man. He was on the floor. The guards had tackled him. I remember the chaos when I walked out."

He nods his head slowly.

"My father rushed me out. He said it wasn't safe." I pull my hand down his lapel before resting it on his thigh.

"He recognized me. I stopped him outside of your house one day months before that to explain who I was and to ask to see you." He reaches to squeeze my hand. "He told me to go to hell and that if he ever saw me again he'd call the police. He wasn't lying."

I twist my hand around his. "He called you Zander. That's why when I said I was seeing a man named Hunter he didn't connect the dots."

"I hate my name." He cringes as he says the words. "I'm Hunter. I've always been Hunter."

"You're Zander." I correct him. "They all call you that."

"My mother calls me Hunter." He drops my hand. "When I was young she'd call me that because I hunted creatures outside. Bugs, spiders, mice. I'm her Hunter."

CHAPTER TWELVE

HE'S MY HUNTER TOO. HE HUNTED ME. HE WATCHED ME FOR years. He was always there. Always in the background of my life.

"Why are you marrying her?" I know the question is ill timed but I can't contain it any longer. I've wanted to ask him that since I saw him at the doorway of my room.

"It's so complicated." He twists his hands together. "I took Coral away and then Ben died because of me."

"Ben?" I stare at his face.

"Coral's dad." He winces as he says his name. "He died of a broken heart."

I don't know how to respond. I can't imagine the pain her parents must have felt in the days after her death. Blaming himself for her father's death just didn't make sense. It was too much weight for anyone's shoulders to bear, even Hunter's.

"His death wasn't your fault." I try to sound reassuring but I can't comprehend everything I've learned since he walked into the room. It's all too much.

"It was." He pushes back slightly so he can turn and face me directly.

"I managed to destroy their entire family when I crashed that car." I see the weight of the words as they cling to him. His expression speaks of such deep regret that it's almost palpable.

"They're blaming you for this." I reach to cradle his cheek in my hand. "I saw that tonight."

He pulls his hand up to cover mine and closes his eyes. "I blame myself for it."

"You have to let it go," I whisper. "It's been such a long time."

His eyes flash open and a darkness flares over them. "It's not that simple." His tone is deep and low. "You can't just let something like that go."

"You can and you need to." I exhale in a rush. If he's marrying her out of guilt, he can change that. He can let that go and end things with her tonight.

"Sadie, you don't understand," he says softly. "I've taken care of them for years now. Since Ben died, I'm the one who takes care of everything."

"It doesn't have to be that way." I want him to see that a future with me is just one conversation away. All he has to do is tell Christina he can't marry her and I can have him back. He can be my Hunter again.

"It does." He stares into my eyes. I can't read what he's feeling. There's too much pain to see past.

"Then I hope you can find what you need with her." I drop my hand from his face and stand. "Just go. Please."

"Just like that?" he spits the question at me. "We can't have anything?"

I smile as I shake my head slightly. "What can we have?" Do you want to be friends? Is that it?"

"I want us to be what we were a week ago." He doesn't move. "I want to make love to you right now."

"Wow." I pull the robe tighter around my body. "You think we're going to sleep together even though you're marrying Christina?"

"The way you say it, it sounds wrong." He rubs his hands over his face.

"The way I say it? It's the truth. You want to cheat on your soon-to-be wife with me." I spit the words out so quickly they're hard for even me to decipher.

"It's not cheating." His tone is dead serious. "It's not like that."

"It is," I say pointedly. "You are going to vow to love her forever. We are never fucking each other again."

"You don't want to understand." He frowns. "You're being close minded."

"I don't sleep with men who are engaged to other women." I pull the words carefully across my lips. "If that means I'm close minded, so be it. To me it means I'm decent."

He drops his hands and stares directly into my eyes. "Not everything in life is so black and white or cut and dry, Sadie."

"This is." I move towards the door. "You're marrying her. You chose her. We are done."

"We're not done, sunshine," he barks. "I didn't choose her."

"You're just splitting hairs." I exhale deeply. "We circle the same thing over and over again. You're marrying Christina. I don't really give a fuck who chose who. All I know is you didn't choose me so I'm going to go find someone who will." I realize how juvenile my words sound. It's as if I'm talking to a high school boyfriend who has asked someone else to prom.

"That's never happening." He jumps to his feet, moving with fluid grace. He wraps his hands around me, pushing me into the back of the hotel room door. "I won't let another man touch you."

"It's not up to you." I push back with little strength. I don't want him to pull away. I'm already aroused just by the scent of his body and the sheer weight of his chest against mine. He's marrying Christina. I can't forget that. I can't want him. He's not mine to have anymore.

"I can't breathe if I think of another man with you," he whispers into my neck. I feel how hard he is. I want to close off my mind, reach down and guide him into me.

"You're with her." I bite my lip to hold back a moan as I feel his hand caressing my thigh. "You're going to leave here and fuck her."

"You're wrong." His lips skirt my neck. His tongue traces a path towards my ear. "I don't want her."

"She wants you," I murmur. "She said she loved you at your engagement party."

"She loves my money." His hand is moving higher. My body is betraying me. He's going to feel how wet I am. How much my body is craving his.

"You can't fuck me." The words hold little meaning as I wrap my hands around his neck before his lips crush into mine.

He pulls me greedily into him. His hand deftly rips open my robe before he pushes it off my shoulders. I shudder at the burst of cool air that grazes my nipples.

"I have to fuck you." I hear the faint sound of the zipper on his slacks being pulled down.

"No," I say without any conviction. I want him so badly. How can I still want him when he's done nothing but lie to me? He's marrying someone else. He's sharing his bed with her. I have to stop this.

"My cock is so hard. Only for you, Sadie." He groans as he runs the lush tip across my now drenched cleft. I'm so wet. I've never been so ready for him. My entire body is aching in anticipation. I'm going to come the moment his cock is inside me.

He pulls my right leg up, bending it before pushing me against the door. I'm so ready. So open. I just need to clear my mind and take this from him.

"I can't stop." He reaches down, pulling his cock over my swollen clit. I shudder at the touch.

"Stop," I whisper into his mouth. "Please, just stop." My voice is unfamiliar and distant.

"You want me so much." He's so close now. I can feel the tip between my folds.

"Stop," I repeat, this time with more volume. "You have to stop."

His body stalls and I lunge my hips forward just a touch. My mouth is telling him to stop but my body wants him so badly.

"Say it again." He reaches to grab my chin in his hand. His eyes bore deep within me. "Say it."

"Stop." I lean my head back against the door as I feel his body retract from mine.

He takes a step back, his cock still reaching for me. I glance at it quickly before looking back at his face.

"I know that you want me," he hisses the words through his perfect lips. "Your kiss was screaming for me. You're so wet."

I shake my head as if that will ward off the truth. He's right. I want him. I want to drop to my knees and take his magnificent cock between my lips until he empties himself within me. I want him to push me back against the door and fuck me so hard I can't feel anything but him within me.

"I won't be your whore." I pull the robe around my body. "I can't."

His eyes are glued to my face as he zips his pants back up, adjusts his suit jacket and then walks out of the room.

CHAPTER THIRTEEN

"You can't go to Manhattan again." Alexa is rummaging through one of my dresser drawers. "All hell breaks loose when you're in that city."

I know she's trying to lighten my spirits but she's right. I can't go back there. The last three trips I've taken there have all ended in disaster. Since I got home yesterday, I've tried to push the memory of Hunter's face as he left my hotel room out of my mind.

"Do you seriously think he's marrying her out of guilt?" She pulls a light blue shirt out of the drawer before holding it in front of her.

"I think so." I scrunch my nose when she looks at me. "That's not your color."

"You're right." She tosses it thoughtlessly over her head so it lands next to the others she's thrown on the floor. "That's fucked, don't you think?"

"That blue isn't your color?" I tease. "You'll get over it."

She pulls her hand to her hip and cocks her head to the side. "Not funny. It's fucked that he's so full of guilt that he's throwing his life away for that bitch."

"That is fucked," I whisper. "The whole situation is fucked. I wish I'd never met him."

"You don't mean that." She swiftly undoes the buttons on her blouse revealing a sheer black bra. "You're in love with him."

"It doesn't matter." I point to a black sweater that is sitting on top of my bed. "Try that."

"Why doesn't it matter?" She pulls it over her head and I'm instantly reminded of how much better my clothes fit her than me.

"You should wear that." I nod at her reflection in the mirror.

"Don't avoid the subject." She pulls the fabric taut, which only accentuates her breasts even more. "Why doesn't it matter that you love him?"

"Alexa." I move behind her, pulling her blond hair back from her shoulders. "He's marrying another woman. I have to stop loving him and let him go."

"It's not that easy." She pats my hand with hers. "Love doesn't disappear like that."

"You don't know that." I pull a thin grin over my lips. "You've never been in love."

"I will be after next Friday." She turns so she's facing me directly. "I'm going out with an older man."

"How much older?" I grimace at the question. I'm always slightly worried about my best friend's choices in dates. I don't want her getting involved with someone too old.

"He's thirty." She winks at me. "Didn't he tell you that?"

I feel my stomach drop. "Who?" I cringe as I ask the question.

"Who do you think?" She cocks her head to the side. "Clive."

I run my fingers across my eyebrows as I let out a heavy sigh. "Alexa. No. Why would you do that?"

"Why would I go out with a hot as fuck guy?" She pulls her tongue across her lips. "Let's see. Let me count the ways."

"Don't." I throw my hand up in protest. I don't want to hear about what she's planning on doing with Coral's older brother.

"He's almost a decade older than you," I whine. "You don't think that's too big of an age gap." I want to be diplomatic but during the brief time I spent with Clive in New York, he didn't strike me as the type of man who chased after girls our age.

"He thinks I'm twenty-five." She smirks.

"He what?" I almost scream the words at her. "You can't lie like that."

"Sadie." She grabs hold of both my shoulders and gives me a slight shake. "I'm not marrying him. I'm going to fuck him."

"You said you were going to fall in love with him," I shoot back.

"With his big, beautiful, thirty-year-old cock maybe." She laughs. "He's got to have more experience than any of the boys I've been with."

"He's going to be Hunter's brother-in-law," I protest. The thought of her in bed with anyone related to Coral is making me queasy.

"He's going to be my fuck buddy for now." She reaches behind me to retrieve the shirt she pulled off earlier. "Don't get all bunched up about it. It's not a big deal."

It's not a big deal. Maybe it's not a big deal to her. It's all a big deal to me. It's my life.

CHAPTER FOURTEEN

"We need to talk." My father's voice startles me. I didn't hear him come into the kitchen. I'd been sitting there in solace eating my cereal and thinking about Hunter, just as I did every other moment of the day.

"About what?" I push the empty bowl away from me and pull a napkin across my lips. "I need to be at work in an hour."

He leisurely pours himself a cup of coffee before he takes a seat next to me. "About Zander Reynolds."

The last thing I want to do today is talk about him. Now that I know the lengths my father has gone to in order to keep Hunter away from me, I'm ready to pounce at the mere mention of his name. "About how you had him arrested?"

"He told you about that?" His voice doesn't convey any surprise at all. He must have known that Hunter would share the history he shared with my father.

"He did." I nod as I trace a diamond pattern over the linen napkin with my finger. "He told me you refused to let him talk to me." I feel a pang of disappointment at the words. Maybe if my father would have given Hunter a chance, things would be different today. He would have fallen in love with me sooner and he wouldn't be on the brink of marrying Christina.

"He's a spoiled brat whose reckless behavior killed someone."

The words carry loathing. Obviously, my father holds the same view about Hunter as Coral's family does. What the hell is wrong with all of them? It was an accident.

"That's harsh," I spit out. "Do you even know him?"

"I know enough." He takes a small sip of his coffee.

"You know nothing." I shake my head as I chuckle. "You're no better than Coral's family."

He slams the mug down so hard that coffee spills over the brim. "What do you know about them? Just what he's told you."

"I've met them." I arch my brow. "I met all of them."

"You what?" I can see confusion cloud his expression. My mother didn't tell him that I was going to see them. She must have been so hurt that he didn't tell her about Coral years ago that she kept this from him now.

"I had dinner with them in Manhattan," I toss out.

He freezes and I can tell that he's working to hold his composure. "Why am I only hearing about this now?" The steely grain to his voice cuts through me.

"The very same reason I only heard about Hunter's desire to meet me a few days ago." I throw back knowing that it's something he won't be able to counter.

"This isn't a game, Sadie." He stands. "You're playing with fire."

I follow his lead and rise to my feet too. "You're all playing with my life, pops," I say sarcastically. "You have been for years."

―――――

"DO you want to go apartment hunting with me next week?" I ask Alexa as she squeezes whip cream on top of an iced coffee.

She licks her lips before she hands it to the waiting customer. "Why don't you move in with me?"

"I want my own place," I answer swiftly. Truth be told I've stayed with Alexa from time-to-time and her more than active sex life has left me with deep memories of the sounds of noises I shouldn't have heard in the first place.

"I've got Wednesday off. You should trade with someone and we can do it then," she suggests before taking the order of another of the dozens waiting in line on this very humid afternoon.

"I'll check the schedule before I leave." I reach for a pitcher of tea to prepare the next drink when I spot him standing by the counter.

He's dressed in a pale blue dress shirt and navy slacks. The arms of the shirt are rolled up and the way he's pushed his hair back from his forehead indicates that he's hot. Of course he's hot. He's sweating which makes him look that much hotter. Maybe if I keep my eyes downcast he'll think I haven't noticed him.

"Sadie. Heads up at three o'clock," Alexa shouts loud enough that everyone at the back of the line can hear her.

I pull my gaze up slowly and he bows his head in response. He points at his watch. "When's break time?"

"I don't have one today," I call back knowing how ludicrous that sounds. If I'm going to lie to him, I need better excuses than that.

He cocks a brow and points at his watch again. "I just need a few minutes."

"Go," Alexa barks at me. "I've got this."

I watch her expertly take orders and then hand the cups to one of the other girls working with us today. I realize if I do go now, I can use the lingering line of people waiting to my advantage. He can't expect me to sit and visit with him endlessly when we're swamped like this.

He nods as I walk around the counter towards him. "There's no place in here for us to talk. Come out to my car."

I hesitate. I don't want to be in a confined space with him. I don't even want to talk to him. What's he going to tell me now? Unless he's here to announce that his engagement is off, there's absolutely nothing I want to hear.

"We can talk here." I stop as soon as we exit the bistro. "Whatever you need to say, you can say here."

He searches the parking lot, his eyes settling on the countless people milling about. "This isn't private."

"Are you still engaged?" I turn away after I ask the question. I don't want to see the pity in his eyes when he answers.

"Yes." He grabs my arm. "I didn't come here to talk about that."

"Are you here to tell me why you lied about owning all those restaurants?"

He stops and raises his brow. "I don't own them. My father does."

"Are you going to explain why you're nothing but a liar?" I spit the words out harshly.

He doesn't respond. He only shakes his head slightly from side-to-side.

"Then I don't want to hear it." I reach for the bistro's door. "Please don't bother me again."

"I have an emergency in New York and I won't be here for a few days." It's as if he didn't absorb anything I just said to him.

"Christina broke a nail?" I ask facetiously. Why do I always revert back to acting like a rejected teenager whenever he's around?

"Someone I care about is very ill." He gazes over my head. His breath hitches as he continues, "I have to be there. I don't want to leave Boston though. Even when you're not talking to me, I feel close to you when I'm here."

"Who is sick?" I shoot back. I know so little about his life other than his never ending drive to make everything right in Coral's family's life.

"I don't know when I'll be back." He ignores the question so effortlessly. It's another lie of omission. He won't let me in. He's never let me in.

"I hope they'll be okay," I offer.

He nods. "I heard you talking to Alexa. If you want to stay at my place for a few days, I can give you back your key."

"I want nothing to do with you." I stifle the harshness of my response. Even though I'm livid with him over everything that's happened the past few weeks I can't recall a time when he looked so haggard and worried.

"We'll talk about that when I'm back." He reaches to kiss me on the forehead.

CHAPTER FIFTEEN

"Did you like the one on Preston?" I pop a cherry tomato into my mouth.

"It was really small." Alexa shrugs her shoulders. "You don't want a roommate?"

I shake my head slightly. "I'm looking forward to living alone."

"In that case, it was the best deal and close to campus." She pushes the spoon in her hand around the rim of the bowl of soup she ordered.

"I'll send an application for that one when I get home." I smile. As much as I was dreading apartment hunting today, it's turned into a fun adventure. Watching Alexa work her magic on all the prospective male landlords we met is the distraction I was longing for. It's been four days since Hunter showed up at the bistro and I haven't heard a word since. I'm beginning to believe that his story about a sick friend is real.

"What's going on with you and Hunzer?" She laughs at her own joke.

"That's a horrible nickname." I bite my lip to hold back a giggle.

"He left a few days ago because of a *sick friend.*" I pull air quotes around 'sick friend.' "It might be a rouse because he's getting married right now."

"He's not getting married." She scoops some soup into her mouth before letting it dribble back into the bowl. "It's cold."

"He might be," I counter. "It's not as if he's good at telling the truth."

"Cory is really sick," she mumbles.

"Cory?" I wince at how close the name is to Coral. Who is Cory? Yet another of Coral's vindictive relatives?

She silently reaches for her purse that is perched on the chair between us. I watch as she scrolls quickly through it before holding it up for me to view.

It's a text message from Clive: **Raincheck? Cory is sick. Pray for us. xx**

"Who is Cory?" I pull my eyes from the phone to her face.

She places it down carefully on the table before she looks at me. "I don't know. I thought you'd know."

"Why didn't you mention this before?"

She pushes the soup away from her. "Maybe because you freak out whenever we talk about Hunter and them."

"Do you think Cory is a man or woman?" My curiosity is peaked and if this person's illness is hitting both Hunter and Clive that hard it has to be someone incredibly important.

"It's like Jordan or Billy." She taps her finger on the table. "You just never know."

"I guess," I respond.

"I bet it's another sibling. Coral's mom does like her names that start with the letter C."

I smile at the statement. I've thought the same thing too. "I asked Hunter about her siblings. He only mentioned Christina and Clive."

"Weird." She reaches across the table to pull my half eaten salad towards her. "If you're done with this, I'm going to finish it."

I nod as my mind races around the mystery of who Cory is.

————

"WHAT DOES GOOGLE SAY?" Alexa is thumbing through a photo album of my brother's she found in the shelf by the television.

I glance up from my laptop briefly. "Nothing about Cory Parker."

"Odd." She pulls one of the pictures from its place and tucks it into her purse.

"My mother's going to notice that's missing." I raise an eyebrow.

"She won't." She laughs as she slams the book shut. "Google Clive and see what that shows."

I nod before I punch his name into the search engine. "Let's see. It says that he owns a company that does some techy stuff, he's single and wow."

"Wow?" Alexa bolts across the room so she's sitting right next to me. "What's wow?"

"Look at all these images of him with women." I scroll through at least two dozen images of Clive at different events, each with a different striking woman on his arm.

"Wow is right," she whispers as she leans in closer to the screen.

"Just think," I tease. "That could be you."

Her eyes dart up to meet mine and I see a flash of disappointment. "He's too old for me."

I laugh at her response. "What happened to his thirty-year-old dick being irresistible?"

"Look at them." She points to the screen. "I'm not anywhere near their league."

"They're dates." I try to offer some reassurance. "Obviously none of them were serious or he wouldn't be chasing after you right now."

"He did say I was different." She sighs. "I don't even know what he means by that."

I push the laptop to the couch beside me. "He means that you're special and unlike any woman he's ever known."

"You're great at this." She laughs before standing. "It's probably the same thing he says to every woman."

"Don't think like that," I push back. "You're always the one telling me not to sell myself short."

"You shouldn't." She bends to kiss me on the forehead. "Don't worry about who Cory is. Hunter is part of your past. You're moving on and into that great new place."

I nod silently.

CHAPTER SIXTEEN

"THAT FELLOW THAT IS ALWAYS LURKING AROUND HERE WAS in looking for you last night," Josephine says as she hands me the schedule for next week. My manager rarely talks to me. I'm actually shocked that she paid close enough attention to Hunter to recognize him.

"Hunter?" I ask even though I already know the answer.

"That's him." She smiles. "I hear Alexa talking about him to you sometimes."

I blush at the mention of our conversations about Hunter. They typically involve Alexa talking about him intimately. I really need to speak to her about reining that in.

"Sadie." She grabs my hand just as I'm ready to walk to the front. "He specifically asked me not to mention he was here."

"What?" I raise a brow. "He didn't want you to tell me he was in looking for me?" That made no sense.

"He did but I don't feel right about that." She drops my hand and throws her gaze back to her desk.

Why would Hunter be looking for me and not want me to know? As soon as my shift was done, I was going to find out.

———

I GLANCE down at the white sundress I'm wearing. It's so humid out and in my rush to get here, I'd thrown on the first dress I could find in my closet. I hadn't realized that the top of my scar was visible until I looked down. Seeing as how I'm already standing in the lobby of Hunter's building, now doesn't seem to be the right time to worry over it. I'll just find out what he wanted last night and be on my way.

"Can I help you?" The doorman rushes over. I thought I was coy when I snuck past him as he helped a young woman move a baby into her car.

"I'm just going up to see a friend," I say casually as I press the call button for the elevator. My mind jolts back to when Hunter and I stood here together. It was right before the last time we'd made love. Right before he'd taken me so hastily and with such raw desire.

"Miss?" The doorman is shaking my arm. "I asked who your friend is."

"It's Hunter." I stop myself. "Zander Reynolds," I say his name with as much calm certainty as I can muster.

"Do you want me to announce your arrival?" He pulls a phone from the pocket of his jacket just as the elevator arrives.

"No," I call back as I step into the lift. "I want to surprise him."

I pull in a heavy breath as I stare at myself in the mirror that adorns the elevator wall. I had taken the time to apply just a bit of makeup before catching a taxi to come here. Even though I know in my heart that Hunter and I are over, my body still craves him. I still want to know that he finds me as attractive as he did during those magical weeks we spent together.

I smooth my hands over the skirt of my dress as the elevator doors slide open. I march with determined steps towards Hunter's door.

I run my tongue over my lips, push back the hair that has fallen over my forehead, and I knock softly on the door.

I turn around wanting to have a brief moment of solace to gather myself once he opens the door and greets me.

I listen as the door slowly opens. The silence is endless before a very small, and soft voice says, "Hi."

CHAPTER SEVENTEEN

I TURN SLOWLY AND MY EYES MOVE DOWNWARD IN WHAT feels like slow motion. Standing at my feet is a small boy. His hair a wild mess of red, his eyes the same brilliant blue as Christina's.

"Hello," I whisper back.

"I'm Cory," he announces proudly.

I smile at the softness of his voice. "I'm Sadie."

He pulls his hand to his mouth and lets out a gleeful squeal. "Are you Princess Sadie? Princess Sadie?" He jumps up and down, his hair bouncing with each movement.

"I'm…"my voice trails. I stare at him in wonder. He's beautiful. So perfect.

"Daddy," he screams loudly. "Daddy. Princess Sadie is here."

I pull my hand to my chest. My eyes gloss over with tears. This is the Cory who was ill. This is the reason. He's the reason for it all.

"Sadie." Hunter is at the door now, the small boy scooped up into his arms. "Come in."

I take a step over the threshold and the apartment looks completely different than I remember it. Toys are strewn everywhere. A child's movie blares over the speakers on the television.

"Cory, Daddy needs to talk to Sadie." He places the boy down on his feet. "I need you to go into your room to play with your train."

"She's Princess Sadie," he corrects. "Call her that."

Hunter taps him on the top of his head. "Princess Sadie and Daddy are going to talk in here. I'll come get you right away."

"In ten?" He holds up both his hands proudly displaying his fingers.

"In ten." Hunter kisses the top of his head. "Go now."

The little boy races down the hallway and disappears into the guest room. His room. He's the reason Hunter wanted me to get my own place.

"I should have called," I whisper. I have no idea what to say.

"No." Hunter reaches for my hand. "Princess Sadie is always welcome here." He manages a small smile. He motions towards the couch and I sit down waiting for him to take a seat beside me.

"You must have more than a million questions." He sits on the coffee table so he's facing me directly. "I can't imagine what you're thinking."

I pull my eyes over his face. He looks different to me now. He's no longer the man who lied endlessly so he could carry on a sordid affair with me all while being engaged to someone else. He's someone's father. He's a dad. "He's so beautiful."

His face brightens. "He's amazing, isn't it?"

"How old is he?"

"Three." He holds up three fingers, mimicking Cory's movements.

"He's been sick?" I twist my hands together. Everything I knew has shifted so suddenly. Ten minutes ago I was coming up here to push Hunter into telling me why he was creeping around the bistro at night. All I want to know now is why he didn't tell me about Cory.

"Very." He pulls in a heavy breath as if he's tempering his nerves. "I was so scared."

"He's alright now?" I want to know more. I want to know everything he can tell me about his son but it's not my place. He shares this child with her. It's obvious he's Christina's son.

"Yes. He had a high fever. It was an infection with a complicated name." He doesn't offer more and I don't push.

"Can Princess Sadie come play trains with me?" Cory pops up next to the couch and I jump at the sound of his voice.

"Maybe in a bit," Hunter pats him on the shoulder. "We just need five more." He holds up one large hand and Cory slaps it playfully.

He scoots back down the hallway before Hunter speaks again. "I tell him bedtime stories about Princess Sadie."

I pull my bottom lip between my teeth to stave off the rushing emotions. "That's really sweet," I whisper.

"He's my life." He reaches to clasp my hand in his. "I can't be away from him."

I smile realizing that the statement makes me care for him even more deeply. "You shouldn't be away from him. He's your child."

He casts his gaze downward as he nods his head.

"I understand now," I say softly. "I get why you're

marrying her now. You want to be a real family." I squeeze his hand as tears well in my eyes.

"If I don't marry her, she'll take him." His voice cracks.

"She can't." I rest my head on his cheek. "You have rights."

"Sadie." He pulls me into a tight embrace. "I can't be away from you either."

I pull back. I raise my hands to cradle his face. "That little boy needs you so much but you don't have to marry her. You're his father. You have rights. Any lawyer will tell you that."

"No." He bows his head. "I don't have any rights."

"Did she tell you that?" I pull back, my anger rising to the surface. I'm tired of Christina using Hunter's guilt to goad him into doing things for her.

"It's the truth." He reaches to cradle my cheek.

"No. That's wrong." I search his eyes willing him to listen to me. I want to break the spell she has over him. I want him to be my Hunter again.

"Sadie," he whispers as his lips brush over mine. "Listen. Please."

"Yes," I murmur, lost in the brief taste of his lips.

"Cory is not my son. I don't have any rights." He stares into my eyes. "She got pregnant during a one night stand. She doesn't know who his dad is."

"How long have you two been together?" I can't connect any of this. "Did she cheat on you?"

"I've never slept with her," he says tightly. "I'm repulsed by her."

"You're marrying her," I spit back at him. "How can that be?"

"She'll steal him away from me if I don't marry her." His

eyes darken. "She wanted me since we were teenagers. Once Cory was born and I reached out to help, she knew she had me right where she wanted me."

"Where's that?" I ask.

"In the palm of his tiny, perfect little hand."

CHAPTER EIGHTEEN

"Daddy, it's been five now." Cory is back, as if on cue. He bounces onto Hunter's lap as I stare at his face, wishing we had just a few more minutes to talk in private.

"Princess Sadie was just talking to me." He pushes the unruly strands of hair back from Cory's face. I stare at the genuine tenderness that runs between them. How can he not be this little boy's father? He calls him daddy. He loves Hunter so much. I can see that.

"We can play trains together." He jumps back to his feet as he reaches for my hand.

"I'll play." I smile before standing.

"This way." He pulls me down the hallway in a rush. I gasp as we enter his room. His name is spelled out in large letters on the wall. A small bed covered with blue linens and an assortment of stuffed animals is across the room. A massive toy train set sits in the middle of all the chaos.

He falls to his knees and I follow suit. I stare at his small hands and feet. He's giddy with excitement. He's everything that Hunter needs. He loves this little person so much even though he's not his father. He would trade his own happiness away to care for him. How could I not love a man who would do that?

"Do you want the red train, Princess Sadie?" He touches his hand to my cheek pulling me from my thoughts.

"What's that?" I reach to cradle my hand over his.

"You're crying. I like the blue train but if it makes you sad, you can have it." He proudly holds a small train engine in his hand.

"No. I like red." I smile through my tears. "I'll use the red one."

He throws both arms around my neck in a quick embrace. "Thank you for coming to play."

I suck in a deep breath as I place the little red engine on the track.

———

"I TOLD Clive it wasn't going to work."

My eyes dart up. "Did you even go out with him?"

"No." She sighs as she sinks down into the couch in my new apartment. "It was destined to be over before it began."

"How do you figure that?" I laugh. I reach to fan out the magazines on my coffee table.

"I was too young for him," she smirks.

"As opposed to him being too old for you?" I raise a brow with the question. "He never called you back, did he?"

"No," she pouts. "I texted him twelve times and not one response."

"Twelve is eleven too many," I counter. "That's almost as much as a stalker."

"No, it's not." She sounds unconvinced by her own words. "I guess he didn't want any of this." She gestures to her body, which is hidden beneath a sweater and jeans.

"I guess." I shrug my shoulders. "Dylan is coming home next week so you can try and tap that again."

"You're kidding, right?" She asks expectantly. I can't remember a time when she didn't chase my brother.

"Yes." I laugh. "He's engaged,"

"To what?" she spits the question out along with her chewing gum.

"A woman I think," I tease. "He's been away a long time though so it could be a guy, I don't know. He didn't tell me the details. He just said he'd be back in Boston at the end of next week."

"Well, fuck that." She pulls her knees up to her chest. "Now, who am I going to fuck?"

"One of the thousands of boys at school?" I offer. "I can think of at least five who would probably do you tonight.

"I've done those." She purses her lips. "Maybe I need to go to Europe to find a fiancé." She says the last word with the playful lilt of a French accent.

"That's a great idea. You should do it."

"I was kidding." She pulls herself lazily to her feet. "I'll be stuck here forever."

"No. You won't." I stand up to pull her into a tight embrace. "There are always teaching jobs in Europe. Think about it. After graduation you could go there and start a brand new adventure."

"I could." A smile pulls at the corner of her lips. "I totally could."

"Start saving." I hold her hand tightly in mine as we walk towards the door.

"Enjoy your first night in your brand new place, Sadie." She kisses me on the cheek. "You deserve this and you're going to find your happiness too."

CHAPTER NINETEEN

"You're not enrolled in classes here, are you?" I tap the top of Hunter's head as I take a seat next to him on the concrete steps outside the library.

"Hardly." He reaches to pull my hand to his lips.

I smile when I realize there's no wedding ring on his left hand. It's been over a month since we said goodbye at his apartment door. Getting a text from him this morning asking me to meet him pushed my mind into all sorts of random places. Most of which involved him proclaiming his undying love and devotion to me.

"I'm moving." His intense blue eyes catch mine. "The day after tomorrow."

"Permanently?" It sounds more like a muted whimper than a word.

"Christina wants us to go to Los Angeles. She says the best pre-school is there. She already enrolled Cory."

"He's three-years-old," I mutter. "It's just pre-school."

"It's not about school." He turns his gaze forward. "I told her I was in love with you."

The wind catches my hair and I reach to pull it back from my face. "Now she's taking you away."

"She's scared." He looks back at me. His index finger pushes a hair away from my cheek. "She'll take him with or without me. She agreed to put the engagement on hold if I moved. At least I don't have to marry her."

I nod. Any joy I should have felt at the news of his broken engagement is muted by the news of him leaving. He has to go. Cory comes first. I've known that now for a month. I felt as though my heart had stalled the past four weeks while I waited to hear anything from him. Although the silence was deafening I secretly hoped it meant that they had worked out an agreement.

"You've taken care of him his entire life, doesn't that count for something?"

"I took care of him because no one else would." He reaches for my hand again. "I'm the only stable person in his life. Christina is constantly running off from this place to that place. If she cuts me off, he'll be left with nannies. I can't do that to him."

"I know." I push closer to him, pulling his arm around my shoulder. "You need to go with him. You have to take care of him. He's your boy."

"You're my angel." His voice cracks. "I don't know how to function without seeing your face."

"You'll remember me." I pull his hand to my cheek.

He pushes a tear across my skin. "Forever."

I lean in to brush my lips against his. "Forever and always."

———

"PROMISE YOU'LL CALL me as soon as you land."

"The second." Alexa's voice is giddy on the other end of the line. "Paris, Sadie. I'm going to Paris."

"I know." I try to temper my voice. As excited as I am for her to be taking this semester off to go explore Paris, I'm also heartbroken. After losing Hunter two months ago and now faced with the prospect of losing her too, my heart is sinking to my toes. My studies and the occasional visits with my mother are all I have left.

"You're going to come visit me, right?"

"I'll be there during Christmas break." I balance the phone on my shoulder as I place three green apples in the shopping basket in my hand.

"I'm boarding. I have to go. I love you." Her voice cracks before the line goes dead.

I stare at the phone before placing it back into my purse. After picking out a few more pieces of fruit and a prepared pasta salad I pay for my purchases.

The air is crisp as autumn settles over the city. I pull my lilac scarf around my face as I rush the few blocks to my building. A quiet evening of studying awaits me.

I fumble with my keys as the lights near the street flicker on. It's only five o'clock in California. I imagine Hunter picking Cory up from pre-school and taking him for an ice cream before they go back to their place to make dinner. Remembering the way they smiled at each other the day I met Cory is the source of my strength these days.

After precariously climbing the three flights of narrow stairs to my walk up apartment I turn the corner, balancing the bag of groceries in my hand while I again search for the key to my door.

I look ahead. The bag drops to the floor. The apples roll around my feet. The plastic container of pasta bursts open.

My eyes are locked on the wall near my door. He's sitting there. It's him.

"Hunter?" I whisper into the dimly lit hallway.

"Sunshine." He jumps to his feet. "You're finally home."

I drop my computer bag and my purse and lunge at him full force. He catches me in his arms, pulling me tightly into his chest. "You're not real," I murmur. "It's not really you."

CHAPTER TWENTY

"It's me." He tilts my chin up with one finger before his lips brush against mine. "Look at you. You're so beautiful."

"How are you here?" I smile up at his face. "How did you find me?"

"I went to your parent's house. Your mother told me your address." His entire face is beaming. "I thought you'd never get home."

"You should have texted me." I giggle at the idea of him sitting on the floor for hours waiting for me to arrive.

"And miss seeing that expression on your face?" His strong hand cups my cheek. "I'd wait a million years to see that."

"How long can you stay?" I push the key into the door. I desperately need to get him inside. I need to be close to him. I need him to hold me.

"Forever." His hand covers mine as he turns the lock. "I'm back."

My heart feels as though it's dropped into my chest. "Cory," I whisper. "You left him."

"No chance." He pushes the door open with his foot.

"He's back at my place here fast asleep. My mother is there watching him."

"How? I thought Christina wouldn't let you take him away?"

We both turn as one of my neighbors steps out of her apartment. I giggle as I realize my groceries and school bag are littering the hallway.

"You go inside. I'll get that." He smiles as he scoops up all of my things from the floor.

I step inside my apartment and cover my mouth with my hand. This is my dream come true. This is what I've waited for.

I spend the next fifteen minutes watching in silence as he sorts through the groceries, tossing the garbage in the bin in my kitchen. He carefully washes the fruit and wipes the remnants of the spilled pasta salad from my bag.

"Hunter?" I say his name. The name I love so much.

He turns and cocks a brow in response.

"Why did she let you take him?" I need to know. I don't want this to be about us. I don't want to fall even deeper in love with him to discover he has to race back to her when she decides she wants him back.

"I'm adopting him," he says it stoically. "She agreed to let me become his father legally."

"In exchange for what?" I know it's a heated question but based on what I've learned about Christina this past summer I know that nothing comes without a price in her world.

"My apartment in New York. A lot of money. Visitation with him once a month."

"You paid her to get him?" The words roll off my tongue before I realize the full impact of them.

"Sadie." He moves so he's standing directly in front of me. "Cory likes to talk. He talks a lot."

I furrow my brow in confusion. "Yes, but what does that
_"

"He talks about Princess Sadie non-stop. Probably
because I talk about Princess Sadie non-stop." He tilts his
head to the left.

I smile at the mention of Cory's name for me. "Yes, but
still. Why would that suddenly matter to her?"

"It was only a contributing factor." He reaches to grab
both my hands in his. "She found her element in Los Angeles.
She was suddenly someone. It wasn't about being Coral's
little sister or Cory's mother. She went out every night and
met a lot of different guys."

"You took care of Cory?" I ask even though the answer is
crystal clear.

"She asked me for the money. She wanted to give him
up." He shudders as he says the words. "She realized that I'd
never really give her what she wanted."

"So you get full custody and she gets visitation?" it seems
too good to be true. It means that he can have Cory and I can
have him.

"I get my dream." His lips brush against mine. "I get my
Cory and my sunshine."

I melt into his arms as he scoops me up and carries me
down the hallway. I point towards my bedroom and he lowers
me gently onto the bed.

"I've waited so long to have you." He pulls at my clothes,
baring my body in just a few seconds. "There wasn't a day
that went by that I didn't imagine your taste, the smell of your
skin, or the feeling of being inside you."

I pull at his shirt but he's too eager. He pushes me onto the
bed, spreading my legs wide. "This is beauty," he whispers
into my folds.

I whimper at the first touch of his lips on my cleft. I feel as though I'm floating as he pulls my clit between his teeth, gently biting it before sucking it gently into his mouth.

"Hunter," I whimper through clenched teeth. "That's so good."

"It's perfect," he pauses. "You're so perfect."

He laps at me greedily while I pull on his hair. I can't stand the intensity. He's so bold and brazen with my body. I've missed this so much. I've missed everything about him.

I push my heels into the bed, raising my hips to meet his tongue. He pushes a finger inside me. I gasp at the sensation. I'm already so close to the edge. He knows how to push me to the brink and hold me there.

"I want to come," I murmur under my breath.

"Now. Please, yes." He breathes into me.

I fall over the edge as I grip his head, pushing his mouth onto me, wanting him to suck me inside of him.

"I have to fuck you, sunshine." He pulls his clothes off quickly. "I've been so hard for so long."

I stare down at his erection. It's so large, so full and so hard. I crave the feeling of it within me. I need to feel it now.

He crawls over my body, his face lingering over mine. I feel him glide the tip of his cock over my slick cleft. I whimper as I try to push my hips off the bed.

"You're going to get tired of me fucking you." He pulls his lips across my forehead. "I can't get enough of you."

"Never," I cry as he pushes into me. I gasp at the intensity. It's so much. It fills me in every way so completely. I feel so whole, so raw, and so open.

He leans back on his heels as he pulls my hips into his lap. His thumb circles my clit. I moan at the sensation.

"Fuck," he groans under his breath. "Nothing is as sweet as this."

I moan in delight at his words, at the very touch of his thumb on my center and his body inside of mine.

He pulls me into his lap. I scream at the feeling of his cock being so deep. It's so much. Too much. "Hunter, I can't."

"You can." He rocks his hips up and down on the bed. His cock is pushing deeper and deeper with each thrust.

I find my own rhythm and push him down. He growls as I take control of him. I lean forward so my breasts graze his chest. I look down at his face. His perfect, beautiful face as I ride him to orgasm. I scream as I plummet over the edge, feeling him release within me at the very same moment.

"YOUR PRESENCE IS REQUESTED for lunch, Princess Sadie." He kisses me on my nose as my eyes flutter open.

"What time is it?" I glance at the clock on my bedside table. "I'm late for class."

"No." He runs his fingers across my forehead. "It's early. I made you some breakfast. You have plenty of time before your first class. I checked your schedule on your computer."

"What day is it?" I run my hand across my eyes. I still feel as though I'm dreaming. Hunter Reynolds in my bedroom can't be real.

"Thursday. You have a two hour break at lunch so I was hoping you could come over for peanut butter and jelly with me and Cory."

"Yes." I pull in a deep breath to hold back a wave of tears. "Peanut butter and jelly is my favorite."

"You're my favorite, sunshine." He leans down to kiss my lips softly. "You are my everything."

PART FOUR

CHAPTER ONE

"I WANT YOU TO COME LIVE WITH ME." HIS TONGUE FLUTTERS
softly over my clit as I brace myself by holding tight to the
now crumpled sheets on my bed.

"No," I whisper into the air so softly that I'm certain he
can't hear it. "No, Hunter, please."

He runs his tongue lazily over my now aching core. "Yes,
Sadie." His breath courses a hot path over my sensitive
tissues. He's made me come so many times tonight. I can't
keep track. I can't move. I can barely breathe at this point.

"It's enough, please." I pull lightly on his hair, trying
desperately to get him to shift his body so I can take him in
my mouth and help him feel the same pleasure he's given to
me for the past hour.

"Never." He pulls my clit between his lips as he plunges
two fingers inside of me. My hips buck off the bed in
response. My body writhes under his touch. There's nothing I
can do to stop the wave of intenseness that is gripping my
body.

"Hunter." His name floats from my lips along with a deep
moan. "It's so much." It is so much. It feels so deep, so

intense, so overwhelming each and every time I come under his touch.

"Sunshine, I love you." His mouth is on mine now, pulling my tongue into his. A growl escapes him as he pushes his cock between my folds.

I arch upward, my hands gripping the sides of his strong hips. I'll never get used to how it feels when he's inside of me. I'll never get enough of our bodies becoming one. I feel his hand slide beneath me, cupping my ass to arch my body so he can bury himself completely within me.

He groans as he finds his rhythm and slowly pushes himself into me with long, easy strokes. His lips cover mine, pulling me into a delicious kiss. I moan deeply into his mouth, savoring the taste of him, wanting to soak in every moment of this. He takes me harder, my body moving in tune with his. I'm nearing the edge again and I claw at his ass, pulling him as far into me as I possibly can.

I come with a loud moan. "You're so good, Hunter. It's always so good."

I feel him smile as his lips glide over mine. "Sadie, I can't..." his voice trails as his body bucks its release into me. He holds tight to my ass, pulling me into him, melding us together.

"That was so... it was so..." I stammer, my breathing heavy and labored.

"Perfect." He rests his large body over me, supporting his weight with his forearms. "You're so perfect, sunshine."

I blush at the words. I never imagined a year ago that I'd find a man to love me like this. Now that Hunter and I have been together for more than six months, the reality is finally beginning to sink in. This stunning, desirable man staring down at me, the man who just made love to me, is my Hunter. He adores me.

I can feel it every time I see him, touch him and kiss him.

"I was serious." He rolls heavily to the side and pulls my naked body into his. I can feel he's still aroused. The thought of even more pleasure causes my breath to hitch.

"That was more fun than serious," I tease as I trace a line down his muscular shoulder. "That was just so good, Hunter. I lost track of how many times I came."

His breath wafts across my cheek before he glides his lips softly over mine. "I love feeling you come. I love watching you. You're so beautiful."

I slide my arms around his waist, resting my face against his chest. "I don't want you to go," I say the words in a hushed tone. I don't want him to. Every night he sleeps in his bed and I sleep in mine.

"You have to come live with me." His lips press against my forehead. "I ache for you at night. It's almost unbearable, sunshine. Please."

It's the same conversation we've had for weeks. His incessant desire to have me in his apartment is shadowed by my fear. I'm scared everything will change if I pack up my life and cart it over to his place.

"I can't." It's a weak argument. I know he'll press. I know it's coming.

"Why, Sadie?" He rolls me over so I'm flat on my back and he's leaning over me. He knows he's intimidating. He knows I can't resist him when I see him like this.

I run my tongue over my bottom lip. I want to reach behind his head, pull his hair and glide my lips over his. I want that. I want to go back to five minutes ago when he was buried deep within me and the world beyond our bodies didn't exist. "You know why, Hunter."

His intense blue eyes scan my face slowly. "You're going

to tell me it's because of school." He cocks a brow and waits for me to respond.

I only nod. Part of it is school. It's easier to get to campus from here. It's quicker and more convenient.

"I'll buy you a new car." The offer is sweet and genuine but it only brings up the core of why I don't want to live with him. He'll insist on taking care of me. I'll become too dependent on him.

I smile sweetly as I cup his cheek in my palm. "You're so generous." He is. He's the most generous and giving person I've ever met. I want to show him that I can make it on my own. I want to savor our relationship just as it is.

"Sadie, sunshine, tell me what it is." He's different tonight. He sees within me. He knows I'm holding back.

"It's just that…" I stop myself. If I open this up for discussion, I'm going to lose.

"Do you love me?" It's a question that he doesn't need to ask me. He knows it. He feels it. Anyone within ten feet of us can feel it radiating from my body.

"More than anything, Hunter." It's the truth. He owns every part of me. My heart, body and soul are his. They'll always be his.

He leans down to claim my lips in a hungry kiss. "Come be with me. I can't waste another day away from you. Please. Do this for me."

"Will you let me help with the rent?" I need to feel valuable. I have to contribute so I don't become like my mother.

"I own the place, there's no rent." A sly grin pulls the corners of his full lips.

"I can cook for you." My face brightens at the thought.

He shakes his head slightly. "You're amazing, sunshine. You're so smart, brilliant, really, but you can't cook."

I stifle in a giggle. He's right. I've tried. "I'll do anything to earn my keep."

"I can think of so many things." He effortlessly shifts his body so he's hovering over me again. I can feel he's aroused. "We'll start now."

CHAPTER TWO

"I LOVE, CORY." IT'S A SIMPLE STATEMENT, BUT IT'S PURE and true.

"He loves you, sunshine." Hunter slips his feet back into the shoes he kicked off before he carried me to my bed.

I tie the sash of my robe around my waist before I settle onto the corner of a chair in my cramped living room. "Have you talked to him about me moving in?" I grimace at the question. The last thing I want is to come between Hunter and his son. If my moving in with them is going to pull them apart in any way, I can't do it.

"He's the one who sent me over here to ask you." He leans down to brush his lips across my cheek. "He told me to come back with you."

I giggle at the idea that Cory is the mastermind behind Hunter's never ending crusade to get me to move in. "Don't put all the blame on him."

Hunter raises a brow and then slowly kneels until he's directly in front of me. "His birthday is next week. He'll be four." He holds up four fingers. "Do you know what he wants for his birthday? There's only one gift that he keeps asking for."

"Another train set?" I ask the question half-jokingly.

"You." He softly pushes his index finger into my chest. "Cory wants you."

I pull in a heavy, measured breath to curb my emotions. I want to ask what he means but I don't have to.

"This morning when I asked him what I could get him for a gift he said Princess Sadie. I want her to be here with me." His voice cracks as the words leave his lips.

I pull my hands up to wrap them behind his strong neck. I softly glide my lips over his. "That's so..." It's so everything to me.

"I'd ask you to marry me again right now, but you'll say no." The wide smile that covers his mouth is breathtaking. "I'll keep asking until you say yes."

I want to say yes. I want to be his wife. It's too soon. I'm scared and he knows it. He can feel it. That's why he doesn't push.

"Promise you'll keep asking." I arch a brow waiting for his response.

"Forever." He rests his head in my lap. "I'll ask every day for as long as it takes."

———

"IT'S SMALL, but it's going to be perfect." The excited expression on my brother's face is foreign to me. Getting used to this new, happier Dylan has definitely been an adjustment.

"You're sure?" I wave my hand around the apartment. "You're both going to be happy here?"

"Leanne and I have been living with mom and dad for six

months, Sadie." He rolls his brown eyes playfully. "I've got to get out of there. This is the perfect solution."

Getting my brother and his fiancé to take over my apartment's lease was perfect for me too. I only had six months left on it but I didn't want it to sit empty and the extra cash that I will save on rent will help a lot.

"When's the last time you talked to dad?" His question startles me. Although he doesn't know all the details about what happened between my father and me, he does know enough to not bring it up.

I shrug my shoulders. "Weeks I guess." It's been months. Ever since I left my parent's house to move into this place I've avoided my dad. The knowledge that he kept Hunter away from me for years is too much for me to bear. Forgiving him is something I can't grasp right now. Maybe someday that will change, but it's hard to imagine.

"He misses you. He asked me to check up on you."

"Did you tell him I'm moving in with Hunter?" It's a pointed question and I cringe waiting for his answer.

"Nope. Not my business, Sade." He brushes past me to look in the bedroom. "I don't know where Leanne's going to put all her stuff." He laughs. "I'll need a storage unit just for her shoes."

I can't suppress a giggle either. "There's a storage locker downstairs. The key is on the counter over there." I motion towards the kitchen. "It's pretty tiny though."

"We'll figure it out." He can't hide the excitement in his voice. "This is the perfect place for the two of us to start our life together."

I smile as my mind jumps to thoughts of Hunter and my life together too. I only wish I could be as excited about my future as Dylan is about his.

CHAPTER THREE

"I'VE BEEN THINKING THAT WE NEED A BIGGER PLACE."
Hunter pulls my suitcase into his bedroom with effortless
ease. I marvel at how he doesn't even break a sweat. It took
me twenty minutes to yank it down the three flights of stairs
at my building. I almost had to have a nap in the taxi on the
way over.

"I don't have that much stuff," I scoff. "Almost everything
I own is in that suitcase."

He laughs. "No, sunshine, that's not what I mean." He
places the suitcase on the bed and flips the lid open.

"What do you mean then?" I'm wary.

"This morning when I was getting things ready for
Princess Sadie's imminent arrival, I realized you don't have an
office here where you can study."

I manage a small smile. "I can study anywhere." I have
the same concern as he has. School is taxing and I need a
quiet space to focus. I just assumed when I agreed to move in,
that I'd be doing more of that on campus.

"No." He reaches to pull some of my clothes from the

suitcase. "I want you to have a quiet place at home. I think we should sell this place and move as soon as we can."

My heart leaps at all the references to us as a couple. I love when he says the word '*we*.' I love hearing it float off his lips.

"Cory loves it here." I know that he does. He seems so at peace here with Hunter. I don't want to barge in and turn his life upside down.

Hunter sits on the edge of the bed and pulls me between his legs so I'm resting against his chest. "Cory's happy wherever his train set is." He smiles and his entire face brightens. He's so handsome. How can a man like this love me?

"I'll settle in here and we'll see how it goes, okay?" I offer.

He cocks a brow and sits in silence. I know he's thinking he's going to get his way and we both know it. "For now," he counters. It's a small reprieve but it means that I'll have time to adjust to living with both of them before we have to take on the task of a move.

"Thank you." I pull my hands through his thick black hair. "I already like being here."

"Sunshine," he whispers softly into my neck. "I need to go away for a few days."

My heart drops as soon as he says the words. He's always traveled. It's been a part of our relationship from the very beginning. The difference now is that he's leaving me here, at his home, with Cory.

"When?" I don't want to know. Please don't let it be today or tomorrow. Please let me have at least one night with him in his bed before he leaves.

"Later tonight." I can't tell if there's disappointment in his tone or not. I know how important his work is to him.

"Okay," I manage. I don't know what else to say.

Suddenly, I've gone from the high of feeling as though Hunter and I are partners, to the trepidation that always comes when I have to entertain Cory on my own.

"His nanny will be by in the morning before you go to school." He pushes me slightly so he can stand and finish unpacking my bag. "If you need her overnight you can call. Her number is on the piano."

I nod in silence.

"I'll be back in two days." The muted sound of his cell phone ringing stops him in his tracks. He walks quickly out of the bedroom as I hear him answer it.

This is my new life. There's no time like the present to jump in headfirst.

CHAPTER FOUR

"WHY DO YOU HAVE TO GO TO SCHOOL, SADIE?" CORY'S pulling on the hem of my sweater as I try to explain to his nanny, Donna, that he hasn't eaten anything for breakfast yet.

"It's really important." I tap him on the top of the head to get his attention in an effort to save my sweater from becoming a stretched mini-dress.

He rubs both hands over his eyes. "I don't want you to go. Daddy said you'd be here with me."

I kneel down so I'm right at his eye level. "As soon as I'm done school, I'm going to come get you and we'll go shopping."

"For a new train?" He tugs lightly on the end of one of my curls.

"No." I tap him on the nose. "For some stuff so we can make tacos for dinner."

"Tacos?" He jumps up and down with my hair still tightly clenched in his fist.

I try to pull free but his exuberance is addictive. I just kneel and watch the pure joy in his face over my choice of a dinner entrée.

"I'll be back at three." I hold up three fingers. "I want you to eat some cereal for Donna and then show her what a good boy you can be."

"I'll do it." He pulls me into such a tight embrace that I almost tumble with him unto the floor.

"You're my favorite guy." I kiss him lightly on the cheek before I pull away.

————

"THERE'S something I have to ask you when I get back." The deep melodic sound of Hunter's voice drowns out all the idle chatter coming from the other passengers on the bus.

"To marry you?" I tease back. "The answer is please ask again next week."

He laughs and I can picture him throwing his head back. "The next time I ask it's going to be so special that you won't be able to resist."

My heart races at the promise of that. I want to say yes. I want to marry him but I'm only twenty-two and I have years of school left in front of me. We haven't discussed how we envision our future yet and until we do, allowing my heart to believe that everything will fall into place is just not smart. I have to take care of it. Even though I now know it was once Coral's heart and she loved Hunter before I did, it's still my life. I want to be a doctor. I need to be. It's as much a part of who I am as loving Hunter is.

"What do you need to ask me?" I doubt he'll tell me. Hunter isn't the type of man who has important discussions over the phone.

"You'll have to wait until I'm back."

The bus lurches to a stop and I peer out the window. Several people rush up to the side waiting to board. I'm thankful that when I boarded a block from Hunter's place that the bus was almost empty.

"Are you on the bus?" The question comes out of left field. I can hear the distaste in his words.

"Yes," I answer back. I can't lie to him. He's heard enough background noise on the call to know that I'm not using one of his cars to get back and forth to school.

"I told you not to do that." There's frustration skirting his tone. "Sadie, I left keys to two cars there for you. Why didn't you take one?"

"I prefer the bus," I lie. The truth was that I didn't feel comfortable driving either car because they both were too expensive.

"Liar," he spits back with a chuckle. "I'm buying you a car when I get back."

"You're not." I try to sound determined. "I can study on the bus. This works well." It doesn't. I hate the bus. It's impossible to concentrate on anything because of all the sudden movements and people milling about.

"Then buy yourself a car." He rarely brings up my trust fund. I know he wouldn't be doing it now unless he was really concerned about my safety and comfort.

"The bus is fine." I want the conversation to be over. This is the first time I've heard his voice since he left and I don't want to mire our time talking about my mode of trans- portation.

There's such a prolonged silence on the other end of the line that I'm certain the call has dropped. "Sadie," he finally speaks. "We're finding a new place next week. As soon as Cory's birthday party is over, we're moving."

I don't try to disagree. It wouldn't matter if I did. He's determined and once Hunter wants something, nothing will stop him from getting it.

CHAPTER FIVE

"YOU'RE BAKING A CAKE?" HE DOESN'T EVEN TRY AND MASK the surprise in his voice.

I turn around to face him as I clap my hands together causing flour to float through the air. "Stop acting like I can't do it."

"It's not an act." He brushes the light dusting of powder from his black sweater. "You can't bake."

I try to stifle a laugh but I can't. "I want to make Cory's birthday cake myself." It's a genuine attempt. This is my third cake today. The other two hadn't worked out but I'm focused and determined and maybe I'm getting a little discouraged.

"I can think of a much better use for your time." He runs his hand down my side until it's resting on my hip.

"What might that be?" My pulse is already racing at the promise of making love.

"This," he whispers the word softly across my cheek as he undoes the button fly on my jeans. "And this." He slides his hand into my panties and runs his fingers over my cleft. "I need this."

I drop the whisk I'm holding in my hand and reach back to steady myself against the kitchen counter. "Yes, please."

"Your choice, sunshine. You can bake a cake or I can touch you just like this until you come."

"We'll buy a cake," I mutter into his chest.

He scoops me into his arms and carries me to the bedroom. He doesn't waste any time pulling my jeans and panties off before he unbuttons my blouse. "No bra." I feel his smile against my skin as he takes one of my swollen nipples into his mouth.

I push my body back onto the bed as I moan. "I love when you bite them," I confess. I want to feel that sharp edge of pain mixed with pleasure. I want to let go and feel everything I can.

He pushes one hand into the bed above my head as he leans down to kneel on one knee. I stare up at him, he's fully dressed, his face awash with desire as he runs his fingers through my swollen folds.

"I'm going to make you come just like this, Sadie." His breath skirts across my nipple before he licks it and pulls it between his teeth.

"Yes," I moan as my hips circle the bed, trying to get his hand to bring me to the edge.

"You want to come." It's not a question, it's a fact. He knows it. He can tell just from feeling how wet I am at the promise of an orgasm. "I'll take you there."

I close my eyes and seep in all the sensations as his teeth course pained bites across my nipple. My back arches at the deep rooted pleasure. He slowly pushes a finger inside of me now as his thumb circles my nub. It's all so much. Every cell in my body is yearning and aching for release. I moan uncontrollably when he slides another finger into me.

"I love how tight you are," he growls into my breast. "You're so wet, sunshine. It's so good."

I can only nod in response. I'm lost in the race to find my release. All that exists for me is his mouth, his voice and his hand.

"You're getting close." He knows it. He can sense it by the way my body is tensing. He slides one more finger in and pumps me slowly. I know I'm going to come. I want to tell him but I can't form the words. I just throw my back into the bed, push my hips up and let out a deep, heavy moan.

"That's it." He coaxes me. His lips now pressed to mine. "Take it. Feel it."

I rotate my hips, pulling another low, slow orgasm through my body. I feel his breath hitch when he realizes I've already come again.

I motion for him to move his hand away. I know he's going to want to give me more. He always does. I can't. It's already so much.

I close my eyes as I feel the bed heave under his weight. He's moving. I can sense his clothes are coming off. I ache when I realize he's going to fuck me now.

"Sunshine, I need this." His deep voice growls into the empty silence of the room.

"I need this," I repeat back and then open my eyes when I feel the tip of his cock at my lips. I hungrily open my mouth as he kneels on either side of my head. I slide it in and move my tongue in a lazy circle over the head. It feels so good. It's always so much for me to take it in. He's always so gentle.

"Fuck, yes." The words skirt off his lips when his hand settles in my hair. He pulls on it lightly, holding my head in place so he can slide his cock in and out of my mouth at his own pace. The head slides slowly, softly and sensually across my lips and tongue. I moan at the sensation.

He ups the tempo and braces himself with his other hand on the bed. I open my mouth wider, trying to take in as much as I can but he's so large, so wide. I moan around the thick root. I can't help it. It feels so good to look up to see his face. To see all the pleasure he's taking from me.

"Take it, sunshine." The words spur me on and I stroke the thickness with both hands, sucking gently on the head as he throws his body back in pleasure. "Like that, Christ, yes."

I take more in. I run my tongue up and down and across the head. I want him to feel how much I need this. How much I love giving him the same pleasure he's giving to me. "Come," I whisper around his cock. "Please."

"Sadie," he growls my name as I feel the first of his heat hit the back of my throat. I adjust my head so I can take it all. He holds both his hands in my hair as he pumps his body into me. I swallow it all while I moan around his cock.

CHAPTER SIX

"You should try and bake a cake tomorrow too." He's behind me and I can smell the fresh scent of soap.

I turn quickly and pull his still damp chest into my body. "That was amazing, Hunter." I know I say it almost every time we make love, but it always is amazing. I love making love with him. I love everything we do together.

"It was beyond amazing." He kisses the top of my head. "I'll run and buy a cake and then we can decorate together before my mom gets back with Cory."

I hold onto his hips not wanting him to pull away just yet. "Can we talk about something first?" I want to bring this up at just the right time.

"Sure, sunshine." He takes a single step back before he pulls his index finger across my jaw so he can tilt my head up.

I didn't want to be staring at him directly when I talk about this. "It's about Cory's mom."

"Christina?" His tone is anxious and frustrated. "What about her?"

"He asked me if she was coming to his party." There I

said it. I dove into the deep end and brought up the one person he warned me never to speak of.

He pulls one of his hands through his hair. "You should have told him to talk to me about that." It's a fair response even if it feels too impersonal for the subject at hand.

"I did and he said you won't talk about his mommy with him." I pull air quotes around the words trying to emphasize that even though Hunter wants nothing to do with Christina, she is still, and will always be, Cory's mom.

"This is between me and my son." The words sting as they leave his tongue. He knows they will. That's why he shot them at me. It's not the first time he's subtly warned me to keep my distance when it comes to how he deals with Christina. It's the first time it has hurt this much though.

"No problem." I try to push past him so I can breathe. Being almost pinned against the kitchen counter while we discuss Hunter's ex fiancée isn't how I imagined I'd be spending my time on Cory's fourth birthday.

"Sadie." I can hear the exasperation in his voice. "I don't want this to come between us."

I don't look at him. I can't. I'm angry with his refusal to address this in any substantial way. "She's always going to be his mom." The words are true. He has to admit them at some point.

"You're going to be his mom," he whispers as his hand glides over the top of my head and back down my neck.

I shake my head. "No, I'm Princess Sadie. Christina is his mom." With that I push past him and walk into the other room.

———

"DADDY SAYS we're going to go on a trip." Cory runs back into his room after brushing his teeth.

"We are?" I feel excitement course through me. Hunter and I have never gone on a trip together and bringing Cory along would give us all a break from the day-to-day stresses of work and school.

"Not you." He taps me lightly on the nose. "Just me and my daddy."

My heart sinks at the pronouncement. "Where are you two going?" I peer quickly over my shoulder to make certain that Hunter isn't eavesdropping on me interrogating his four-year-old.

"Someplace fun." He shrugs his shoulders as he walks over to the small, white bookcase in the corner of his room. "Will you read me a story, Sadie?"

"Daddy will." Hunter's booming voice carries through the silence in the room.

I hesitate before turning knowing that he likely heard me asking Cory about their trip. I feel like an outsider. "I'll see you tomorrow, sweetie." I reach to kiss his forehead.

"Goodnight." He rushes past me to jump into Hunter's arms. "The one about the caterpillar, daddy."

"That's my favorite." Hunter carries him to the bed, neither of them acknowledging my presence at all.

CHAPTER SEVEN

"It's not a big deal, sunshine." I hear his footsteps enter the room before he even speaks. I consider pretending I'm asleep for a minute. I'm exhausted and the idea of hearing about why he chose to not include me in his trip plans is wearing on me.

"You're right." I don't pull my gaze from my tablet. I have a test tomorrow and with all the stress of moving in and worrying about Cory, I haven't had time to prep yet.

"I'm right?" There's definite surprise in the question.

"Sure." I don't turn around. I just don't have the energy to face him. For the first time since I've been here I just want him to go to sleep.

I feel the bed heave as he sits down. "You're not alright with this so stop pretending that you are." The words are meant to provoke me. If he wants a fight I can give him one but I'm not in prime form. He's going to win.

"I am." Does that sound sweet enough? The immature part of me wants to take off for Paris to see my best friend, Alexa, once Hunter leaves with Cory. That's so grown-up of you, Sadie.

I hear the rustle of his clothing and I know he's getting undressed. Shit. He's going to be sprawled beside me in all his naked glory in the next minute and I have to ignore that. I need some sort of impenetrable shield for my overly active libido. "Don't you want to know where we're going?"

I just shake my head. Nope. I'll pretend I don't care. Maybe if I don't speak anymore he'll get the hint and leave me alone.

"You're really pissed, aren't you?" He's reaching for my arm now. He wants me to turn around so I can probe him about his secret trip with his son.

I sigh heavily making sure it's loud enough for him to hear. "I have a big test tomorrow, Hunter." I grab my tablet and turn over. I'll just stare at his face. I won't look down. "You would have given me a heads up about your trip with Cory if you wanted me to know."

"Sadie, it's not like that." He reaches to grab the end of my ponytail. "It was a last minute idea."

"You don't have to explain a thing." I scoot down to the end of the bed and pull myself to my feet. "I'm going to go study for a few hours. Sweet dreams."

He doesn't say a word as I walk out the door.

———

"SADIE, WAKE UP." Cory is standing in front of me, tapping me on my cheek. "Get up."

I shake myself awake and realize that I'd fallen asleep on the couch. I panic as I search for my tablet to see what time it is. "Cory, my tablet," I beg for him to help me.

"I took it," he announces proudly. "I'll go get it."

I stumble to my feet and race into the kitchen. I draw in a heavy breath once I realize how early it is. I still have time. I'll shower and use the time on the bus to finish studying.

"Here it is." He hands it to me and my breath stops. I have to pull my hand to my mouth to quiet my breathing.

"Cory." He's taken a picture of himself and it's staring straight back at me. "This is amazing."

"Daddy helped me." He beams brightly. "It's for when I go away. So you can see my face."

I pull my hand to my chest and close my eyes briefly. This is what it feels like to just let go and let life takeover. This is what it feels like to let him in and love him.

"I love it, Cory," I whisper as I kneel down to kiss his cheek.

"I love you, Sadie." He throws his arms around me. "I'll miss you."

"I love you too."

CHAPTER EIGHT

"THANKS FOR MEETING ME HERE, MOM." I GIVE HER A BRIEF hug as she reaches my table in the bistro.

"Are you still working here?" She surveys the small space, her eyes pouring over all the college kids gathered around the tables. It's late afternoon and that's when Star Bistro springs to life when classes are in session.

"I'm here two afternoons a week." I've thought about asking her to come down when I was working but she'd always frown on my uniform whenever she caught a glimpse of it when I lived at home.

"Why?" The question is ripe with innuendo. She's always made it clear that she didn't want my brother or me working at any 'menial' job as she called them. It was likely the reason Dylan was trying so hard to follow in our father's footsteps. He'd been trying so hard that he kept tripping and falling.

"I like it here." I'm not going to offer more. I know that she wanted to see me to discuss my current living arrangements. I can sense it every time she's called me the past few weeks.

"I'd order a coffee but I remember it being bitter." She

spits the words out loudly. I don't flinch. I'm not going to allow her relentless need to be negative to push me into a confrontation.

"You can stop for a martini when we're done," I say the words too sweetly. I need to temper my reaction to her. Getting her riled up will only result in one thing and that's a scene with her crying and me feeling sorry that I upset her.

She scans her phone before she throws her gaze back to me. "Your father wanted me to talk to you." The words catch me off guard.

"Why?" I spit the question out without thought. I've avoided him for so many months. Now is the worst possible time for me to be thinking about him.

She pretends to swat away an errand piece of lint from the top of the wooden table. "It's about him."

"About dad?" I'll play dumb for a few minutes to bide myself some time.

"No, him?" Is it so hard for her to say his name?

"Dylan?" Strike two. I'm running out of possible males.

"Your father has a problem with that man. Zander," she seethes. I actually see her lips retract enough that her gums show. She looks like an attack dog readying to pounce on its prey.

"What about him?" I don't know why I'm asking. She's going to tell me regardless what they both think of him.

She stares at me, her eyes never flinching. "You're living with that man and his child."

"I'm aware of that." If she's going to open the door and start this, I'll gladly follow her through.

"Do you know how that looks to your father?" The disdain in her tone makes it very clear that she doesn't think it looks attractive or acceptable either.

"I don't care." I don't. Why should I pretend that their opinion matters?

"Sadie, he has a child with another woman. Your father says he's one of them," she whispers the words in what she intends to be a hushed tone. Judging by the fact that almost everyone in the bistro turns to look at the vile harshness in her voice, I'd say my mother needs to work on her whisper techniques.

"One of them?" I repeat the phrase back to her hoping she'll hear it coming from me and recognize how completely horrific it sounds.

It flies right over her perfectly styled hair and into the ether. "Yes, one of them. Coral's people."

"Is that what we're calling them now?" I honestly can't believe she just said that. Did my mother honestly just refer to Cory's family as 'Coral's people'?

She nods frantically. "That's who they are."

"I don't know what that means," I begin before I stop myself mid-sentence. "Mother, what's going on? Why the problem with Cory's family?"

"Don't you get it?" The smirk on her face is unsettling. This is my mother. Isn't she supposed to be the person who loves and protects me? Isn't she supposed to want me to find my true happiness?

I shake my head slightly. "No, I don't get it."

"Your father thinks they're just using you," she says the words with so much conviction.

I'm going to have to point out that there's nothing any of them can gain from using me. "How so? How in the world are they using me?"

"It's your heart." She waves her finger in the air towards my chest. "Your father thinks they're using you to get rid of all of their guilt."

We're back to that again. How many people are going to insist that Hunter loves me because he still feels guilty about Coral's death? "That's ridiculous."

"You don't know everything, Sadie." She stands to leave. "You should ask Zander for the truth."

I can't believe she's resorting to that tactic. She's used it to manipulate people for years. "You want me to believe there's some deep, dark secret you know that Hunter hasn't told me yet?" It's almost laughable but I try to conceal my amusement.

"There is." She turns on her heel.

"Good to see you too, mom," I call after her. "Tell dad to fight his own battles next time."

CHAPTER NINE

"CAN I ASK YOU SOMETHING?" I STAND IN THE DOORWAY watching Hunter bend down in all his custom-fitted-suit-glory to pick up Cory's toys from the living room floor.

"Anything." He drops everything he's scooped up in his hands and turns to face me. "Sunshine, ask me."

It's been so long since he's called me that. Since the awkward encounter we had in bed about his trip with Cory, we haven't really talked. With my heavy exam schedule and his persistent need to be at a new restaurant that's opening in midtown, we haven't had time together at all.

"Do you think about her when you look at me?" It's a question I've never asked directly. I haven't had to. He's always made me feel loved and adored just for me. It's never been a question of whether that love was directed towards Coral's heart or me.

"Who?" It's the answer I wanted. I didn't want him to automatically assume that she was the woman I was speaking of.

"Coral." I can't look at him directly when I say her name.

I can't. I'm not sure I'll ever be able to get myself to that point.

Tugging me into his body, he sighs before he answers. "No, never. Not once."

I wrap my arms around his waist, wanting to pull strength from him. "My mother said something about her." I don't want to confess everything she said. I don't want him to think that I put any weight in the words that she spoke to me.

"You saw her?" He doesn't try and hide the surprise behind the question. Naturally, he'd ask. I've complained to him for hours about how she's been completely unaccepting of my relationship with him. I was shocked when she gave him my address all those months ago when he came back to Boston.

I nod and cling tighter to him. "At the bistro. She wanted to meet me to tell me that my father disapproved of my living with you and Cory." I hate the sound of the words coming from my mouth. I hate that she made me doubt this beautiful man even if it was just for a moment.

"She's just being your mom," he offers while his hand runs up and down my back. "They both want what's best for you."

"You're the best for me." I feel no doubt in the words at all. He is. He's always been the best thing in the world for me.

He pulls back from our embrace so he can rest his hands on my shoulders. "What else did she say?" The question accompanies a raised brow. He's invested in this now. He's going to push until I tell him exactly what she said.

I fidget slightly from foot-to-foot trying to find the strength I need to tell him. "She's just delusional about us." There. That feels right.

"Delusional?"

"She thinks you're hiding something from me," I say it with a chuckle. It sounds absurd and I know it. I hate that I had to repeat those words to him.

"Like what?" His finger playfully pulls on my hair. "Did she say what it was?"

I stop and stare right into his eyes. I see the mask within them. It's the same mask that's always there when he's holding something back. "No," I answer cautiously. Why isn't he laughing this off? Why isn't he telling me it's ridiculous and that she knows nothing about him that I don't know?

"So she didn't elaborate at all?" What the hell? Elaborate on what if there's nothing to hide?

"Why would she elaborate on nothing?" I feel my shoulders tense beneath his touch. This conversation has gotten so far off the track I thought it would be on that I can't think straight. Is there a secret? Is he actually hiding something that my mother knows? How is that even possible?

"I don't think she likes me." He pulls a thin smile across his lips. "Actually, I'm sure she wishes I'd disappear."

I want to tell him that it doesn't take a brilliant mind to see that, but I'm not going to engage him in anything until I get to the bottom of this. "That goes without saying, Hunter." I want the part of the conversation that focuses on my mother's dislike for him to be over. He's sidestepping and right now he's tripping over his own two feet.

"Is there something?" Being direct is the only choice I see right now. I'll ask, he'll answer and we'll put to this rest.

"Something that I'm hiding from you?" Bingo. There is. He wants to volley the questions back and forth to avoid whatever it is.

I just stand in silence studying his face. I hone in on his eyes and that's when they drop. He can't hold my gaze. He won't hold my gaze. The man, who promised to love me forever and vowed never to keep secrets, is holding something within him that feels like a ticking time bomb.

CHAPTER TEN

"I went to the store before I got home from work." He motions towards the kitchen. "I got everything you like so you won't even need to leave the house until we get back."

"I have to go to work and school." I also have to go and talk to my mother. I don't add that last part in because frankly I don't give a fuck at this point. I can tell by the way he's racing away to California with Cory and the fact that he's been avoiding me since we talked about my mother, that whatever the secret is, it's not going to be something I'll embrace.

"Sadie!" Cory comes running into the living room. "I'm taking this for my mom." He holds up a colored picture of a kangaroo with his name neatly spelled next to it.

"She's going to love that." I reach down to tousle his hair. "Did you pack everything?"

He nods excitedly before he scoots back down the hallway to his bedroom.

"I'm sorry it took me so long to tell you that we were going to see her." His voice is low and calm.

"I don't know why you thought you had to hide it." The

words are pointed and direct and meant to sting. I hate this veil of secrecy that's surrounding him. "I brought up on his birthday that I thought they should at least talk to each other."

He shuffles his leather shoes on the hardwood floors. "I thought you'd want to come along."

Of course I would. I ached to be invited and it had nothing to do with seeing Christina. I would have avoided that if he'd asked me to go to see her with him and Cory. Just the joy of going anywhere with them was what I wanted and I knew if I was there, with them in California, I could give Hunter the emotional support he was going to need after seeing Christina again.

Cory's back in the room with his small backpack slung over his shoulder. His bright blue suitcase is skidding behind him on the floor. "Let's go, daddy." He pulls anxiously on Hunter's hand coaxing him towards the apartment door.

"You'll call me if you need me." The words sound so hollow and empty when he says them now. It's not like before. There's a weight hanging in the air between us. I know that he's aware that I suspect. He has to be. I can see it in his eyes.

"I'll be fine." I move towards the door. "I hope it's a good trip."

He leans down to brush his lips against mine before he pulls on the doorknob. "I love you, sunshine. Always."

"DAD." It's so empty and heavy coming from my lips. I didn't want to call my mother to ask her to meet me again because I was fearful that would give her a chance to prepare for my questions. I wanted to appear out of nowhere. She's never been good under pressure.

"Sadie." He only nods in response before he opens the door wide enough to let me in. I haven't been home since I moved into my own place last fall. It's exactly the same. Everything is prim, proper and in its place, including my parents.

I don't reach to embrace him. That's never been part of our relationship. I know he cares for me. Deep within my heart I know he truly loves me but the wedge that was put there when I found out he had kept Hunter from me for all those years is unyielding. He lied about something as fundamental as my heart.

"Is mom here?" I'm hopeful that I can get this over quickly and be back in Hunter's apartment before it gets too late. I'm falling behind in my studies and an empty place means extra study time over the course of the next few days.

He studies my face as if he's about to launch into a tirade about the merits of running away from the man I love. I know my father doesn't approve of Hunter. He's the one who once had him arrested. "I'll go get her."

I breathe a heavy sigh of relief that I've dodged one uncomfortable confrontation tonight. Now all that's left on my agenda is getting my mom to spill the beans. I have to find out what she knows about Hunter. I hate living with him not fully understanding what's going on and what he's keeping from me.

"He's trying to protect you." The words reach me before she appears at the top of the staircase. She looks elegant even wearing her pajamas and a silk robe. It's rare to see her without her makeup. It's been years since that's happened and I'm stunned by how youthful she looks.

"Daddy?"

"No. Zander." She's standing in front of me now. I can see

past the barrier she usually has surrounding her. There's worry skirting the edges of her beautiful brown eyes.

I follow her lead into the large sitting room. She takes a spot on an ornate sofa and I settle in next to her. Although the home I grew up in is elegantly designed and decorated, the one thing I always longed for was the coziness that comes with having a family who showed affection.

"What is it, mom?" I can't let my pride shelter me this time. I need the truth. I've been struggling for days with the knowledge that Hunter is hiding something.

"It's about the boy." She's staring down at her robe, her pointed red fingernail tracing a line along the fabric's intricate design.

"Cory?" I offer his name. He's an important part of my life. I want him to be just as important to my parents. In a perfect world, they would embrace him and Hunter but perfect worlds are only found in fairy tales and other people's homes.

She nods silently. I hear her breathing become heavier. She's struggling with whatever it is she needs to tell me.

"Please, mom." I reach to touch her hand and this time she doesn't instantly recoil from my touch.

"It's about the boy's father." Her words hit me like a high speed baseball. She didn't say Hunter, or Zander. She didn't call him by his name.

"Hunter?" I offer. "You mean Hunter?"

"No." She pulls her gaze up to meet mine. "His real father, Sadie."

CHAPTER ELEVEN

"How...how do you know?" I struggle to get the question out in one breath. I didn't think anyone knew that Hunter wasn't Cory's biological father. Hunter told me himself that Christina had no idea who that man was.

"Your father told me." Of course he did. My father knows every detail of Hunter's entire life.

I squeeze her hand harder this time. "They don't know who the father really is." That's what Hunter told me. It's the truth. He told me that Christina had so many one night stands that she couldn't pinpoint Cory's father.

"Did he tell you that?" Her brow furrows as she scans my face. I see concern there. Real, genuine concern flashes over her expression. I can only remember seeing it once before. It was years ago when I was so ill during those months before my heart transplant.

"Yes." I see no reason to not be direct with her. I feel as though she's offering me everything she knows. I want to do the same.

She pulls her gaze down and her eyes flit back and forth

slightly almost as if she's searching for something in her lap. "Sadie," she begins but stops herself.

"Mom," I whisper as I lean in closer. "Please, just tell me."

"They know who it is." Her voice is so soft. I struggle to make out each word. "They all know."

"Hunter knows?" I can't believe that. Why would he keep something so important from me? Why wouldn't he share that detail?

She pivots her body so her shoulder is touching mine. "Sadie, I don't know who he is. I overheard your father talking."

That's all I need to hear. I bolt to my feet and turn to walk out of the room.

"Sadie," she almost screams my name into the silence of the house. "Stop."

"Why?" I freeze and turn to stare at her. "I'm going to talk to him."

"He won't tell you anything." She pulls her hands through her hair in utter frustration. "I've asked. He won't say."

"This is ridiculous." I almost chuckle at how ludicrous this is. My family knows important information about the child I live with and they refuse to tell me. "We're a family." I feel the need to point that out to my mother. "We shouldn't have secrets."

She only shrugs her shoulders in response. "I don't know anything."

"I'm going to ask daddy." I turn on my heel again to march out of the room in search of my father.

"Maybe it's time you ask Zander," she calls after me. She was right. Maybe it was time I ask him what the hell was going on.

CHAPTER TWELVE

I SEARCHED THE HOUSE IN VAIN FOR MY FATHER BEFORE finally waving the white flag of defeat and leaving. I spent all of the time on the bus on the way back to Hunter's apartment replaying that conversation with my mother over and over again in my mind.

I dial Hunter's cell as I walk through the door and there's no answer. I don't leave a message because I know he won't want to talk about something so serious over the phone.

I glance at the clock on my tablet. It's just after eleven, which means it's only five in the morning in Paris. Alexa told me to call her whenever I needed her. I don't know if I've ever needed her more than I do in this instant.

I listen intently as her cell rings three times before she answers with a gleeful, "Bonjour."

I giggle inwardly knowing that she's spent the last half of the year struggling to learn even the simplest French phrases. It's not for lack of trying, but her focus seems to be centered on the men there instead of learning the language.

"You're awake?" Why am I surprised by that? Of course she is.

"Wide awake, Sadie." I instantly feel comfort when I hear her say my name. I miss her endlessly and I've spent a small fortune talking to her each week. "What's up?"

"Hunter." I don't see any reason to tiptoe around the reason for my call. Alexa is bold, direct and isn't going to pull any punches when it comes to telling me what I need to do about Hunter.

"What's he done now?" I know she doesn't mean it, but the disappointment in her voice stings tonight. When he kept his engagement to Christina a secret, it was enough to tarnish his image in Alexa's eyes for good. I'm not sure how she's going to react once I tell her that he's keeping something equally major to himself.

"I think he lied to me about Cory's dad." It's so foreign to hear myself say the words. Do I truly believe that Hunter lied to me about that? Would he do that?

"What makes you think that?" It's a logical question.

"My mom mentioned something about it and...." my voice trails as I recline back into the comfort of the couch. "He's just been acting strange lately."

"Zander's being weird?" The use of his legal name isn't lost on me. "That's hard to imagine."

"Funny," I say the word without any meaning. "I can tell he's holding something back. I'm not sure."

"Where is he? Why aren't you riding his cock right now?" I blush even though she's thousands of miles away from me. Her brash demeanor hasn't changed a bit.

"He's in California visiting Christina," I grumble. I hate that he went there without me.

I hear Alexa shuffle before she speaks. "Did he take Cory with him?"

"He did." I feel as though she's unintentionally rubbing salt in the open wound that is my heart. "Without me."

"How the fuck did that happen?" Her tone is raised now. I know she's mentally adding to the list of reasons why she hates Hunter.

I pull in a heavy breath. "He didn't ask me to go along. Actually, he didn't even discuss the trip with me."

"That's fucked." It's abrasive and it's unfortunately, completely true.

I wish she were here. I could use some quality Alexa time face-to-face. "How am I supposed to find the truth if no one is willing to tell me?"

"You've got to be straight with him." Her tone is more muted now. "Just tell him you know and he's going to cough up the details. Simple."

"I'll do it as soon as he's back." I have to. This is tearing me apart inside. It's too reminiscent of when he was engaged to Christina and hiding that from me.

"Good girl."

CHAPTER THIRTEEN

"WE HAVE TO TALK." I'VE PRACTICED SAYING THOSE FOUR simple words for the past day now. When Hunter did finally return my missed call the other night while he was away, I didn't mention anything about Cory's biological father. He'd told me how much he loved me on the phone and it broke my heart. I need this man to be transparent with me. I need him to trust me with everything in his life if this is going to work.

He turns slowly from where he's seated by the table. He's just finishing his coffee after getting Cory ready for a play-date. "You're so serious, sunshine. Is this about how I fell asleep before you got to bed last night because I'm ready to go right now?" He cocks both brows and I melt instantly at the suggestion that we make love. I wish it were that easy. I wish I could take off my clothes and jump on his lap right now.

I reach out my hand to him, hoping he'll take the lead and follow me to the couch. "It's very serious, Hunter."

He's up on his feet in an instant, grabbing onto my hand before he pulls me into his chest in a tight embrace. I pull my arms around his waist, wanting to soak in this moment. I love everything about him. He's so strong, so protective. He's such a beautiful person both inside and out. He takes the initiative to pull me by my hand to the couch. I nestle in very close to him, my hand resting on his thigh.

"Are you okay?" There's so much genuine concern and love woven into the words. He really does care for me. I know it. I can feel it. If we can climb over this hump, we'll be happy again. I can sense it.

I shake my head. I'm not. I need to tell him that I know about Cory's biological dad and I'm hurt that he kept it all from me. "Not really, no," I manage to say in barely more than a whisper.

His blue eyes scan my face very slowly. "Are you ill? Has something happened to someone?" They're both expected questions. He has no idea that I have a clue that he's been lying about Cory's father.

"It's nothing like that." This is it. I have to just blurt it out. "It's about Cory."

"Did he do something? What did he say to you?" The questions feel awkward and misplaced. Cory is an innocent, tender little boy. Granted, he sometimes said things that made my heart ache. Things about how much he misses his mommy and wishes he could see her more.

I pull a faint smile over my lips as I think about the tight hug he gave me before his nanny rushed him off this morning to a playdate. "Cory's perfect." I believe those words. He's human but he's the most amazing little human being I've ever met.

"You know, don't you?" His voice is deep and low. How can he possibly know that?

"Know what?" I want clarification. I need to hear it from him. I have to hear the words coming out of his mouth.

He pulls his gaze down into his lap. "That question I was

going to ask you when you were on the bus a couple of weeks ago. You know that I want you to be Cory's guardian, right?"

The words bowl through me with lightning speed. I fumble to grasp onto them. Did Hunter just say he wants me to be Cory's guardian? "What?" I can't manage anything beyond that right now. How did this go from my needing to know about Cory's biological father to us talking about me being his guardian?

"Did Donna tell you? I know she overhead me talking to my attorney about it. Shit. I wanted to tell you myself." His eyes lock on mine and I see happiness deep within them.

"No." Again, the words just aren't there. I can't form any cohesive thought. How am I supposed to respond to this? It's just another secret that he's kept hidden from me. Cory's nanny knew about this and I didn't? How did this wall of secrets suddenly appear? Everything changed when I moved in or maybe there have always been things he's held from me and now that I'm here and closer I can finally see them.

"You'll do it, right?" There's so much expectation hanging between us right now.

I fumble in my mind, trying to claim words that will make sense when they tumble off my tongue. "What does it mean?" I have to understand what he's asking of me.

His brow furrows. I can tell he's looking for an answer himself. He reaches to grasp both of my hands in his. "It means that if anything happens to me, Cory can stay here and you'll take care of him."

It's not that simple. What about Christina? What about the man she slept with that night? The man who helped to give him his life? What about them?

"Sadie? Why aren't you saying yes?" He squeezes my hand slightly and I recoil at the touch. I can't agree to that. I can't agree to take Cory away from his real parents if something happens to Hunter.

"Who is Cory's real dad?" I wince the moment the question leaps from lips. I was thinking it. I didn't want to pounce on him like this. Not now. Not when we're stuck in the middle of a conversation about what will happen if I lose Hunter.

He bolts to his feet in an instant as his large hand runs through his hair. "Sadie." My name leaves his lips in a rush. There's anger circling him. I can see it. I can feel it in the air.

"Hunter. I know." I don't really know. Why would I say that? I want to know. I need to know.

"You don't know anything." The words are harsh and terse. He mutters a curse before he turns on his heel, pulls his suit jacket from the back of the couch and walks out of the apartment.

CHAPTER FOURTEEN

"IT JUST ISN'T WORKING." HIS VOICE IS LOW AND SHAKY. "She's not happy so something has to change."

I nod. Maybe it's a sign from the heavens. Maybe the fact that my brother is moving out of my apartment just a month after moving in is a clear sign that I need to go back there. After our talk yesterday morning, Hunter hadn't come home until late in the night. He'd slept on the couch and raced off to work before we could even talk this morning. He's avoiding me. He actually made a decision not to speak to me. How can I possibly stay there with him and Cory any longer?

"It's fine, Dylan." I try to smile. "I may be moving back in."

"Why?" It's something anyone would ask. Anyone but my brother, that is. He's never cared about what happens to me. We've never had a very close relationship. We've always just been two people who happened to share the same DNA.

"It's not working with me and Hunter." I have to pull in a heavy, measured breath to keep myself from sobbing as I say the words. How can it be? How can Hunter and I be this fucked up?

He takes a sip of coffee from the paper cup I brought him. "I thought you were crazy about that guy? Mom said you were nuts over him."

I lean back in my chair for stability when I hear him mention our mother. "She actually said something to you about Hunter?"

"She calls him Zander." He rolls his brown eyes and smiles. "You'd think she'd give that up if he wants to be called Hunter."

I laugh. "A lot of people still call him that." They do. It's hard for me to see him as Zander but all of Cory's family calls him that. It still feels as though people are talking about a completely different person when they say that name. Maybe he is a different person than the one I thought I knew. Maybe Zander isn't who I wanted him to be after all.

"Do you want to talk about it?" The question may as well have been asked in a foreign language. It's as if a stranger just walked up to me and asked me to confess my life story to them. I've never confided in Dylan.

I glance back at the counter to see how many people are waiting. That may be my out. Suggesting that Dylan meet me on my lunch break at the bistro meant I had to fill in almost thirty minutes of time with him. He only just got here and already I'm completely uncomfortable. "It's okay." It is okay. I can't tell Dylan what's going on.

"We're family." He reaches across the table to rest his hand over mine. "Talk to me."

I stare at his hand. It's a man's hand. When did my brother become a man? When did he grow up enough that he would want have an actual conversation with me?

"Mom hasn't told you?" I know the question's answer before I even ask it.

He leans back in his chair and his hand leaps from mine.

"I know Hunter isn't Cory's dad."

I've never heard Dylan say Cory's name before. He's never acknowledged his existence. "He's not. That's common knowledge." It's not meant to sound so insensitive, but it does.

"I didn't know until mom told me," he counters. "She said Hunter didn't tell you some stuff about Cory."

It sounds so simple and innocent when it comes from my brother. I wish that were it. I wish that Hunter was hiding just stuff. It would be refreshing at this point if the biggest secret hanging between us was the fact that he gave Cory an extra serving of dessert or bought him a new toy train engine without telling me.

"I'm here." He taps his finger on the edge of the table. "Family is everything, Sadie. It's everything."

"What's going on?" Something isn't adding up. My brother doesn't just blurt out sentimental statements about family and love. That's not the Dylan I know.

"Leanne is pregnant." His voice cracks before he continues, "I'm going to be a dad."

My breath catches and I almost leap from my chair. "You're kidding?"

"I'm not." He shakes his head from side-to-side. "We just found out last night. Can you imagine, Sadie? Me a dad?"

I can't. I can't imagine it at all. I can't imagine Dylan holding a beautiful little baby in his arms. "Dylan," his name escapes my lips in a rush. "I can't…"

"We have to fix our family." He stands and moves to kneel next to me. "I want my baby to have a real family. Let me be your brother again."

I reach to hug him, burying my face in his shoulder. I need this. He has no idea how desperately I need a family right now.

CHAPTER FIFTEEN

"WHERE'S CORY?" I COULD TELL HE WASN'T IN THE apartment the moment I came through the door. The silence is deafening.

Hunter doesn't turn around as he answers, "My mom took him for a few hours. He wanted to go down to the park so she said she'd keep him company."

"I'm just grabbing some stuff so I can study." It was only a half lie. I was actually taking some of my things so I could head over to my old apartment. After Dylan's announcement about the baby and his plans to move out, I'd gotten all the details. They'd left yesterday for a rental house so if I wanted my place back, it was empty and available as of right now.

"Sunshine, I'm sorry."

The words hit me all at once. I'm not sure what hurts more. Hearing him call me sunshine or the fact that he says he's sorry even though he still hasn't confided in me about Cory's biological father.

"I'm sorry too." I'm sorry I'm going to run away. I'm sorry I can't live here with you anymore. I'm sorry I'm not worth trusting. I'm just sorry.

I wait for any response and he sits silently at the table, his face buried in a stack of documents.

"See you." I throw the words carelessly at him as I turn to walk down the hallway.

"He's been in prison."

I almost trip over my feet as my body lurches to an abrupt halt. "What?" I whisper through the pained silence that engulfs the room.

"That man. The one who slept with Christina, he's been in prison," he says the words so slowly that I wonder how much control it's taking him to temper all of his emotions.

"Cory's father?"

He stands and turns all in one swift movement. "Don't call him that. I'm Cory's father."

I feel my heart drop at the sight of him. He hasn't shaved, his hair is a mess. It's obvious that he's been stuck in worry judging by how tired he looks.

"I'm sorry," I whisper. "You're Cory's dad."

He nods as he walks past me. "I only found out when Cory was ill months ago."

Only months ago? Cory was in the hospital before I even knew he existed. Hunter had told me then that he didn't know who Cory's father was. "You found out then?" I want to understand. I need to.

He sits in a chair in the living room, his knee shaking slightly as he talks. "A few weeks later."

I move to sit across from him on the couch. I can sense that he doesn't want me close. I can see that he's struggling. "How did you find out?"

"The doctors had so many questions when Cory got sick. It's happened before." There's a veiled sob within the words.

"I didn't know." Of course I didn't know. I barely know

anything about Cory's past other than the few fragments that Hunter has thrown in my direction.

"When we were living in California last fall I found out who he was." He doesn't raise his eyes. He still won't look at me.

There had been weeks then when we didn't talk. He'd wanted to make a clean break from me when Christina forced him to take Cory to live with her in Los Angeles. "Christina told you?"

He nods. "She knew all along."

"What?" I spit the word out much louder than I want to. I hate that Christina was manipulating things again. I hate that she is still causing Hunter so much pain and frustration.

"Did he know he has a child?"

He instantly pulls his gaze to mine. "He doesn't have a child. He donated his sperm when he fucked her that one time."

The words are too harsh coming from Hunter. He doesn't talk like that. He's not that way. I can't respond. I don't know what I'm supposed to say.

"She gave in and told me his name because we needed to get to the bottom of what was wrong with Cory. I contacted him and he gave up his family's medical history. That should have been the end of it." His tone is clipped and decisive.

"But it wasn't." It's not a question. I can tell by the look on his face that this is far from over.

"No." There's sarcasm skirting the word. "It's not over. That fucker is trying to ruin my life."

CHAPTER SIXTEEN

"How?" I leap from the couch to kneel before him.
"Hunter, please. Tell me what's going on."

He leans forward, his hand cupping my jaw. "I've only
ever tried to protect you and Cory."

I nod. I reach to cradle my hand over his. I've been so
desperate for his touch. I've missed feeling his hands on me.
"I need to know."

"I'll never let anything happen to you." He closes his eyes
briefly as if he's chasing away an image of something dark
and sinister.

"I know." I do know that he's always tried to protect me. I
also know that by keeping this from me, it's created a wedge
between us that is slowly destroying both him and me.

He pulls his hand from my face and balls it into a fist in
his lap. "Once he realized that he had a son, he started
demanding things from me."

"Things?" I correct myself immediately. "You mean
money?"

"He's a greedy bastard, sunshine." He pushes my hair
from my forehead. "He's so much like Christina."

"You gave him money to stay away from Cory?" I don't want the question to sound as judgemental as it does. I don't want him to think that I'm assuming anything. I can't really understand the position he's in. All I can understand is the depth of his love for Cory.

He caresses my cheek again. "I just want him to go away and leave me alone."

"You said he was in prison?" I shudder at the thought of Hunter dealing with anyone in prison. "Why? What did he do?"

"Armed robbery, assault, there's a lot." His jaw tightens. "The guy was a fucked up mess from the start. He thinks he's hit the lottery now that I'm Cory's dad."

I feel a rush of anger course through me. I know that he had to pay Christina a lot to get her to agree to let him adopt Cory. I can't imagine what this other man was asking of him.

"What about the adoption?" He hasn't spoken of it since he first mentioned it months ago when he came back to Boston.

"He was going to petition the court to get his name on Cory's birth certificate." He bows his head down. "We're still negotiating that."

Negotiating that. They're negotiating Cory. The thought makes my stomach turn.

"He belongs with you." I rest my head in his lap. "He's your boy." I just want the world to disappear. I don't want to think about how these people are trying to manipulate Hunter by using the love he has for Cory.

He strokes my hair. "No, he belongs with us, sunshine."

I feel a rush of emotions as the gravity of the situation hits me. "That's why you took him to California? It was because of all of this?"

"Christina demanded I bring him." I feel the tension in his

thighs as he says her name. "She told me if I didn't, she'd give Peter my address here."

"Peter?" I repeat the name back. "That's his name. The name of the man..." I can't call him Cory's father anymore. I can't. A real father wouldn't use his son as a bargaining chip.

"He's out now." Hunter reaches down to pull me up so I'm resting in his lap. "I don't want him to find us."

Suddenly all the pieces are falling into place. "That's why you want us to move?"

"We're going to move." He runs his hand over my shoulder. "I want us in a place that Christina doesn't know."

We're running. We're hiding. He must feel real fear. "We can stay at my apartment." It's a weak offer but it's something.

"Your apartment?" He shifts his body so he can see my face. "Your brother lives there, doesn't he?"

"No. He moved out," I whisper. I don't want to do this. I don't want to talk about Dylan when we're focused on what's going on with Cory's parents.

"You were leaving me, weren't you?"

"What?" I pull my gaze up to his.

I feel his hands tighten around my waist. "Just now. You weren't getting things together to study. You were going to go back there, weren't you?"

I won't lie. I can't. "Yes."

"Sadie. No. Please." He pulls me into his chest. "Never. You can't leave me."

I reach to cup his cheek in my hand as I rest my lips against his. "I'm not. I won't. I promise."

He glides his lips over mine and I melt in the sensation. I've missed kissing him. God, how I've missed this. I love the taste of his lips, of his breath. I need this so much.

"Sadie, sunshine," he groans into my mouth. "I want you."

"Hunter." His name leaves my lips as he unbuttons my sweater and pushes it from my shoulders.

"Let me fuck you." It's not a request. I can feel how aroused he is. I can feel his steely erection pressing against me.

"Please, Hunter," I say in a breathless whisper. "I need it."

He growls as he picks me up and stands in one swift motion. "Now." It's one word but it contains all the pent up need and want we've both been feeling for weeks.

He pushes me onto the bed before he pulls the remaining clothes from my body. I don't have time to reach for him before he's on his knees at the edge of the bed, my calves in his hand. He pushes my legs up, bending them at the knee, spreading me wide.

I gasp as he plunges his tongue into me, lapping at my wetness. He's not gentle. He's hungry and needy. My hands drop to his hair, pulling at the roots, controlling his tempo. I grind my hips into him, needing to come. I have to orgasm. I feel it building inside of me. It's so strong, so much.

"I've missed this," he purrs into my folds before he pushes a finger deep within me.

"Eat me, Hunter," I moan through clenched teeth. "Like that."

He groans and I'm rewarded with him sucking hard on my clit. He slides another finger into me and I circle my hips to take it in.

"It's so good." I can't control it all. I feel the pleasure rush through me. I feel so close already.

"Come." It's a single command.

I arch my back as the rush pulls through me. I almost cry

out because it's so much. It's been so long since I've come like this. It's been so long since I've felt Hunter pleasing me.

"I'm going to fuck you." His voice is unrecognizable. It's so deep. There's so much want in it.

I watch him race to get his clothes off. He's so hard, so ready. He lunges at me. His body hovering above mine. His dark hair falling into his face. He looks so needy. He wants me so much.

I moan uncontrollably when he plunges fully into me with one buck of his hips. The biting mixture of pleasure and pain almost takes me over the edge again already. "Hunter," I scream out his name. "Hunter."

He grabs my hips and pumps himself into me, each thrust harder and faster than the last. "Fuck, I've missed you. Christ."

I love the sound of his voice like this. It only makes me want more. I push back, trying to pull all of him within me. He's so large, pulsing, wanting.

"I'm going to fuck you forever, sunshine." Each word is louder than the last. He's lost in the pleasure. His uncontrollable grunts and groans only spurring on my own desire.

"God, please." I push my hips farther into him. "I'm so close."

He moves faster, his cock ramming into me over and over. So much, so fast, and so good.

I scream loudly as I come hard. He slows and pumps his body into mine. I hear my name softly glide off his lips as he fills me with his own intense orgasm.

CHAPTER SEVENTEEN

"I WANT YOU TO TAKE ONE OF THE CARS." HIS BREATH RUNS hot over my back and I feel my nipples instantly harden. We've been in bed for the last few hours leisurely enjoying each other's bodies. Making love again has helped me feel closer to Hunter than I've felt in weeks.

"You're trying to get rid of me?" I giggle as I ask the question. I may have thought that when I woke up this morning but he's proven to me now that he can't live without me. The hunger in his body when he took me shows me that he still wants and needs me.

I hear him chuckle softly. "You have to be with me forever. My life is nothing without that."

"I can't be without you," I confess. "I hate the thought of us apart."

"You'll marry me then?" I can hear the smile in the words.

I twist quickly around so I'm facing him. I run my finger over his brow. "Is that a proposal?"

"Will you say yes if it is?"

I purse my lips together and shake my head slightly.

"It's not a proposal yet then." He laughs. "Cory told me you're going to train him to be an artist."

"He what?" I pull back and cock a brow. "I'm training Cory to be an artist?"

"That's the word he's spreading around." I can tell that he's trying desperately hard to hide his amusement.

My eyes open wide as I realize what he's talking about. "I'm taking him to the art store this afternoon. That's what you mean?"

He nods softly. "You're teaching him to paint a giraffe."

I smile at the mention of Cory's latest interest. His love of giraffes is quickly overtaking his fondness for toy trains. Today we're going to an art store near campus to get him supplies so he can paint some pictures of his new favorite animal.

"He's going to teach me," I correct him. "I'm just letting him choose his implements of creation at the art store."

"You're going to be an amazing mom." He pulls his gaze down but not before I see tears welling in the corners of his eyes.

I reach to tilt his chin back up. "If I'm half a good of a parent as you are, I'll be really lucky." I mean each and every word. He's an amazing dad. He's willing to sacrifice so much for Cory.

"You'll take the car then?" It's a statement that's faintly veiled as a question.

"Why? Cory loves the bus." He really does. It's always an adventure taking him with me on the bus. He loves interacting with everyone we meet and he always brings a smile to the people around him. Who wouldn't have their spirits lifted by a beautiful little boy with red hair?

He bends his elbow so he can rest his head in his hand. I

stare at the way his arm flexes. "Sadie. I have someone tracking Peter's movements."

My eyes dart to his. "Why? Where is he?"

"In Memphis right now. He's got family there."

I feel a shudder race through me when I realize that Hunter really does feel threatened by this man. "Isn't there something you can do? Can't you call the police?"

He tries to raise a smile to his lips but I can tell the worry is overshadowing everything else. "He's dangerous, volatile and I don't trust his motivations."

I respond without any hesitation. "You're worried about what he's going to do, aren't you?"

He pulls me into his chest. I feel his strong arms surround me. "I love you and Cory too much to take any chances."

CHAPTER EIGHTEEN

"You might as well just hire us a bodyguard," I tease as I enter the kitchen.

He raises a brow without even the hint of a smile on his face.

"No." I reach to grab hold of the counter. "You're not serious?"

"I haven't yet." He hands me a cup of coffee. "If he gets any closer to Boston, I'll have no choice."

"Hunter." I lean back against the granite of the countertop. "There has to be a way to make him go away. Isn't he on probation or something? How can he just roam around the country?"

"He's served his time. He's allowed to live his life according to the courts." He shrugs his shoulders offhandedly as if I'm supposed to believe this isn't eating him alive inside.

"His name isn't on the birth certificate. He has no rights." I feel the need to point that out even though I'm certain Hunter has already thought of everything.

He walks over and brushes his hand across my chin. "I

love when you're on fire like this. You're so strong even in the face of a threat."

"I'm not threatened by him," I lie. The truth is that since Hunter told me about Peter earlier, my heart has been racing.

"Taking extra precaution right now is smart, sunshine." His tone is direct and stern. "You can't risk yourself or Cory."

"I would never do anything that would put Cory in danger." I'm mildly offended by the suggestion that I would. He knows I adore Cory. He knows I would do anything to keep him safe. I'm the one who cuts his food into such tiny pieces because I'm fearful he'll choke.

He effortlessly glides his lips across mine. "I trust you completely with my son. There isn't anyone I trust more."

"Just give Peter what he wants so he'll disappear," I plead. I want this to be over. I don't want the shadow of this stranger to be chasing after us a minute longer.

"He has proof that he's Cory's dad now so he's demanding a lot more."

"Proof?" I scoff. "What proof?"

He closes his eyes and draws a heavy breath. "Christina helped him with DNA when he was released. She got involved with him again."

I feel a rush of rage through every cell in my body. "She wouldn't do that?"

"She did." His voice cracks. "She gave him some of Cory's hair from a hairbrush she had with her and Peter ran the test."

"This is a nightmare," I say as my eyes scan his face. "Hunter, we have to do something."

"We are." He pulls my hand to his lips. "I am. I'll give him whatever he wants. I'll do whatever it takes to protect my family."

———

"ARE these all the colors you want?" I survey the small paint cups in our basket before looking over at Cory.

"That's it." He points one of the paintbrushes he's clinging to in my direction.

"Your giraffe is going to be purple?" I have to work to stifle a laugh. Every color he's chosen is a hue of purple. Obviously it's his new favorite.

"Purple's best." It's simple. I like it. He's right. Right now, purple is best.

"Paper." I point towards a wall covered in samples of papers and canvases. "We need to pick some of that."

He races away from me and I feel a shot of panic course through me. *"Don't let him out of your sight, sunshine."* Hunter's words to me just before we left the apartment bolt to the front of my mind.

I take off after him and I almost run squarely into the back of a woman he's talking to.

"Sadie." His voice is filled with joy as he bounces up and down. "It's your mom."

I stand silent as I watch the woman turn. "Sadie." A wide smile overwhelms her face.

"Mom?" It's much too loud. The shock I'm feeling isn't about her being in this space, it's about the smile. My mother rarely smiles unless it's in an effort to impress one of her friends.

"You must be Cory." She turns and bends down to grab his hand.

"That's me." He ignores the offer and wraps his arms around her neck.

She hesitates only briefly before pulling him into a tight embrace. She wobbles on her heels and I have to reach out to steady her balance. I'm tempted to pull my smartphone from my bag just to get a picture of this. This was something I never thought I'd see.

"How did you know she was my mom?" The question is directed at Cory but I anticipate my mother putting her two cents in before he has a chance to answer.

"She comes to the park." He pulls back from their embrace and grabs her hand. "I talked to her."

"Wait. What?" My attention has turned to my mother now who is still standing with her back to me.

"I was curious." The words float from her mouth and are meant for me even if she's not going to turn around.

I take the lead and walk around her to stand behind Cory. I rest my hands on his shoulders. "You've met him?"

"Not officially." Her gaze is set on his beautiful little face. "I go to the park sometimes and sit on a bench. He came to talk to me."

"She told me you were her daughter, Princess Sadie." I jump at the mention of my nickname. He rarely calls me that anymore.

"When?" The pieces of this puzzle aren't fitting together.

"A few weeks ago," my mother offers. "I saw you and Hunter with him at the grocery store one day. I followed you to the park."

"Mom," I spit the word out in utter surprise. "You should have just called me."

"And said what, Sadie?" Her eyes finally settle on my face. "I want to meet the child you live with?"

I cover both of Cory's hands with my ears." Try to be sensitive."

He shakes his head pulling my hands into his. "She some-times brings me candy."

I'm angry. I'm angry that she's been forging a relationship

with him and I haven't heard anything about it. "Where's the nanny when this is going on?"

"I explained to her who I was," she says flippantly. "She understands discretion."

"Hunter won't like this." I struggle to hold onto Cory's hand as he plays with a row of paintbrushes sitting on a shelf next to us.

"Daddy knows her." Cory points to my mother.

"What?" I bend down so I'm eye level with him. "Daddy knows her?"

"They talk at the park sometimes." He nods his head before he kisses my cheek. "Daddy says she's not a stranger."

"I'm not sure about that," I whisper in a muted tone.

"I didn't want your father knowing." It's a confession I didn't see coming." I asked Zander to let me tell you."

"Hunter," Cory blurts out. "Call him Hunter."

We both smile at this declaration.

"Hunter it is." She reaches to tap him on the top of his head.

CHAPTER NINETEEN

"I FOUND OUT TODAY THAT YOU AND MY MOM ARE BESTIES." I try not to let a laugh pop out with the words.

His fork drops onto the plate. "We're what?"

"You and Sadie's mom. Besties." Cory pipes up.

We both stare at Hunter and his eyes drift from me to Cory.

"He didn't tell me." I reach out my palm and Cory slaps it with his. "He's excellent at keeping your little secrets."

"It's the candy," he confesses.

Hunter and I both burst out laughing.

"He will do anything for candy." Hunter nods in Cory's direction. "Your mother told you?"

"We saw her at the art store. Apparently she's taken up painting again." I hear the words and I'm still shocked by the meaning. My mother gave up painting when I was very ill. The fact that she's taken it up again speaks volumes about her state of mind. She loves it. It's always been something that she wanted to do.

"Cory recognized her?"

"He practically ran into her arms." I smile at Cory as he picks at the sweet peas on his plate.

"I like hugs." He doesn't break his gaze from his plate.

"How long have you known that she sees him?" It's not confrontational. Since I've gotten back from the store I've been slowly absorbing the fact that my mother sought out a connection with Cory and with Hunter. It's sinking in how profound that really is.

"A few weeks." He looks down, sheepishly. "She wanted to tell you in her own time. I didn't push that."

"It's a pretty big deal." My tone is serious. "Was that what you thought I was talking about when I told you I went to see her?" I suddenly realize that Hunter must have assumed my mother told me about her stolen visits with Cory in the park.

"Exactly that." He tips his head towards me. "She's really trying."

I know he feels that. I'm still trying to catch up to everything that's happened today. "I want her to know Cory."

"She knows me." He pulls on my arm. "Today she said my name."

"Yes." I reach down to run my hand along his forehead.

"Why didn't she tell him who she was sooner?" It seemed as though today she was finally ready to share that she was my mom.

"I introduced her as a friend. I didn't want small ears to tell you before your mom was ready." He motions towards Cory.

"Daddy, my ears aren't small." He taps the edge of his fork on the table in mild protest. "I like Sadie's mom."

"I'm really glad." I feel my breath skip. Maybe Dylan was right. Maybe family did mean everything.

———

"PLEASE DON'T WORRY, DONNA," I say into my phone. "I've got this."

"You're saving my life, Sadie." I can hear the appreciation in her tone.

"Just take the time to get better." I hang up the phone and realize that now that Cory's nanny is sick, I'm on duty for the day. I'll only miss one class and Hunter will be back by the time I'm expected at the bistro.

"Where's Donna?" Cory pops around the corner still dressed in his pajamas. "She's going to take me to the park."

"Get your clothes on, mister." I clap my hands together. "It's just you and me today."

He jumps up and down, squealing in glee. "This is the best day ever."

It was. I was going to do my best to make sure that every day from now on would be the best day ever for Hunter, Cory and me.

CHAPTER TWENTY

"PUSH ME HIGHER." HIS LEGS KICK FRANTICALLY AS I PUSH on the swing.

"Higher." I give the swing a hard thrust and move out of the way as he glides into the air.

"So high," he screams at the top of his lungs. I reach into my pocket for my phone. I want to take a picture of this for Hunter. I want him to see the joy in Cory's face.

"My phone," I mutter under my breath. I left it on the counter. I remember putting it there before I slipped a sweater on. Dammit. We'll just have to come back later this afternoon so I can recreate the moment for Hunter.

"We should get ice cream." Cory points towards an ice cream vendor near the edge of the park.

I fumble in my jeans pocket hoping I have some money.

"It's my treat." My mother's voice is behind me.

"Sadie's mom," Cory giggles as the swing slows.

"We have to come up with a better name for you than that." Part of me wants to embrace her. I want to thank her for being here, for coming to see Cory.

"Grandma is nice." She pulls her lips into a tight smile. "He can call me that."

I stop on my way to retrieve Cory from the swing. "What?"

"You're going to marry his father." Her tone is calm and controlled. "I'll be his grandmother."

"You're my grandma!" Cory struggles to get out of the swing. "I have another grandma?"

I arch a brow in her direction.

"You do." She races past me to pull him free of the restraint that is holding him firmly in the swing. She cradles him to her chest as he kisses her cheek. I can't do anything but stare at the two of them.

"How did you know we were coming?" He's pulling on her hand leading her in the direction of the ice cream vendor.

"I was hoping, " she says to him before she turns to me. "I want to do better this time, Sadie. I'm trying to make up for all my mistakes with you. "

I watch as she races along behind him, her designer loafers picking up sand as they scurry together through the dust.

"Sadie, what do you want?" Cory calls back towards me as my mother pulls a bill from her wallet.

"Nothing." I can barely form the word. I feel as though I've stepped into a dream.

"My grandma is having an orange ice pop." Cory points to my mom. "I'm having grape."

"It's purple." I point at the ice treat he's holding in his hand.

"It's my favorite."

I follow as the two of them walk towards a bench near the edge of the grass. I settle in next to Cory listening as he tells my mother a story about giraffes.

"We should take him to the zoo tomorrow, Sadie."

"I have school tomorrow." I wish I didn't. Right now I just want this moment to last. I want to stay on this bench with these two people for days and days.

"I can take him. Do you think Zander would mind?"

"Grandma." Cory taps her knee through the beige slacks she's wearing. "It's Hunter."

"Hunter." She reaches to hold his hand in hers. "Sadie will ask him if we can go to the zoo."

"Are there giraffes?" His entire mouth is stained purple from the ice treat.

"Lots of them."

I giggle when I notice that her tongue is now a bright shade of orange. I can't ever remember my mother like this. I don't know the last time she was so carefree, so happy and so willing to embrace another person.

"Let's go now." Cory's up on his feet and bolting across the playground before either of us can react.

We both jump and I race after him, the sound of all of our laughter filling the air.

CHAPTER TWENTY-ONE

"WHO THE HELL ARE YOU?" I'M STARTLED BY A MAN'S VOICE behind me. I tense as I feel my elbow being pulled back. I have to struggle to maintain my balance.

I turn sharply trying to break free of his grasp. "Let go of me."

"That's my boy, isn't it?" He points with his free hand towards Cory who is now back near the swings. My mother is frozen behind me. I can see the fear on her face.

"Get Cory, mom." I call to her in panic. "Take him, go."

"Sadie," Cory screams when he realizes the man is grabbing me. "Stranger, Sadie. It's a stranger."

Peter lets go of me and lunges towards Cory. I have no time to react. I jump from my feet and onto his back. We both tumble to the grass.

"Stay away from him," I seethe. "You're not going near him."

"Shut the fuck up." He pushes me to the ground, his hand around my neck. "That's my kid."

"He's not."

I register my mother's voice calling for help in the distance. I can hear Cory's screams.

"I'm taking him." He's pulling his heavy frame back up.

"Like hell you are." I reach to grab his legs and yank as hard as I can. He teeters before falling forward. "Run, please," I scream into the air. "Mom, take him." I can't see anything. I can't tell if they're still close.

"You're a little bitch." He's clawing at me, trying to break my hold on his legs. "You're ruining everything."

"Leave him alone." My voice is so unfamiliar. It's so high pitched and filled with fear. "I have money. I can give you money."

He flips us both over until he's sitting on my chest. The pressure is so much. I can barely breathe. His large hand grabs hold of my neck and he squeezes.

"Please," I whimper as I flail beneath him. "Leave him alone."

"How much?" His dark eyes bore into me. He's unshaven. His clothes are dirty and mismatched. He's breathing heavily, rage coursing over his expression.

"Millions." I try to talk but my throat is so compressed. "I have millions. You can have it all."

"You have millions?" He squeezes harder and I choke. I can't cough. I can't talk. I can barely breathe.

I nod my head frantically. I feel as though my eyes are going to pop out of my head. Please let me go I want to say. Please leave us all alone.

"Sadie." I hear Hunter's voice. I hear it. I close my eyes. I'll think about Hunter. I'll remember what it felt like the first time he kissed me. I'll think about his arms. I should have said yes. I could have married him.

"Fuck," Peter's voice booms through my ears. I open my

eyes slightly. I don't have the strength to lift the lids any higher. My arms fall to my sides. I can't breathe. I can't.

I watch Peter's fist rise above my face just before I hear Hunter's voice calling to me. "Sadie. No. God. No."

"You stupid little bitch," Peter growls. "You fucked up everything."

I close my eyes as the pain of the blow barrels through me.

———

I HEAR A SIREN. I taste blood.

"Cory," I try to whisper but I can't find my voice. My eyes flutter open slowly.

"Please, please." Hunter is rocking me. I'm resting in his lap. I can feel his sobs running through me.

I move my hand to his. It's so heavy. I pull it across the fabric of his pants. "Hunter." My lips move but I don't hear anything. "Hunter."

He jumps when my hand touches his. "Sadie, sunshine."

"Cory," I try to say louder. "Where is he?"

"Sadie." He only repeats my name, his body still rhythmically rocking back and forth as he cradles me in the grass.

I try to push away from him but I have no strength. My body is so heavy. There's more blood. I can taste it. It's bitter. I try to reach to touch my face but my hand doesn't move. It's resting against Hunter's.

"Sir, please." There's a woman's voice now. She's close. I can feel her touching me.

"I can't let her go." Hunter's voice is filled with so much sadness. He's crying. I can feel it through me.

"We need to look at her." She's insistent. I see the flash of a glove as her hand reaches to cradle my wrist. She's taking my pulse. I'm fine I want to tell her.

"Let her be okay, please, let her be okay," Hunter's voice cracks. "Is she going to be okay?"

"We need to take her in." She's trying to pry Hunter's arms from around me but he won't let go.

"No." He struggles to stand while he's holding me. "I'll take her."

"Sir." Her voice is more insistent now. "Let her go."

I try to squeeze his hand. I need him to know I'm okay. Everything is spinning so fast though. I close my eyes again.

CHAPTER TWENTY-TWO

"I MADE YOU THIS PICTURE." CORY CLIMBS ONTO THE COUCH beside me and hands me a purple hued painting.

"Is there a giraffe in it?" I try to smile but my face doesn't cooperate the way I want it to.

"Just you." He taps his hand on my leg.

I glance down to see a stick person with a very large face and an enormous purple mark on their cheek under their right eye.

I have to pull my hand up over my mouth to control my need to giggle. "This is very good. It's lifelike."

"You got that thing there." He tentatively touches the welt under my left eye. "She's got that thing too." He points to the paper.

"It's brilliant." I reach to pull his head into my chest. "I love it."

"You saved me." His words are barely more than a whisper as he pulls my hand into his. "The stranger was going to steal me. You saved me."

My eyes well with tears. It's been three days now and I

haven't talked with him about it at all. This is the first time I've seen him since the attack in the park. I didn't want Hunter to bring him to the hospital. I couldn't subject him to that.

"You would have saved me if he was trying to steal me." I work to keep my voice at an even temper. I know he has to be traumatized by what happened. Even though my mother scooped him up and ran from Peter, I know that he still must have been terrified by what he saw.

He finally looks up at me, his brilliant blue eyes resting on the bruise on my face. "You're a ninja."

I laugh out loud at the proclamation. "A ninja? That's cool, right?"

"The coolest." He nods before leaping from my lap. "I'm thirsty." He runs into the kitchen.

I stare at the picture as my mother sits down next to me. "I was so scared." She pulls her arm around my shoulder. "Sadie, I'm so grateful you're okay."

I reach to embrace her. I need to have her arms around me. I can't imagine what would have happened to Cory if she wouldn't have been in the park that day. "Thank you for being there for him."

"He's my grandson." I see her gaze drift behind me towards Hunter. "He will be once you finally say yes."

I nod. "I will."

"Dad and I are going home now." She motions towards where my father is sitting across from us in a chair. His unexpected declaration of love at the hospital when I woke up hasn't been spoken of since. I know that he loves me now. I know that he understands that I love Hunter.

"I'll call you tonight." I squeeze her hand.

My father bends down to run his lips across my forehead before they leave.

"Do you want something, sunshine?" Hunter asks from where he's sitting on the edge of the coffee table. "I can get you some water or juice."

"No." I pat the spot next to me. "Come sit with me."

"I can't refuse that." He snuggles in next to me, carefully pulling me into his chest. "Does this hurt?"

I shake my head slightly. "It's not your fault," I whisper the words slowly.

I feel his breath hitch and his breathing stalls. "It is. I can't stop thinking about it."

"You have to." I trace my finger along his thigh. "It's over. He's in jail again. He's not coming back."

"When I saw his fist." His body trembles. "I just knew. I couldn't protect you. I ran so fast."

"You came to get us," I try to reassure him. "You came to the park as soon as you knew he was in Boston."

"I was so panicked when you didn't answer your phone, Sadie. All I got was that voicemail saying you were taking him to the park." He pulls me even closer into his chest. "I thought he'd taken you both away forever."

"I'm sorry I forgot it." I've felt horrible since I realized that he'd tried to call to warn me that day. He knew Peter was looking for Cory and he wanted to tell me to stay inside with him.

"No." He kisses my forehead. "I wish I had been there."

"I'm okay." I tilt my head back to look in his eyes. "We're all okay."

"We're going to be okay." His finger brushes against my swollen cheek.

I nod before I sink my cheek back into the fabric of his shirt. "Did you talk to your lawyer?"

"Earlier," he offers.

"Well?" I tap his hand wanting more information than that.

"In a few months, Cory will be mine. I'll be his father, legally. In every way, he'll be mine."

"Ours," I whisper into him. "He'll be ours."

CHAPTER TWENTY-THREE

"Princess, wake up."

I open my sleepy eyes to see Cory's face not four inches from mine. I smile at the sight. "I fell asleep."

"You had a nap like babies do."

The words are so sweet. I glance behind him to the clock on the nightstand. It's almost dinner time. I slept most of the afternoon away.

"We have a surprise." He can barely contain himself. He's literally shaking with excitement, the red hair on his head bouncing as he shifts from one foot to the other.

"You and daddy?"

"Me and Zander." He pulls his hand to his mouth as he lets out a big laugh at his own joke.

"Where's daddy?" I try to sit and I'm bowled over by a sudden feeling of dizziness. The doctor was right when he told me to take it easy for a few days.

"Come." He holds out his tiny hand and I reach for it. He waits patiently as I slowly pull myself into a sitting position before I tentatively try to stand.

"Is it a good surprise?" I follow his lead as we leave the bedroom and walk out into the main living room.

"The best." He nods as he glances back at me.

I'm greeted by the sight of dozens of small white lights and Hunter standing in the middle of it all. He's wearing the same tuxedo he had on the first night I saw him at my parents' house. He looks so different now. He's so much more handsome. I can see the kindness in him, the compassion that is always resting in his soul.

"Wait here." Cory bolts from the room and races down the hallway.

I shrug my shoulders as I stand and stare at Hunter.

"Do you remember when I pretended to forget my coat at your parents' house?"

The question draws a smile from deep within me. "I was just thinking of that night."

"My life began that night. You came down those stairs and I knew one day we'd build a life together. I knew that we'd have a family together."

"You wanted another woman's number, remember?" I joke through happy tears.

"I wanted you."

"Then you came to the bistro the next day."

A smile spreads across his perfect lips. "You were so shocked to see me. You were so beautiful."

I laugh. "I had on a dirty apron and my hair was a mess."

"You were the most beautiful woman I'd ever laid eyes on." He breathes a heavy sigh. "I just sat and stared at you while you worked."

"Then you were there at the restaurant that night." I float back in my mind to the night I went to the birthday dinner for Alexa's friend. "You and Jax."

"I wanted to take you home with me that night."

"I wanted to go home with you," I confess. "I wanted you to kiss me."

He smirks, "I asked you if you wanted to. You turned me down." He reaches for his chest. "I was heartbroken."

"I will never break your heart." I pull my own hand to my chest. "Never."

"Sadie," Cory's voice calls to me from behind.

Just as I start to turn he walks past me dressed in a tuxedo that's identical to Hunter's.

"Now, daddy? Now?" I can tell he's trying to whisper but his excitement is getting the better of him.

"Now." Hunter reaches down to kiss him on the cheek.

I watch carefully as Cory pulls a small box from his pocket just as Hunter kneels on one knee. Cory leans back, pulling himself onto Hunter's bent leg. "Princess Sadie, will you please marry us?" He opens the box and there's a brilliant diamond ring inside. Two large pear shaped diamonds are crafted together.

I stand in silence, staring right into my future.

"Yes, yes, yes," I say as I race across the room and into their arms.

EPILOGUE – ONE YEAR LATER

"How will the baby know that I'm her brother?" Cory rests his head against my stomach. "Will you tell her when she comes out?"

I glance over at Hunter sitting on the foot of the bed. "If you talk to her now, she'll know your voice."

"No." He laughs. "That's not true."

"It is." I rub my belly, enjoying the very small bump that has appeared. It's still five months until our daughter arrives and already I'm anxious to know what she looks like. I want her to have Hunter's beautiful blue eyes. I want her to be as caring and loving as he is.

"All you have to do is rest your head on Sadie's tummy and talk to Olivia." Hunter moves to sit next to me now.

"You show me, daddy." Cory obviously needs a bit more convincing.

Hunter slides his tall body across the bed until his head is resting lightly on my stomach. He cradles my waist, pulling me into him.

"Listen carefully, champ." He pulls Cory's head back down.

I reach to cradle both of them in my hands.

"My sweet baby, Olivia," Hunter's voice breezes over the fabric of my t-shirt. "Your mommy, daddy and big brother are waiting for you."

"I'm going to show you how to draw," Cory's voice is faint.

"Daddy is going to tell you all about the day he married your beautiful mommy. She looked so beautiful."

"She did." Cory's head nods against my stomach. "We had so much fun that day."

We had. Our small wedding four months ago had been perfect. Only our families were there and Alexa had flown back for the celebration. It was simple, quiet and perfect.

"Sadie is going to be a doctor." Cory rubs his hand over my tummy. "I'm going to be one too so I can work with her."

I smile at the idea. This week Cory is determined to be a doctor; he's even taken to carrying my stethoscope around the apartment, listening to his own heartbeat.

"We love you very much." Hunter squeezes my side. "We all love each other very much."

"We do," Cory adds. "I won't share a room with you though."

That brings up a belly laugh from both me and Hunter.

"Cory." Hunter touches him on the head to get his attention. "We have a surprise for you."

I glance at Hunter and throw him a look. I thought we were going to wait until closer to moving day to share our surprise.

"What? Tell me." He's on his knees now, shaking the bed as he trembles with excitement.

"We're moving," I blurt out and that draws an animated frown from Hunter.

"Where? To Disneyland?" Cory jumps to his feet.

I shrug my shoulders at Hunter. Neither of us anticipated that reaction.

"To a new house," Hunter says excitedly. "A big house. You'll have a new room. Olivia too."

He pulls his hand to his face. "And a dog? Can I have a dog?"

I cock a brow waiting for Hunter to answer. "A dog too. We're going to be one happy family."

"We already are." I reach to pull his head closer.

"We already are," he whispers as his lips glide over mine.

ALSO BY DEBORAH BLADON
& SUGGESTED READING ORDER

Hush

Bare

Wish

Sin

Lace

Thirst

Compass

Versus

Ruthless

Bloom

Rush

Catch

Frostbite

Xoxo

He Loves Me Not

Bittersweet

The Blush Factor

THANK YOU

Thank you for purchasing and downloading my book. I can't even begin to put to words what it means to me. If you enjoyed it, please remember to write a review for it. Let me know your thoughts! I want to keep my readers happy.

That's all for Hunter and Sadie. As sad as it is to say goodbye to characters, all good things must come to an end. Thank you so much for making this series such a success. I really mean it.

There are exciting things in the wings, so stay tuned to my website for more information www.deborahbladon.com.

If you want to chat with me personally, please LIKE my page on Facebook. I love connecting with all of my readers because without you, none of this would be possible. www.facebook.com/authordeborahbladon

Thank you, for everything.

ABOUT THE AUTHOR

Deborah Bladon has never read a romance hero she didn't like. Her love for romance novels began when she was old enough to board the bus, library card in hand to check out the newest Harlequin paperbacks. She's a Canadian by heart, and by passport, but you can often spot her in New York City sipping a latte and looking for inspiration for her next story. Manhattan is definitely her second home.

She cherishes her family and believes that each day is a gift for writing, for reading, and for loving.

Made in United States
North Haven, CT
12 April 2022

18178580R00196